2 SHANES

LEE TULLOCH

The Text Publishing Company
171 La Trobe Street
Melbourne Victoria 3000
Australia

First published 2001
This edition 2001

Printed and bound by Griffin Press
Typeset in Stempel Garamond by J & M Typesetting
Designed by Chong

National Library of Australia
Cataloguing-in-Publication data:

Tulloch, Lee.
Two shanes.
ISBN 1 877008 04 4.
I. Title.
A823.3

This project has been assisted by the Commonwealth Government through the Australia Council, its arts funding and advisory body.

Australia | **Council**
for the Arts

Praise for Lee Tulloch and *Two Shanes*

'This is a Manhattan cocktail made with the merest hint of Martin Amis strained over early Jay McInerny; stirred with Vegemite jokes, *Crocodile Dundee* stereotypes and a suspicion of Bazza McKenzie.' *Weekend Australian*

'Tulloch has always shared Armistead Maupin's skill for writing quirky characters…[she] has an infallible bullshit detector.' *Sydney Morning Herald*

'Just as she deconstructed the lofty world of fashion in *Fabulous Nobodies*, Tulloch also takes swipes at the superficiality of the acting industry and the art of "cool-surfing"…She is merciless in her treatment of the so-hip-it-hurts New York culture of branding and posturing.' *Age*

'A high-spirited comedy of mistaken identity…Tulloch has always approached the glamour world from a socio-cultural perspective, gently pinning back fashion's butterfly wings and skewering it with humour.' *Vogue*

'A hip, relaxed third novel, driven by New York's fascination for anything Antipodean…Tulloch has a sharp eye for character and cultural differences' *Who Weekly*

'An entertaining comedy of errors.' *Marie Claire*

'Clever and original…hilarious.' *Examiner*

LEE TULLOCH WAS BORN IN MELBOURNE AND CURRENTLY LIVES IN
NEW YORK WITH HER HUSBAND, PHOTOGRAPHER TONY AMOS, AND
THEIR DAUGHTER, LOLITA. SHE IS THE AUTHOR OF THE CRITICALLY
ACCLAIMED BESTSELLERS *FABULOUS NOBODIES* AND *WRAITH*.

TEXT PUBLISHING MELBOURNE AUSTRALIA

For my husband, Tony Amos.

Shane: 'Gracious gift of God'.
A form of the name John.
Variants: Jack, Eoin, Seon, Sean, Shaun, Shawn.

Shane Dekker bought a stale egg-and-bacon roll at the crummy supermarket a few blocks from 67th Street beach.

With his surfboard under his arm, he trudged back to the ocean across the remains of a car park, barren except for the waist-high weeds that defied the crumbling tar. Weathered piles of trash flapped in the north-northwest gale that was blowing the waves flat.

Train tracks had more height.

He sat on the boardwalk, legs dangling, and ate, tucking his head into his collar. His ears were burning from the cold and bits of blackened bacon kept dropping out of his roll as he fumbled with frozen fingers. He tried to imagine that he was back in the dunes at Gunnamatta, his eyes squinting in the December sun, the water evaporating off his hot, bare skin, and munching on an oozing Burdekin's meat pie.

He couldn't believe they called *this* a beach.

The sea was the colour of green disinfectant, the wet sand the grey of a cat's litter box. He sat between two jetties. It was after eight in the morning and even the fishermen had stayed in bed. Behind him were blocks of abandoned car parks and broken roads going nowhere he could imagine. Ugly high-rise buildings loomed on either side. It looked like some genius city planner had said, let's dump all the poor people over here, give them a nice view of the sea. Except he bet that no one was looking at the water right now. They'd all be watching the television, playing with their Nintendos, or beating the shit out of each other.

Tiny shards of ice stung his cheeks, stuck in his eyelashes.

He wiped a fleecy glove across his brow.

Only a dickhead would come to New York for the surf.

Two hours later, the A train screeched out of Rockaway Avenue station and then stopped suddenly, the back carriages buckling against one another and causing an elderly man who was making his way along the car to be flung into an abrupt sitting position.

'Oops. Sorry, folks,' came the crackling apology of the guard over the speaker system.

Shane woke with a start. He'd been sitting with his head resting against the window, eyes closed, still thinking of Gunnamatta, the waves he'd surfed since he was a kid. One of the best beach breaks in Australia, the long cool barrel of water rolling over you, sucking the hair right off your head, the wax out of your ears, your eyes out of their sockets through the back of your skull, the tunnel closing in at the other end, you crouched low and flat, no time for thought, tasting ocean, shooting for the air, making it and coming off the peak like a fucking champion, or losing it and being shredded on the reef below…That was the thrill. Paddling out with the warm air on your neck, the salt drying on your cheeks, the set to yourself. Death or honour. And never knowing which it would be.

Fuckin' amazing.

He opened his eyes and squinted. *Gunnamatta my bum.* Here he was in New York City in the dead middle of winter, sitting on the crowded A train at 10.15 on a Saturday morning, dressed like he was on his way back from the bloody Antarctic, swaddled in a fur-collared jacket, fleecy gloves, beanie down low over his eyebrows, thermal socks, steel-capped boots, his six-foot-four concave board between his legs.

He'd spent an hour paddling around at Rockaway on green sludge, the wavelets so close together they had about as much power as water sloshing in a glass. As he sat on his board, waiting for a tube that never came, he knew that across the Atlantic Ocean, straight across, on the Basque coast of Spain, lay Mundaka, one of the longest left-hand barrels in the world, Spanish women in yellow bikinis, sangria, heat as thick as tortillas, wads of cash in your hand from teaching chicks to surf.

Instead, here he was, getting tubed all right, in the New York subway system. Shooting down a tunnel in a dirty train instead of the crystal barrel of a wave.

The train pulled into the Utica Avenue station and grey-looking passengers shuffled on and off. Shane was big in his ratty jacket, the long surfboard in its silver cover a shield. People hesitated when they saw him, and stared. Sitting opposite was an old woman, her bare hands clutching the handle of a cart full of crushed soda cans. The way she folded into herself as she sat, she resembled one of her aluminium scavengings. She glared at him, as if he were the cause of all her misfortune.

Shane screwed up his face and scowled back.

You think your life's bad, old lady? I'm stranded in this fucking rathole, twelve thousand miles from home, with less than a hundred bucks in my pocket. Surrounded by water, the Hudson River, New York Bay, the fucking Atlantic Ocean, and not a decent wave anywhere. The ocean with about as much swell as the sewage farm at Werribee and cold enough to turn your balls inside out.

Fuck. He remembered now that he'd left his wax on the boardwalk. Where the hell was he going to find wax in Manhattan? He felt in his pocket and brought out his plastic Metrocard instead. You had to say one thing for New York. You could take the subway from Manhattan straight to the beach. The fare was only one dollar fifty, one way.

Even he could fucking afford that.

'Stand clear of the closing doors! Stand clear of the closing doors!'

At West 4th Street, Cheyne Burdekin slid between the doors and pushed himself into the middle of the crowded subway car, clutching his copy of *Backstage.* He found himself wedged between an Orthodox Jew holding a tiny book close to his face and a man in a Santa suit with a briefcase chained to his wrist. What was so precious about its contents? Cheyne wondered. A confidential dossier of the elves' remuneration package?

He smiled at his own wit. A girl with hair like a red acrylic bathroom mat thought he was smiling at her and gave him a frankly appraising look. He locked eyes with her until she blushed and looked away. A wrinkled brown woman in a beret was reading aloud from the Bible. Two Chinese kids stood in the doorway, tongue-kissing.

'Stand clear of the closing doors!' The subway guard's voice was ragged with frustration as the doors refused to close. The culprit was a shabby-looking guy with a backpack and a surfboard who was trying to manoeuvre his board around the amorous couple as he got off. The tail of the board whacked an old man on the shoulder and its nose poked the chest of a messenger who was making a last-minute dash through the doors.

A *surfboard* on a subway! Cheyne watched as the surfer turned around and gave the messenger the finger. He was struck by the immaturity of the gesture. The guy looked to be late twenties, Cheyne's own age. But there the similarity ended. The surfer was obviously a fuckwit. Where did you find a wave on Manhattan at eleven on a Saturday morning?

The doors finally closed and Cheyne had to grip the pole tight not to be thrown around by the jolting train. He loved it, the crush, the smells, the yelling and singing and lost tempers. Just yesterday, an old woman in a faded print frock and plastic poncho evacuated a flood of piss in the middle of the subway carriage and each person in the car started doing a little dance so as not to get their shoes wet.

This was the life. Holed up in a tiny apartment in Greenwich Village, living on hot dogs from street carts and whiskies from bars straight out of forties *film noir*, babes all over you, no one knowing or caring who your father was, no one knowing or recognising *you*. Not like Sydney, no strangers stopping you on the street and asking for your autograph. This was his little window of anonymity before all hell broke loose. And hell would break loose once he won his first role.

The girl with the red hair was looking at him again. He slid his eyes around the carriage and noticed other people staring too. He was used to it. He ran a hand across his face. Even though he was fair, his stubble always grew in black as coal. His body hair was like that too, and his eyebrows. He put his hand to his right eyebrow and felt the scar that cut the brow in two, the result of a cricket accident at school.

It was always spoken of as an *accident*, but Cheyne knew it had been a deliberate attempt to wipe him out of the competition. The bowler was full of remorse and said the ball had been greasy and had just flown out of his hand. Then, as the school nurse fluttered around with compresses and Mercurochrome, he whispered in Cheyne's bloody ear, 'Howzat *Pie Boy*?'

His mother, Gloria, had insisted Cheyne see the plastic surgeon she was fucking, and the quack botched the job. 'Look what's happened to my beautiful boy!' she sobbed when the results were unveiled. Well, he *was* beautiful but he liked the scar. It made him look…roguish. Gloria went off to Bali for the month to recover from the shock, which was another reason to like his new flaw. Besides, he'd always felt uncomfortable being perfect.

'Serves yourself right for playing a poofter sport,' said his dad, Murray, who preferred Rugby League and the races, when he wasn't making public appearances as the Pie King promoting Burdekin's Homestead Pies. He called Cheyne a poofter, too, when he declined his father's offer of an executive job in marketing and announced he wanted to be an actor. 'I suppose your mother put you up to this,' Murray Burdekin complained. In fact, his mother hadn't had any influence, but she was pleased. What femme fatale in a Versace suit and bronze stilettos wouldn't want a movie-star son?

Not that fame was what Cheyne really wanted. His father was famous and what good did that do him? A quadruple bypass and gout so bad they had to wheel him up to the ninth hole. A wife who spent all her time in the compound in Bali molesting teenage surfers.

It was respect Cheyne wanted, people staring at him in the street and saying, *Look, there's Cheyne Burdekin, the movie star, I love his work,* not *Look, there goes Pie Boy.* And the easiest way to get it was by turning up and reading a few lines to a casting director.

And it had been easy. Easy in Australia and easy here, where he'd found an important agent the first day off the plane, three weeks ago. Valerie Bone. Tough as an old boot, workaholic, never out of the office, even on a Saturday. He was going to have a meeting with her now. Exciting news, she had said.

The train thundered into the 42nd Street station. Cheyne took the stairs two at a time. People were looking at him, definitely looking. Wondering who he was.

They'd all know soon enough.

Finley Rule scowled at the forest of bound Christmas trees propped up against the cyclone fence on West 4th.

'Say, mister,' she said to the burly guy in the fuzzy Santa cap. 'Can you move those things?'

'Ten dollars a foot,' the vendor said.

'I don't want to *buy* a fucking tree. I just want you to move them.'

'What the fuck's wrong? I've got a licence, lady.' He frowned at her and shook his head. 'You're too short to be a cop.'

'Look,' she said, exasperated. 'See those posters taped to the wire? I want to rip them down. Some of your trees are in the way.'

He considered the posters. They were letter-sized, printed with the scowling face of a girl with choppy black hair. Across the bottom of the page the words WARNING: BREEDER were stamped in red ink. The picture wasn't clear but you could tell the girl was in her twenties, kind of pretty. The tree-seller turned back to Finley. 'That you?'

'No.'

'It sure looks like you. You an actress or something? On TV?'

'No!' She put her arms around a six-foot fir and hoisted it in the air. 'Now, help me, will you?'

He shrugged and complied. Finley jumped and grasped the wire with her fingers, pressed her combat boots into the fence for balance. She reached and tore down two posters, then edged along the wire and pulled away the rest. Three giants playing basketball in the court on the other side of the fence stopped and whistled.

Finley gave them the finger and jumped down.

'I still say that's you,' said the tree man, pointing to the scrunched-up posters.

Finley stomped off and shoved the twisted paper into the nearest trash can. Thanks to that bitch Natalie she was late for work now. Not that she'd usually care, but she wanted to get a head start on rearranging her surfing shrine before the customers arrived. In the pocket of her army jacket was a photograph of world champion Sunny Garcia she'd cut from *Surfer* magazine. She'd slip that in a frame and move Kelly Slater back a bit. Not *too* far. Despite his semi-retirement from the world surfing circuit, she still had the hots for him.

She ran down the stairs into the West 4th Street station and pushed past a woman ambling along with multiple shopping bags from Balducci's food store. Finley never had time for Christmas shopping. She was too busy selling things. Who would she buy for anyway? Only Blossom, who demanded a stocking of bones on Christmas morning.

She thought about jumping the turnstile and eyed the clerk at the ticket box. The woman glared at her as if she could read her mind.

She sighed and reached into her pocket for her Metrocard. She hated spending the dollar-fifty when it was so easy to sneak in for free.

She lifted her hand to swipe the card and felt the force of something large and padded push her aside.

'Hey!' She looked up angrily, expecting the cocky challenge of a homeboy in a puffy jacket, and caught a flash of silver. She turned, surprised.

A surfer with a board under his arm!

She watched him take the stairs two at a time. She couldn't see his face, just the back of the beanie he had pulled down over his hair. He was tall, broad-shouldered. No one she recognised. She wanted to call after him but her mouth wouldn't move.

She'd never seen a surfer in the subway before, although she knew the A train went directly to Rockaway beach. She'd heard of guys taking the train in summer, when the big swells came. But not in winter. It was almost fucking snowing! This guy must be a true enthusiast. Or a lunatic.

She was impressed.

Before she could follow him, she was pushed into the turnstile by a harassed-looking woman with two children in tow.

'Are you goin' or comin'?'

Finley swiped her card, looking back over her shoulder.

The surfer was gone.

But she could smell the sea.

Valerie Bone sat under the framed Al Hirschberg caricature of herself and lit a cigarette. In the caricature she was puffing on five cigarettes at once. This morning she stopped at one.

She leaned back in her burgundy leatherette chair and surveyed her newest client. There was no denying he was spectacularly good-looking. One of those open faces that still held a hint of what the ten-year-old boy would have been like. She ticked off the particulars as if she were checking through a shopping list. (Which she was, in a way.) Wide-set, shallow green eyes, the kind that photographed well. Humour behind them. A strong nose, not too fleshy. A big smile, slightly crooked. Lips of even thickness, just short of feminine. Wide jaw and neck. Cowlicks. Dirty blonde hair that he kept flicking out of his eyes. Big, six-two according to his resume, not pumped-up but hard-bodied, the kind that goes to fat if he gets lazy. Maybe a bit straight-looking, but the broken eyebrow helped. A hint of strain under his eyes, which could go either way—stressed or debauched. She'd bet on debauched. He was Australian, after all. Weren't they all degenerates? She could think of two Aussie actors who fitted that description right off the top of her head.

Lara Dinardo would love him.

She pushed the cigarette pack at him. He shook his head. He was looking at her very calmly but the way he was picking at his nails showed he was nervous. He was wearing a very nice navy wool coat, something Italian or even Japanese, something bought in SoHo, she thought. Rich kid, for sure. He hadn't even blinked when she'd found him a place to stay for $1700 a month. He'd made some money off a sword-and-sorcery TV series he'd done in Australia last year but cash disappeared fast in this town, up your nose or down your throat. She wondered how he'd react if the money dried up and the jobs failed to materialise. Of course, it was *her* job to make sure that never happened. But she rather fancied he'd be even better looking with a few more shadows under his eyes.

'Well, darling,' she said, grasping her cigarette between yellow thumb and finger. 'I've sent your material off to Lara Dinardo who's casting *The Importance of Being Earnest*. You know the play?'

He smiled confidently. 'Of course.'

'We're talking about a Fox Searchlight film, not the Miramax one. Set in contemporary New York, directed by the Grimley brothers. I don't need to tell you how hot they are. They did that roller derby *Cherry Orchard* off-Broadway last year. It was wonderful, darling. It went so *fast*. Poor old Chekhov must've been bucking in his grave.'

She pointed her cigarette at him. 'Now, the reason I think you might be perfect for this is that it's a Gen X take on that dusty old Wilde play. They're not looking at anyone over twenty-eight so you just scrape in. They want "ethnic" casting, too, which means Latinos and blacks and maybe the odd Chinaman. I figure Australian is ethnic too, don't you, darling?'

The young actor leaned forward in his chair. 'But isn't Wilde satirising British manners in the play? What's the point of it being set in New York?'

'The point is they can suck in American audiences. Now, for God's sake don't get intellectual on them! You don't look it, so keep your mouth shut.'

'I think I can do that.' He gave her a grin. It was really charming the way it twisted to the right. She found herself wondering if other parts of his anatomy twisted the same way. Enough of that, she corrected herself. You're sixty-nine. An interesting number, but far, far too old to indulge in erotic speculation about young men.

'You're not prancing around some sound stage in a loincloth now, darling,' she retorted.

'I've got no problem doing Wilde,' he said, a bit pompously.

'Forget about doing Wilde, young man. You're doing *Grimley*.

Don't ever lose sight of it.' She jammed her cigarette back in her mouth and shuffled through some papers on her desk. 'Now I want you to go straight to the nearest video store and find a film called *All's Well That Ends Well.* You saw it?'

'The Shakespeare play?'

'Yes, the Grimley version. They specialise in reinterpreting the classics. This one was hip-hop, in black face, something about corrupt cops in the urban jungle. Very topical. Indie thing. IFC money. Won a Spirit Award in 1999, maybe for screenplay. Go get it *now.* I want you to study it. Watch it twenty times. Get a *feel* for these Grimleys. Don't know them myself but these transplanted Brits are tricky. Lara's going to review your stuff and call me. I'll try for an audition as soon as possible. We might as well strike while the iron is hot, darling.'

'My iron is always hot,' he smirked.

'I don't doubt that,' Valerie said. 'Just take my advice and don't go waving it around all over the place.'

There wasn't any surf on Manhattan, this was a known fact. There wasn't even one of those indoor swimming pools which produced artificial two-foot waves every thirty minutes for kids with boogie boards. Finley did know of a Japanese restaurant that sent little boats of sushi bobbing around the perimeter of the room on the swell from a bonsai-sized tsunami. But that was about it. Even the most desperate surfer couldn't find a wave on the East River. Unless he made them in his bathtub.

So why was Wipeout doing so well? A surfwear shop on an obscure Tribeca street, in a neighbourhood famous for obscene rents and restaurants where movie stars supped? It couldn't just be the Christmas rush.

Finley crossed her arms and looked around the store at the Saturday lunch-hour crowd, the boys roaming through it with their skateboards, the girls trying on Hawaiian-print flares, the lawyers ogling the new photograph of Sunny Garcia she'd given pride of place in the shrine to surfing greats, the stockbrokers fooling around with the Brian Davenport with the devil's-head hologram on the deck, the investment analysts clipping on snowboards while their limos idled on the kerb. None of these people had ever caught a wave, but here they were, in the boondocks, going home with neoprene wetsuits and $38 tie-dyed tee-shirts with tiny Wipeout logos on one sleeve. Interior decorators came in with measurements for boards to hang over Fifth Avenue fireplaces. It was wild.

'Hey, where do I try this on?' A thickset guy was waving a pair of Mooks pants at her. She pointed to the back of the store. There was one fitting room, enclosed in vintage fifties plastic shower-curtains. She watched him amble away.

Notably lacking in the store were any surfers. She'd met a few guys who surfed Ditch Plains in summer, older guys, in their forties, from Florida or California, making too much money here to go home, but missing whatever it was that surfers missed about flying headlong off a wave into the sand and being dragged, spluttering, into the undertow.

Stewie, the store manager, was watching her from beside the cylindrical fishtank that ran from floor to ceiling in the middle of the store. He claimed to have competed at Maverick's in 1993 but she didn't believe him. He was so pudgy she was sure if she ever poked him she would leave an indentation. Besides, he had the Hawaiian-shirted, receding-haired, mangy-goateed look of a David

Crosby fan. He owned a board but he wasn't a *real* surfer. She thought she'd recognise one in a shot—broad-shouldered, freckled, sand in his eyelashes, the smell of pot in his tangled hair. She thought wistfully about the surfer who'd nearly knocked her over that morning. Why didn't guys like that ever come here? Because, she reminded herself, the store was fifteen miles from the nearest wave.

She rang up another sale on the register, a pair of board shorts, threw them in a bag and tossed it on the counter for the customer to pick up. It was December, for Christ's sake, what did he need with board shorts?

The other sales girl, Hiromi, appeared on the opposite side of the register, her chin in a pile of shirts she was carrying. She looked like a character out of a Japanese *Anime* cartoon, with her white hair in high pigtails, her lightning-flash tee-shirt, her red plastic miniskirt and high, clumpy black boots. Although she was born at the NYU Medical Centre, she would sit through old *Godzilla* movies and sob. It was some kind of collective-memory thing.

'Hey, Finley, how many leashes have you sold?' Hiromi dumped the tee-shirts on the counter.

Finley and Hiromi amused themselves by running a competition every week to see who could get rid of the most leg leashes, the spirals of tubing that attached a board to a surfer. The plastic leashes, one would suppose, were virtually useless to anyone without a surfboard. But Finley devised all sorts of uses for them, and sold them as restraints for children or convinced customers they were Christmas tree decorations.

'Three,' Finley calculated. 'Pitiful.' She eyed a group of girls making fish faces at Mr Stripey. 'I've been telling the suckers it's a new way to exercise their abs. But they're not going for it.'

Hiromi folded her arms across the fluorescent lightning bolt on her chest. 'Well, I lose again. I've only sold one.' Hiromi always lost. She didn't actually try. It was Finley's thing.

Finley idly picked up a fuzzy tee-shirt. '*Yech.* Who'd wear these things? Listen, Hiromi, tonight's Blossom's birthday. You want to come out with us after you finish here? I've got a cake.'

'It's like a pain in the butt but I've gotta go to some thing for my cousin at the hotel.' Hiromi's family owned a small hotel in midtown. She didn't work for the piddling $5.25 an hour. She worked because it was credible to work in a surf shop. Even one with customers who couldn't tell a lump of board wax from a bar of soap.

'I'll save you some cake then.'

Hiromi screwed up her nose. 'Count me out.' She remembered last year's confection: slabs of raw beef layered with liverwurst. Decorated with whipped cream and sprinkles.

'You'll be sorry,' Finley said. 'I've got a nice fat sheep's liver this time.'

'Hey, can you help me?' asked a guy with a briefcase, holding up a Rip Curl spring wetsuit on a hanger.

Finley looked him up and down slowly. 'I don't think so,' she said.

Cheyne left Valerie's office in the theatre district and walked all the way down Broadway to the Village, deep in thoughts about *The Importance of Being Earnest,* the mysterious Grimley brothers, screenings at Sundance, glowing *New York Times* reviews, the covers of *Talk, Interview, Vanity Fair* ('CHEYNE'S REIGN'), development deals with Miramax, his own 'people' (publicist, business manager, personal assistant), partying with Gwyneth, dining with De Niro, hanging out in sleazy Irish bars with Steve Buscemi…

The Blockbuster on lower Broadway had *All's Well That Ends Well.*

'Good choice,' said the kid at the checkout. He was narrow as a string bean under his tight Radiohead tee-shirt. 'You know the directors are twins?'

'No, I didn't,' said Cheyne.

'I'm trying to get a script to them.'

'You're a screenwriter?' Cheyne asked, picking up the video and pocketing his credit card. With his freckly face and unruly ginger hair the kid looked as if he had only recently graduated from alphabet flash cards.

'Yeah. All I need is for someone to buy a script.'

These Americans are bloody amazing, Cheyne thought. If you said something it was true. I am a screenwriter. I am an actor.

'Are you an actor or something? You look familiar. I know I've seen you in something. Don't tell me…' The kid scratched his head. 'You're Australian, right?'

Cheyne made a grimace. Was it that obvious? 'Yeah.'

'I love Australian movies. What about *Proof*? Shit, that was good. It really bums me out when they dub them in American. Like, you know *The Road Warrior*? Well, the only version they've got here is the American one. It stinks. Say, you weren't in *Kiss or Kill* were you?'

'No,' Cheyne said, peeved. Two years before, he had spent a miserable five months in the rainforests of Tasmania shooting six episodes of *Taliesin the Great*, a sword-and-sorcery epic about a sixth-century Welsh magician. It was a co-production between the American network TNT and an Australian outfit called Petulant. It had been a hit in Australia. But in America it had screened last May over three consecutive nights on TNT. The show's ratings had been less than luminous, thanks to it going head-to-head with the final of a real-life series in which a plane was (deliberately) crashed into a mountain in the Andes and the survivors left to battle it out for the opportunity to star in a rap video with Eminem. But this kid must have seen some of it. He looked the sword-and-sorcery type.

'Don't worry, by the time you bring the film back, I'll have remembered. I've got an encyclopedic memory for film. And music. It'll come to me. If I guess right, do me a favour and tell the boss. He thinks I'm a flake.'

'All right. It's a deal.'

'Blender,' said the kid.

'Blender?'

'It's my name. Ask for me if I'm not out front. Oh, I'm only here until seven. Got another job at night. Sputnik records. You know it? It's on the Bowery.'

'No, I don't. My name's Cheyne.' He held out his hand. Blender reached over the counter and shook it.

'Shane? That's your name? Ha, ha—you've just given me a clue.'

'You have to work out how to spell it first.'

There was no doubt Duke Kahanamoku needed attending to. Somehow he'd flipped his frame and landed on Cliff Robertson, pushing the Big Kahuna off his *Gidget* perch and into the well-documented bosom of Pamela Anderson.

It was three in the afternoon and the customers had been playing with Finley's surfing shrine. She sighed. Midget Farrelly was face-down on Tom Carroll and Mickey Dora had crashed into the little diorama she'd made of stills from *The Endless Summer*, tipping it sideways and smothering a grinning Cheyne Horan with the sand she'd scooped from the children's playground at Washington Market Park.

She picked up the famous Australian surfer by the edge of the frame and shook the sand off him. She was admiring his burnished shoulders, the way his wetsuit was peeled down past his hips, when someone behind her coughed.

'Um…' A voice mumbled, apparently masculine.

'What?' She blew on the glass.

'D'you have any Sex Wax?'

'Sex Wax?' She didn't turn around. It was unbelievable some of the lines guys came up with.

'This is a surf shop, isn't it?' His tone was vaguely irritable. Funny accent.

'What does it look like?' Finley laid Cheyne Horan down and contemplated getting a dustpan and brush. 'A juice bar?'

'It looks like a pooncy clothes store.'

'*Pooncy?*' She didn't recognise the word.

'Yeah. Only wankers'd wear this stuff.'

She wiped her hands on her camouflage trousers and turned to face her customer, intrigued now. She had to admit the sweatshirts were a bit overdesigned, with their fluoro plastic inserts and swing tags that looked like Hawaiian licence plates. She made a mental note of the word 'pooncy'. You always needed more ways of saying 'crap'.

He was tall, in a beefy plaid jacket with a matted fake-fur collar, and a black woollen cap pulled down to his eyebrows. She felt immediately suspicious: he looked familiar. Deadbeat or sex offender? It would be easier if men came out of vending machines, clearly marked. 'What did you say you wanted?'

'Sex Wax.'

'Sorry, pal, we don't do that sort of thing here.' Sex offender, she decided.

'No, that's not what I mean!' Agitated, he pulled his cap off his head and waved it around. His hair sprang out like grass flattened by a sleeping farm animal. It was the oddest thatch of texture and colour, light and dark, straight and kinky, an undergrowth of rusty bracken scattered with yellow straw. She wondered how it had got that way. There was a salon in her block that specialised in freakish extensions, purple feathers sewn into lime-green tresses, long silver switches woven with real mousy brown locks. But this guy didn't look the self-decorating type. There were no telltale piercings anywhere above his collar; the fingers seemed to be tattoo-free. There was no *pose* about him, which disturbed her.

He put a hand to his head and raked some straw off his face. His eyes were hazel, under straight brown brows, a frank expression in them that reminded her of wide-open doors. She registered his strong jaw with approval. She wasn't so sure about the stubble. It made him look grubby, like a root vegetable that had just been dug out of the soil. She leaned imperceptibly forward, to peer at his fingernails. Clean.

'Bad accident, that,' he said, following her gaze to his right hand.

'Oh?'

'Grey nurse.' He rubbed the knuckles.

'In a hospital?' She had a vision of a woman wielding a thermometer in a uniform that needed a good wash.

'No. Grey nurse. A shark.'

He held out his hand. She could see now that there was a white scar across it, puckered like a too-tight seam.

'Fucker bit me.'

'A *shark* bit you?'

'Yeah. It was after my watch.'

'It was trying to eat *a watch*?'

'Nah. It was attracted to the silver band. Thought it was a fish.'

'It didn't take your whole hand?'

'Punched it on the nose. That got rid of it.'

'You punched it?'

'I've punched a few sharks in my time.'

Finley felt her interest in him ratchet itself up a few notches. Someone who punched sharks was not someone to be taken lightly. 'You do it for a *living*?'

'For a living?' He scratched the back of his neck.

'Well, there are all those crocodile wrestlers and snake wranglers on TV...'

'Oh, I see what you mean.' The sun lines on his face converged at the corners of his eyes like minnows nibbling at bait. His mouth smiled and he moved the weight off one foot to the other. But he didn't elaborate.

'So what *do* you do?'

'I surf.'

'Really?' As soon as she said it, she realised how she sounded. Too eager.

He smirked. 'Yeah, when there's surf.'

'It's just we don't get many surfers around here,' she quickly explained. 'Just guys who fantasise.'

'Yeah, I know the type.'

Now, she realised she had seen him before. 'Hey, weren't you at West 4th this morning? You almost knocked me over.'

'I did?'

She was finding conversation a challenge. Most guys who came into the store wouldn't shut up about themselves, their cars, their jobs, their Christmas bonuses, the way they liked their ribs cooked, their batting averages in Little League, selling her a line when she was the one supposed to be doing the selling. This tall, scruffy, bramble of a person was different, standing there, not moving, not swaggering down the back of the store to check out the Brian Davenports, but waiting, she thought, for her to ask the next question. Like he was secure in his skin.

She bet his skin tasted like salt.

'Where are you from?'

'Melbourne,' he said. She thought there was an edge of defensiveness in his voice.

'*Melbun?*'

'Yeah. Melbourne. You know, Australia.'

'Oh, cool,' she nodded, as if she knew where he meant.

He scratched his head. 'This is really weird. I mean, to have a surf shop down here. I couldn't believe my eyes when I saw it in the phone book.'

'It's not that weird.' She felt obliged to defend it. 'The A train down Church Street takes you straight to Far Rockaway in Queens.'

'For what that's fucking worth.'

'Oh?' She'd never actually been to Far Rockaway, although she once went to Coney Island to the Mermaid Parade and had her picture taken with King Neptune. 'Well, there are waves in the Hamptons. Ditch Plains.' She felt she should sound knowledgeable at all costs.

He pouted. 'You call that surf?'

'So you've been there?' she asked.

'Taught board-riding last summer at Montauk.' He folded his arms across his chest. There was a silence while he looked at his feet.

'Are you a champion or anything?'

'Nah. Just a grunt. Been doing it since I was five. A late starter.' His eyes crinkled as if he were peering into the sun. She noticed now that his voice had a rising inflection on the last syllable, as if every statement were a question.

'Do you travel around the world…surfing?'

'Mostly.'

'It must be incredible.'

'It depends.'

'On what?'

'The waves.'

'Of course, the waves.' She smiled, radiating warmth, although he frowned back, as if he thought she were teasing him. But it had always seemed infinitely glamorous to her, a life that relied on the pull of the tides.

'So—are you here for long?'

'Not if I can help it.'

'That bad?'

'Been here a few months and it's really fucked.'

She was starting to like the way he spoke, get into the rhythm of it. Everyone always said things were fucked, it was the answer to every question, but the way he said it…it made being fucked sound like a fascinating possibility.

'You think this is bad? Try New York in August.'

'No thanks.'

Out of the corner of her eye she could see the hulking figure of another customer ambling towards her holding something on a hanger. She snapped at him, pointing to the fitting room.

She turned back to her surfer. 'I'm Finley,' she said, holding out her hand.

He reached out and took it. His hand was warm and rough. She thumbed the shark bite wistfully. 'Shane,' he said.

'Shine?'

'No, Shane.'

'Like Cheyne Horan?'

'No. S-H-A-N-E.'

'I've got a picture of him over here.' She gestured at the cabinet behind her.

'You did that?'

'Sort of. Except it's a mess right now.'

'So you surf?'

'Not exactly.'

'Oh,' he sounded disappointed.

'But I'd love to learn.'

She thought he might offer to teach her, but instead he said dourly, 'Got to start when you're a kid.'

She felt stung by that. 'Well, nice to meet you,' she said grimly and half-turned away. She could feel him standing there, not moving.

'The wax,' he said. 'I came in for board wax.'

'Down the back.' She didn't look at him, turned back to the shrine.

'It's fucking freezing, you know.'

'What?' She counted five brown plastic hula girls. There should be six…

'The water.'

'What water?'

'At Rockaway. You wouldn't like it.'

'Why should I care?'

'I'm not going to go to all the trouble of taking you surfing, just to have you wimp out on me.'

She turned and looked up at him in surprise. He was squinting down at her. A smile, she thought. 'There are plenty of wetsuits around here,' she suggested.

'I can see.'

'And boards. There's a Rusty I'm dying—'

'Too fast.'

'I can make you dinner afterwards.'

'No,' he said, crouching down and handing her the renegade hula girl. 'Breakfast.'

It was after five when Finley sneaked out of Wipeout. She'd been smiling ever since she met the surfer. This had caused a few comments in the shop. Finley never smiled. At best, she grimaced.

Feeling upbeat, she treated herself to a subway ride three stops back up to West 4th Street. She skirted quickly past the Christmas tree seller, who was binding a small spruce for a customer, and ducked into MacDougal Street, where she found a giant birthday card for Blossom depicting a wrestling superstar. The shop windows and cafes were swagged with spruce and holly. Under the street lamps a few snowflakes danced like lint. It was sickeningly picturesque. She felt like she was trapped in a snow globe.

She turned into Bleecker and dashed down Sullivan, pushing past a walking group staring up at the decorated townhouses.

Shit!

Her mood suddenly blackened. Across Houston Street, she could see the pale brick wall of the church of St Anthony of Padua. An illuminated life-size creche was attracting a few passers-by. Also attracting them was a small figure in a red coat who was standing in front of the nativity handing out leaflets.

Finley took off across the street, dodging traffic. 'Give me those fucking posters!'

Natalie shook her arm out of Finley's grasp. 'Why should I? I think they look *swell*.'

'It's...slander!'

'That you're a breeder? Changed your mind?'

'No! It's fucking ugly, that's all.'

'Well, I'm sorry,' Natalie smiled and handed a sheet of paper to a woman in a fur. 'But I want to warn other women out there.'

'Other *dykes*.'

'OK, so I've embarrassed you. It could have been worse. I could have *killed* you, you know.' Natalie fumbled in her shoulder bag for her cigarette case. She was wearing matte red lipstick and a red forties-style wool coat, her hair rolled under in a dark pageboy, looking like a pint-sized version of the heroine of one of the old screwball movies she loved to watch on TV.

Without saying anything else, Finley snatched the ream of paper from under Natalie's arm and turned downtown into Sullivan Street. She crossed the road and stood in her doorway, pulling a chain of keys out of her pocket.

'Wait!'

She could hear the clatter of Natalie's granny shoes on the pavement behind her as she tried to catch up.

'Shit!'

Finley turned around. Natalie was staring, dismayed, at the spilled cigarette case on the wet sidewalk, dimly illuminated by a street-lamp. The cigarettes were scattered around her like dead soldiers on a battlefield. Finley watched as she crouched down, trying to scrabble them together. A kid on a skateboard came out of nowhere in the dark and almost ran over her outstretched hand.

Natalie jerked her hand to her chest. Finley went to her aid, bent down and passed her a broken cigarette.

Natalie looked up, bit her lip. 'Have you got a light?' Then she gave a choked laugh. 'Isn't that the first thing I asked you? Ever?'

'No, you asked me if I wanted a *toke*—'

'You *remember*.' Natalie stood.

Finley remembered, all right.

She had met Natalie on the set of an indie movie so independent the producer was paying for it on his Visa card. They always said that if they didn't intend to pay *you*.

Natalie was catering for the crew. Finley was a 'featured extra'. It was the first call she'd had in months. It was all bullshit, this acting thing. Cameramen, electricians, makeup people, other actors, directors—*if* you were lucky, *if* they noticed you—all pushing you around. Not to mention the disinterested agents, indifferent casting directors, scathing critics, the bank clerks who sneered at you when you extracted your last six dollars on earth…It was hard to imagine that she ever cared. The extra cash was easy money. But she might just as happily earn it dog-walking.

Finley's role involved walking five paces along the street, dropping her shopping bag in horror and running three and a half paces onto the road where the lead actor was lying covered in soy sauce.

Twelve takes later, Finley went in search of a bottle of water.

'Here, have a toke,' said Natalie, who was standing behind a trestle table on the street, serving food. She handed Finley a smouldering, twisted cigarette paper.

'No thanks,' said Finley. 'I'm straight edge.'

'The "edge" I like,' replied Natalie. 'But I'm not so sure about the "straight".'

Finley now looked dispassionately at Natalie, who was grinding the broken cigarette underfoot vehemently. What had she been thinking? She'd never been lesbian before in her life. Even at high school, she'd been the one in the equipment cupboard with the boys, no time for crushes on the girls' basketball champion or the female lead in the school play. She'd called them Lezzos, not unkindly, just a tag, like the members of the football team were Jocks.

After every third bust-up with a guy she'd think, it would be so much easier with a girl, there'd be no gender war, no clashing of X and Y chromosomes, you could just sit over a pot of herbal tea and talk about the conflict rationally, like sisters. She knew a few Lipstick Lesbians, walking into bars in couples, very beautiful, very cool, all the heads turning. The *men* lusting after them. That could be a distinct advantage of becoming a lesbian, she thought. The effect it had on men.

She lit a girl's cigarette once or twice, but she never went any further. She liked the idea of lighting a woman's cigarette, there was something very Weimar Republic about it. She had gone to see the Screaming Celines at the Meadowlands once and had let another woman feel her up in the mosh pit, but when two boys joined in she hadn't objected, so she imagined that didn't count.

She had to admit she liked the admiring looks she and Natalie attracted in SoHo on Saturdays, holding hands. It was afterwards, between Natalie's leopard-print satin sheets, when she wasn't so sure. Natalie reminded her of a workman pushing a load of bricks uphill. She toiled. Finley found her mind wandering all over the place—places inhabited by boys named Ben and Mark, among others.

And now there was this person called Shane.

'Anyway,' Natalie was saying, brushing a glob of tar from the hem of her coat. 'I'm over you. Everything's *swell*.'

'Then why are you putting these posters up all over town? That doesn't look very "over" to me.'

Natalie frowned. 'Because I wanted you to get the message.'

'Oh, yeah?' Finley folded her arms. The sleeve of her army jacket rode up over the Celtic 'F' tattooed like a dagger over her wrist. 'What message? You wanted to pass on your grandmother's recipe for spoon bread or something?'

'Don't be a jerk, Finley.' Natalie reached out and touched the tattoo delicately. 'I always loved that.'

Finley pulled her sleeve down. 'What message?'

'Don't be like that.'

'Like what?'

'Cross. I should be cross at you. You changed your phone number.'

'It's fucking freezing out here, Natalie.'

'Can I come up?'

'No.'

'We could be friends. Don't you miss my meatballs?'

In fact, Finley did, though she wasn't going to admit it. 'Just lose those posters, OK?'

Natalie looked remorseful. 'OK. I want to show you something.' She started rummaging around in her bag again. 'Here—' she extracted a white card from her bag and waved it at Finley. 'Read it.'

Finley looked at the card. 'What is it? The number of some lesbian help line?'

'Read it!'

Finley could hardly make it out in the dark. It was the name and number of a casting agent. 'So? I've got a drawer full of these. I could rip them to shreds and have my own ticker-tape parade.'

'The Grimley brothers!' Natalie said triumphantly.

'What are you talking about?'

'The woman on this card is casting a new version of *The Importance of Being Earnest*. The *Grimley* brothers. It's a big deal.'

'I'm retired.' Finley said. 'I'm over the hill.'

'No, you're not. You're only twenty-five. Even I'm older than that and I'm not going to lie down and die *yet*. Anyway, wait until the casting agent gets the parcel I've sent her.' She gave Finley a wide smile. There was a smear of dark lipstick on her teeth. 'I once catered a Masterpiece Theater production of that play. You'd be great in it. You'd—'

'What parcel, Natalie?'

'I sent her the poster of you.'

'You *what*?'

'Well, everyone says you do look awfully cute in it.'

'Natalie! You try to get even with me and paste my picture up all over town with a warning for all the dykes to stay away from me because I'm a *breeder* and then you send it to a *casting agent*?'

'I sent her one of my menus, too. The production's going to need catering. I'm just waiting for her to call me. You can thank me now. I'm waiting to be embraced.'

Finley crumpled the card in her pocket. 'There's no way I'm going to get this.'

'What's wrong with you, Finley? I give you a swell opportunity like this and you turn it down?'

'I don't want to get into that acting shit again. I'm happy as I am.'

'No, you're not. You're never happy. You're the least happy person I've ever met.' Natalie took a step towards her and Finley flinched. Natalie slipped a hand into Finley's jacket pocket. She took out the card, smoothed it and pressed it back in Finley's hand. 'I'm sure the woman is going to be excited about you.' She patted Finley on the cheek. 'It's called projection.'

Finley watched Natalie tap-tap away, slowly this time, dignified.

Cheyne sat at the scarred oak bar and ordered a Samuel Adams. They had Fosters, but it was made in New Jersey.

God knows he needed a drink. It had started to drizzle after he left Blockbuster, so he ducked into a diner, and then a bookshop and then a clothing store where he'd bought a scarf to wrap around his face. It was dark and freezing outside. The bar had beckoned. He had been attracted by its tawdry neon sign, the way the 'B' and the 'A' were illuminated but not the 'R', like something out of a cheap crime novel.

He felt the warm pulse of alcohol hit his bloodstream. He felt good. This was the real *New York*! The bar was crowded, people standing behind his stool, every table taken. He listened to the accents, silently mimicked them, the way they rolled their Rs and made their vowels explode. Americans talked like they were punching the air with their words, not hesitant and half-embarrassed like Australians. Australians always inflected the last consonants of their words as if they sought permission from the listener to continue speaking. Thank Christ he'd gone to a good school and had most of the colloquialisms beaten out of him. He didn't want to sound like his father.

There were three women at the end of the bar with their arms around one another, massacring the theme song from *Fame*, if it was possible to massacre it.

'I'm going to live for-*everrrrr*!'

He emptied his glass.

'Hey! You!' The heavy brunette in the middle was waving at him. She held up a glass of champagne to the bartender and nodded. 'A drink for the handsome stranger,' she slurred.

He tried to wave it away. 'No thanks.'

'Hey! Do you think I'm a pig or something?' She had her hands on her hips, offended.

'No, no.' It was easier to comply when women got all stroppy. 'I'll have that drink, bartender.'

Stroppy. One of the more expressive Australian words.

The bartender placed another beer in front of Cheyne and raised his eyebrows. 'Better you than me, bud,' he whispered.

'So, what's your name?' the brunette called out. He looked over at her. She was attempting a seductive pout. He thought she resembled a sea cucumber.

'Cheyne,' he said, scooping up some peanuts into his wide hand.

'Shane? Like Shane the cowboy?'

'Yeah.' He left it at that. People always thought he was 'Shane'. The only other Cheynes he'd heard of were surfers. Morons, as far as he was concerned.

'My girlfriend thinks you're English.' She nudged the smaller blonde, who blushed.

'I'm Australian,' he said reluctantly. Just admitting you were Australian seemed to get New Yorkers excited. The effect it was having on the women right now.

'Oh my God!'

'*Really*?'

'Like the Crocodile Hunter? I *love* that guy!' enthused the small blonde.

'Who's the Crocodile Hunter?' Cheyne was only vaguely interested.

'You know, that Steve Irwin guy. He's on the Discovery Channel practically every night, wrestling crocodiles. He's *sooo* cute in those little shorts he wears.' She picked up her champagne glass and held it up. 'I think Australia's the greatest place in the world!'

'Oh, you've been there?' he asked.

'No, but she wants you to take her.' The brunette was getting bolder.

'*Tonight*,' said their companion, a dishwater blonde.

'Stop it!' The small blonde giggled and slapped the bigger blonde on the hand.

'Yeah, but that flight.' The dishwater blonde waved off her friend's hand and knocked over her glass. 'How long is it? *Exactly*?'

'Twenty-two hours minimum.'

'No way! Man, that's too much for me!'

'You get used to it,' he said.

'We wanna hear you talk,' the brunette pouted, her fleshy face in her hands. 'Say something now. Like *kangaroo*.'

'Kangaroo,' he said in his best Brooklyn accent.

'Hey, buddy,' the old guy sitting next to him joined in. 'I couldn't help overhearing. You from Australia?'

'Perceptive observation.'

The old guy missed the sarcasm. 'Australia's the country with the crocodiles, right?'

Cheyne groaned.

'Yeah. I seen them on "Wild Discovery". The grandson likes to watch it.'

Cheyne took a swig of his beer.

'You got them koala bears, too. Right?'

'Right.'

It was pointless setting him straight. What would he care that

Australia had theatres and galleries and restaurants, that it wasn't all dwarf-tossing and sharks snatching swimmers in mid-stroke? The world was full of cafes and shops and theatre companies doing *Chicago*. Americans liked to think that there was still a place in the world, albeit one that was conveniently remote, where nature was still natural and the natives spoke the same language, where no petty grievances against American cultural imperialism flourished and the inhabitants displayed a charming lack of sophistication, reminding Americans of the 'pioneering spirit' they had lost sight of amid the gunfire, dead children and drugs.

Let them believe it.

Cheyne put some notes on the counter and stood up.

'Hey, don't leave!' The brunette curled her lips at him.

'She thinks you're the most handsome man she's *ever* seen,' giggled the bigger blonde.

He picked up his video. 'Sorry, girls. I've got to go home and feed my crocodile.'

'Wow!' whispered the little blonde and gulped some more champagne.

Finley was still clutching Natalie's posters when she put her key in the lock. For Blossom's sake she forced a smile as she stepped into the apartment.

The impatient dog took a flying leap at her and pinned her to the wall, which wasn't all that difficult given that the dog weighed 130 pounds, five more than her owner. Finley extricated herself from Blossom's embrace, threw the posters in the nearest trash basket and showed Blossom her birthday card.

'Happy birthday to you! Happy birthday to you! Happy birthday, dear Blossom, happy…Wait a minute, baby, just hold on!'

Blossom sat in the middle of the floor, whining and thudding her tail on the seagrass matting, as Finley prepared the liver-and-cream cheesecake, ignoring the little parcel of excrement Blossom had left outside the kitchen alcove in protest at Finley deserting her all day.

Finley switched off the apartment lights. The candles on the cake—six of them—flickered weakly in the breeze from a propped-up front window, but Finley could still see the waterfall of drool glistening from Blossom's black muzzle and the eager, gummy redness of her eyes. Finley blew out the candles, plucked them out of the cake and put the plate on the floor. Blossom demolished it in two gulps. 'Wanna go to the playground?' Finley said with her usual intonation. 'Wanna go outside?'

Blossom fell back on her haunches and barked twice. Finley picked up the plate and turned the lights back on. The room was the usual disaster, records and books piled against the walls, her clothes stacked in old boxes, the futon and its quilt dominating the floor, covered in black dog hairs. Someone had once said to her, *you'd never imagine a girl lived here*, and she supposed they were right. She didn't believe in interior decorating. It only confused you about who you were.

Blossom was thumping her tail by the door. Finley put on her jacket and gloves and attached Blossom's collar. It looked like a circle of barbed wire. She clipped on the lead and shoved some plastic bags into the pocket of her jacket while Blossom strained and panted and pushed her blunt nose against the door.

They took their usual circuitous route to the dog run on Houston Street in search of spindly trees for Blossom to anoint and stopping to look in the occasional store window, at hunks of salami, displays of cheese and some half-hearted attempts at Christmas decorations.

The neighbourhood had once been Italian: the occasional men's club, a baker or two, the hand-made mozzarella shop held on stubbornly against the fragrant evolution of boutiques selling scented candles and jars of mango body scrub. The realtors called it SoHo, but because it was on the western fringe Finley dubbed it WoHo. She thought the name suited it. *Woe Ho. Woe* because of all the internet millionaires who had moved in and pushed the rents sky-high.

There were a lot of people on the street, even though there was ice in the air. Blossom spotted a rodent on the lawn at the New York University dorms but Finley held her back. The dog was huge, but Finley's arms were strong from swimming and boxing and the Mo Bo classes she took at a gym on Lafayette Street.

When they reached the dog run it was deserted. Most of the dog owners were probably cosily inside getting dressed for Christmas parties, she guessed. Finley let Blossom off her lead. 'Look, baby,' she said and took a pink tissue-wrapped parcel out of her pocket. She threw it to Blossom and let the dog nuzzle it open. Blossom galloped off to the end of the run shaking the new ball between her jaws.

Finley found a dry *Village Voice* and sat on it. She shrugged down on the seat, her hands in her pockets. Blossom rummaged around the trash can for a while and came back with the ball. Finley lobbed it at the wall. She did this rhythmically for several minutes.

'Nice dog,' said a male voice behind her. 'What is it?'

Finley didn't look up, dug her fists deeper in her pocket. Barneys were always using Blossom as an excuse to come on to her. '*She's* a bull-mastiff.'

'Oh?' The man sounded interested. Not in the dog. 'Can I pat her?'

'Not if you want to retain the use of your hand,' Finley replied. That usually got rid of them.

The guy ignored her and walked around to the gate of the dog run. He opened it.

'She's crossed with rottweiler,' Finley warned.

'No worries,' he said. 'Dogs like me. Come here, possum.'

Blossom dropped her ball and turned around. The guy crouched down and clicked his fingers. Finley took a sideways look at him in the half-light of the street lamp. He was wearing a dark navy coat, a scarf, but no hat or gloves. The end of his sweater sleeve was pulled down over one hand. In the other he was carrying a video from Blockbuster. His hair was long, straggly, fair but not blond. He was in profile and his right eyebrow, she could see, was split in two by a scar so that it looked like one of those drawbridges opening.

'Come on, girl. I won't bite.'

Funny accent. Probably British. He had a nice face, a *very* nice face now that she looked more closely, but he smelt vaguely of beer and it was comforting to know her box cutter was strapped around one ankle. She wiggled her right combat boot to check it. You could never tell anything by looks around here. He could have been a street criminal or a famous artist, stopping by to cut your throat or paint your portrait.

Blossom started trotting towards the guy, wagging her heavy tail.

'Nice doggy.'

Suddenly Blossom launched herself at the kneeling figure from six feet away. She flew low to the ground to conserve her velocity and landed with a thud on the stranger's chest before he knew what hit him.

'Blossom! *Sit!*' Finley jumped up and tugged at the dog's collar.

Blossom sat.

'Look, if you don't mind, I'd rather she didn't sit on *me*,' Blossom's victim pleaded from beneath her.

'I did warn you. You said dogs liked you.'

'Dogs do. *Whales* I'm not so sure about.'

Blossom growled.

'It won't help if you insult her.'

'Look…can I just get out from under here?'

Finley hoisted Blossom by the collar while the subject of the dog's attention dragged himself by his elbows to a sitting position. He scrambled to his feet and brushed some gravel off his coat. It was an expensive coat. She revised her estimate of him downward from homeless person to internet entrepreneur.

'You should keep that dog on a lead.'

'Look, yuppie scum, this is a dog run. It's the only square inch in the neighbourhood where she can be let off the leash. So fuck off out of here.'

'*Yuppie* scum?'

She didn't like the way he was smiling at her. Smug. She loosened her grip on Blossom's collar a little. 'You dot-com people think you can take over the city. You come here from London or wherever and fill the restaurants with your fucking cigar smoke, push up all the rents so that people who have lived here twenty years can't afford their places anymore. You should go home, all of you. You should just *go home*!'

Blossom gave a deep, rumbling growl.

The stranger raised his hands and backed away. 'I'm leaving, all right?' But he was still smiling. 'I'll take your advice and get the first plane back to *London*.'

Finley gave him the finger. Blossom twisted out of her grasp and ran off to chase a squirrel.

She pretended to look for Blossom's ball but was surreptitiously watching the stranger striding west along Houston. He didn't turn around. That's that, she thought. He's tall, he's incredibly handsome, he's foreign and he was trying to pick me up. And I told him to fuck off.

I probably am a lesbian.

Then she thought about Shane.

I am *not* a lesbian.

'C'mon, Blossom,' Finley called out to her. 'Enough.'

Blossom bounded back. The trail of the squirrel had apparently gone cold.

So has the trail of that guy, Finley thought, looking along the crowded street.

It had to be there.

Shane stumbled along Houston Street in the dark trying to find the door to his loft building. He'd stopped at a bar somewhere in the Village after the surf shop but he wasn't *that* fucked up. He knew the door was green.

It was after 6.30. The Saturday-evening traffic was bumper to bumper, going nowhere fast up Sixth Avenue. A skinny dog, like the kind you find scratching around in the dirt in Bali, was snuffling along the sidewalk, looking for scraps.

'Pooch!' Shane called out, but it ignored him.

The mottled brown-grey of its coat reminded him of his cattle dog Mavis. He'd had to leave her behind at his parents' little weatherboard house on Railway Parade, imprisoned by a chain-link fence. All day, in that yard with no grass, the only moment of

companionship the once-a-day appearance of the old codger banging
a can of Pal with a dented spoon.

When he got to Mundaka he'd send for Mavis. That was in his
plan. He'd need her to sit in the sand with his towel and cash, protect
his stuff from those slimy Spanish bastards.

He watched the skinny dog scuttle across the road and under
some scaffolding. He recognised the scaffolding: he had to be on the
right block. He turned and looked up at the building in front of him
and observed the blackout curtain pulled across the bank of fifth-
floor windows. Exactly the way he had left it.

But the green door was not green. It was covered with a rash of
posters, red and black. No wonder he couldn't see the fucking thing.
Someone had come and put them up in the hours he'd been pissing
his life away over a few weak-as-piss Budweisers. What did they see
in that stuff? He longed for a VB.

He scratched at one of the posters where it was covering the
keyhole. It was a poster of a girl. She had a big, cross mouth and
black hair that flipped out over her ears like a Dutch girl's cap.
WARNING: BREEDER, the poster shouted at him. What the fuck did
that mean? Was she breeding some kind of poxy disease, like AIDS
or TB? As far as he knew, the girls here were clean. Too clean to his
way of thinking, when you got down to it, which hadn't been often
enough lately. You only had to take a perve at their bathrooms,
cupboards full of deodorant and douches and bottles of lotion to
cover the smells. And all those scented candles burning away, like
offerings to the goddess of feminine hygiene. All orifices sterile,
scrubbed and flossed, and condoms under every pillow. Not like the
girls at home, hair under their arms and golden threads on their legs,
sweating like pigs in the back of the van. Sand mixed with cum,
wiped away with a towel.

This girl looked familiar, though. In fact, she looked like the girl he'd just met in the surf shop. Funny name. Like a fish. *Finley*, that was it. He scratched at the poster with his key. Nah, it couldn't be her. The girl he'd met was kind of grumpy but she didn't look like this. When she almost-smiled it was beautiful.

He managed to get his key in the lock. The hallway was dim and narrow, the cream-painted walls were scuffed and gouged in hundreds of places. The smell of old urine was pervasive. The floor of the freight elevator was covered in dust balls.

But when he reached the top floor, and the elevator doors opened, he staggered out into a space that he still couldn't believe. Three thousand square feet, all one big loft, windows right across the front. It was fucking amazing, worth at least seven grand a month, he had been told. Not that he had been asked to pay a cent of it. The stiff who owned it was named Dirk R. Runkle, a photographer of bottles of dishwashing liquid and cans of soup, who'd gone to London for six months. Shane had lucked into it—the only piece of fucking luck he'd had since he'd landed in this big sewer—through Brian Davenport.

Davenport had driven him into the city, shown him the loft, explained the deal, which was nothing, really, just make the place look lived-in, don't touch the equipment, make sure the windows are closed in a storm. Yeah, he thought, this'll do. New York City: there are worse ways to spend winter.

Fucking Brian Davenport.

Shane met him in the water at Bell's Beach last Easter, after the competition.

Come over to the States, pal. Lots of money to be made in summer teaching city dudes to surf. Big tips, like golf pros get. The waves are great. The women great-*ful*. You Aussie guys always score big-time. I guarantee a wage, give you a roof. You can fuck off south in winter or stay with me, shaping boards. What about it?

For a minute, Shane thought the guy was queer, coming on strong like that. But he learned he was just American, putting the spin on everything.

The spin is that this beach on Long Island, Montauk, is the place to get rich. Fuckwits spending one hundred grand and more on rentals for the summer. Houses with pools and big fences so you don't ever need to put your feet in the cold ocean, or ever see it. Except that surfing's the thing this summer. They all want to do it. Or paddle around with their boards, pretending to do it. Big fat guys with expense-account guts. Scrawny ones who've been sitting at their desks all year. Even a famous film producer or two, refining his technique away from the prying eyes of Malibu.

The Brian Davenport Surf School and Surf Shop was situated in a low-lying compound tucked at the back of the dunes, on the highway. You couldn't miss it because of the boards stacked like lazy teenagers against the porch. And the sports-utility vehicles cluttering up the parking lot. There was a juice bar, a yoga school and an Aveda spa. Davenport's making money hand over fist. Not only the shops, but the surfboard business. And other things Shane reckoned he was dealing on the side.

The Davenport hacienda had to have had fifteen bedrooms. Shane slept in the bunk in the garage with all the motorbikes. There was another guy in one of the bunks sometimes, Randy, a board shaper, who was visiting from the Baja California operation. He left foam dust on his pillow.

Brian always referred to Shane as 'Shane the Australian'.

Right from the start, Shane hated it.

He hated the wankers he taught. He hated being tipped, even

when it was in clumps of twenty-dollar bills. When you accepted a tip from someone, you accepted your inferiority. Australians didn't like tipping, they believed in being equal. He couldn't get used to it.

Then there were the women. He didn't like women who came on this strong. Even the scrubbers back home, you knew they'd do it with you at the drop of a towel, but they played all coy first. These ones, they grabbed you by the balls and then complained if you mussed up their hair. They fucked like they were running through their shopping lists in their heads. And they expected you to pay for everything afterwards, boring things like drinks at a bar or meals at bistros. You had to sit with them and *listen*.

'Say something Australian, Shane,' they'd giggle. 'Let's hear your funny accent!'

'How about this?' he'd reply. '*Fuck off!*'

They loved him.

And then there was Brian. Brian was a great bloke all right, king of the waves. Knew every real estate guy on Long Island. A model wife called Cassie, always parading around in a brief bikini, making eyes at all the surfers, hanging out for it, a baby attached permanently to her hip. A couple of ex-wives, a few more kids in California, one teenager a junior champion.

Busy Brian. Great Bloke. Made sure you were paid weekly, from the till, whatever you calculated. The honour system. Insisted you get fucked-up with him. Took you out in public, put his arm around you. *Buddy.* When you complained about the waves, he cut you off, saying, 'Wait for hurricane season, Shane. Not unusual for it to be eleven, twelve foot off the point.'

So he waited, like a knucklehead. Could have left for Mundaka, there and then.

Instead, he comes off a piddling three-footer into the hard

sand at Ditch Plains in September, ends up in Southampton Hospital with a ruined cartilage and with an awesome medical bill. Brian is cool about it, says he can work it off next summer. Except there isn't going to be a next summer, no fucking way. It's all bullshit. Be stuffed if he is going to spend another minute in the water with those banker wankers who think learning to surf will be as easy as repossessing family homes. All those fatsos throwing cash at him, the only time they ever manage to stand up is when their boards are flat on the sand.

So Brian Davenport closes his surfing school for the winter and goes down to Baja California, where he pays Mexicans to glass the boards he shapes. Boards with pissy little holograms on the deck. As featured in *Martha Stewart Living*.

Now Shane has no money and no cartilage in his left knee. He doesn't want to stay around Montauk in the cold, doesn't want to go with Brian to Baja and work his arse off shaping boards to pay back a debt he doesn't think he owes in the first place. So two months later he's in the city fucking *freezing*.

It was all Brian's fault.

He'd been conned.

Bloody hell, Cheyne thought as he hurried along Houston Street, not daring to look back at the girl and the dog that had attacked him. That chick's a *lunatic*.

Military outfit, savage dog, tattoo of an 'F' on her hand and some kind of obsession about yuppies.

He'd never been called yuppie scum before, but in his heart of hearts he worried that he deserved it.

He glanced across the road at the illuminated creche outside the old church, turned north into Sullivan and stopped a few doors up at a townhouse next to an Italian restaurant. The building was neatly painted; ivy tumbled from wooden boxes under each window. He put his key in the lock of the red door, its brass knocker threaded with ribbon and sleigh bells. The bells tinkled as the door closed behind him. He jogged up the narrow staircase. The floorboards underneath him groaned as he thudded onto the second-floor landing. The person in apartment 2B cracked their door a fraction and then closed it, either satisfied that Cheyne wasn't a stranger or alarmed by his menacing size.

Cheyne fumbled with the lock to his third-floor apartment, still not used to handling keys with cold hands. Inside, he threw down the video, tore off his sweater and went to the bathroom for a piss, a long stream of acid that he would have happily directed at that snippy girl rather than the porcelain.

He washed, pulled off his sweaty tee-shirt and studied himself in the bathroom mirror, checking for flaws, something he did two or three times a day. He flexed his biceps, he prodded his triceps, he examined his skin for blemishes. It was a ritual that soothed him. His muscles hadn't lost definition, his skin was still tanned, although covered in a faint rash from wearing wool. All in all, he was still a fine specimen.

He poured himself a Coke from the fridge and took it with him to the sitting room. The red light was flashing on the answering machine.

'Listen, mate, it's Phil. I hope I've woken you up, you evil wanker. I've got a joke for you: this couple needed money so they decided the wife could go out and work the streets. She comes home at three o'clock in the morning. The husband asks, "How much did

you make?" The wife says, "Two hundred dollars and fifty cents."
He says, "Who paid you the fifty cents?" She says, "All of them."
No, seriously, I'm not going to talk long as this is costing me a
fucking fortune. Call me back in a few hours when you've finished
rooting whichever starlet you're rooting this week. Have I got some
news about Avalon for you, mate! You better call me pronto. Well,
did a fucking brutal show last night. Audience of insurance salesmen.
Been on the town all night. It's 10 a.m. and I'm fucked. Beautiful
day here, not a cloud and so on. I hope you're jealous. Got to get
my beauty sleep. Bye, shithead.'

Cheyne erased the message. Phil Loop was one half of an anarchic
comedy duo, Loop de Loop, in residence at a small suburban Sydney
theatre. Cheyne had known him since school but he regretted giving
him his New York number. Phil called every second day, working
hard to make Cheyne homesick. Well, mentioning the name Avalon
was more likely to put him right off the place.

He threw some cushions off the sofa and sat down, but the
flowery fabric rose up as he sank deeply into it, making him feel like
a big weed being smothered by a bed of greedy petunias. The building
had once been an eighteenth-century townhouse, now divided into
two apartments on each floor, and the rooms were minuscule. His
bedroom was barely big enough for the double bed, which his feet
overhung, although the front room, which looked on to Sullivan
Street, was bigger. He supposed some people might call the place
'charming', with its sloping parquetry floors, white marble fireplace
(working), heavy oak doors and plaster ceiling roses, but he hated it.

He'd sublet it from another of Valerie Bone's clients, an actor,
Simon Garten, who'd gone west to do a sit-com. Garten hadn't kept
a cushion unruffled or a skirting board unstencilled. Pink cabbage
roses bloomed all over the walls, china spaniels guarded the fireplace,

picture frames filled with photographs of men embracing adorned the mantel. All other available surfaces were filled with house plants that trailed and twined from their brass pots and came with copious instructions on when to water and prune.

He felt like a giant in a fairytale princess's bedroom. But he had to grin and bear it. According to Valerie Bone, he was damn lucky. A prime location for only $1700! Why, she said, you couldn't get a damp basement on the Lower East Side for less than two grand a month. Simon hadn't wanted to rent his place to a stranger, there were the plants to consider, which was why the rent was so low. So Valerie had found him Cheyne, a nice, well-mannered Australian.

'Think of all that nature, darling,' she said she had told Simon. 'He'll know how to water a fucking African violet.'

In fact Cheyne had already, in a week, killed two of the violets and the other five didn't look too healthy. He wondered if Simon would notice if he replaced them with new ones. He couldn't remember if the ones that died were pink or purple. Maybe Simon gave them names. He wouldn't be surprised.

He downed his Coke and roughly brushed the silk curtain aside to look out the window. He felt the Coke kick in and his heart start racing again. It was Saturday night. It was Greenwich Village. He was young and unattached.

What the fuck was he doing inside then?

If it was 7 p.m. Saturday in New York, it was 11 a.m. Sunday at Sydney airport.

The immigration officer thought he'd seen the girl before. He came across a few pretty blondes in a day's work, most of them off to Bali in their sexy little sundresses, coming back a few weeks later with their hair beaded and braided, barefoot, half-washed, half-zonked out of their brains.

But this one wasn't going to Bali, he could tell. She was dressed for cold weather in a black padded vest over a black high-neck top and glossy black lycra pants with red stripes down the legs. He'd been watching her since she was way back in the line, standing there with her red-and-black duffle over her shoulder. (It was too big for cabin luggage, it should have been checked in, but he guessed she would flirt with the guys at the desk and get away with it.)

He had first noticed her inhumanly yellow hair, the colour of dry straw, the way it was shoved carelessly through the vent in the back of her black baseball cap. And then his eyes had travelled down her body, taking in the long, tubular thighs, knotted into slender knees, and the high globes of the calf muscles twitching above rumpled black socks and black and red trainers with soles the thickness of mattresses. There was something about the way she stood, listing slightly against the weight of her bag, elbow on hip, knees bent, that suggested she was still in half-stride, that at any moment she might bound to the front of the line and spring over his cubicle in her eagerness to get to the plane. An athlete, he thought, or a dancer, to have spectacular pins like those.

'Were you in the Olympics?' he asked her when she handed over her Australian passport, ticket and departure card.

'No bloody way,' she said, but smiled with a mouth full of white teeth, indicating she found the comment flattering.

He opened her passport and looked at the identification. AVALON ELLIOT, born MARYBOROUGH, AUS, 17 NOV 74. In her photograph her hair was brown and wavy. He checked the expiry date: the photograph was eight years old.

He openly examined the face under the baseball cap. Her skin was buffed a deep bronze, and her ice-green eyes with their spiky black lashes jumped out from the dark palette like startled creatures in a rainforest. Her lips were on the thin side, but she'd generously outlined them in brown and then smeared pearly gloss right out past the edges. The teeth inside were small and dazzling, probably capped. He looked down at the old photograph again. She had a nicer face eight years earlier. Now, there was something freakish about it, the way the features had been chiselled to a point, like a fox.

'I broke my nose, if you're thinking I look different,' she volunteered unexpectedly. Her voice was flat and gravelly. 'Three times since I was a kid. Had it fixed last year.'

'Nice work,' he lied. It looked like the surgeon had sliced off bumps from the bridge and left the tip of the nose stranded.

'Yeah. George Paphitis did it. You heard of him? The best bloke in Brizzy they say. He's a Greek, he still did an ace job but.'

The immigration officer, who was of Macedonian decent, smiled to himself. *Scrubber*, he thought. Rough as houses. Looks great until she opens her mouth. They're all the same, these Aussie girls. Gorgeous bodies and faces until they're twenty-one and then they turn into their mothers.

He checked the departure card. She had ticked the box beside RESIDENT DEPARTING PERMANENTLY. 'You're leaving us for good?' he asked.

'Yep. I'm going to New York.'

'Oh? You're in business?' He was fishing. He told himself it was his job. She might be a drug courier, dressed like that.

'*Show* business,' she corrected him.

'Really?' *Icecapades*, he thought. She's a skater for Disney for sure.

'I'm an actor,' she said importantly. She beamed at him. 'I can tell you're thinking you've seen me before.'

'What have you been in?'

'Well, I had a lead role in *Taliesin the Great,* that mini-series on Ten earlier this year. I was Rhiannon, Warrior Nymph. The one with the blonde hair,' she added unnecessarily. 'You must have seen it.'

The immigration officer shook his head. 'The wife probably saw it, though.'

'And I do some stunts, on the side. I was in that Jackie Chan picture shot in Melbourne, had to fall off Flinders Street Station onto a tarp. Got a role in *Star Wars*. And I'm in the Sunburst Dew ad with all the sky-divers.'

'That I've seen,' he said, impressed. 'Pays well, does it?'

'Yeah,' she said. 'Paid for my trip to New York.'

'That's a dangerous place for a pretty girl like you.'

Her eyes sparked at the compliment. 'Are you kidding? I'm a fourth dan in Karate. I can beat the shit out of any of those fuckers but.'

'And you're going to be in a movie or something?'

'Dunno. Maybe. I'm going to be with my boyfriend.'

'Lucky him,' said the immigration officer. He stamped her passport and handed it to her.

'Too right.' She shoved the documents in her duffle. 'I bet he's fucking stoked.'

'Is he an actor too?'

'Yeah, he is.'

'Anyone my wife would know?'

'She'd know him, all right. Cheyne Burdekin is his name. But it's kind of a secret from, you know, the gossip columns, so don't tell anyone.'

The immigration officer wasn't interested, anyway. He didn't understand why the girl standing in front of him would leave a great place like this for anywhere, least of all a pornographic sewer like New York. Not that he'd been there. But he'd read about it, in the *Telegraph*. When he was a kid, everyone talked about going back to Europe, students went to London or Paris, the old folks revisited their peasant lives in Sicily or Skopje. But all of them came back, singing the praises of a country where it didn't cost to walk on the beach and the government paid for your holidays. It was different these days, he admitted, but it was still a bloody fantastic place. The whole world wanted to live here; we had to fight to keep them out. And yet Australia's own children, all these ungrateful bastards, grown tall from a lifetime of good food and fresh air, educated for free in the best system in the world, were leaving the country in droves. What was wrong with them?

'What's wrong with you?' he said out loud.

'What?' She looked startled.

'Sorry,' he said. 'Nothing.'

'Oh, OK.' She showed him her teeth again. 'If you've got a spare piece of paper round here, I could give you my autograph.'

He pointed to her departure card. 'I've already got it.'

Kendra Spitz watched as the new tenant creaked along the hallway and disappeared down the staircase. Satisfied that he was descending the stairs alone, she closed her door silently.

Padding across the parquetry in her designer flip-flops, she passed through the white sitting room with its red and lime accents (Eames sofa, red, Jeff Koons plastic elephant, lime, on a pedestal) and into the kitchen, where she poured into an antique milk glass the tisane of parsley root and elderflower that had been seeping in a pot for the requisite ten minutes.

She took the warm glass into the white bathroom with its feature wall of Chinese lacquer and placed it on the old porcelain wash basin a dealer had rescued from a psychiatric ward in Pennsylvania and sold to her for $13,000. She put an approving finger into the long, tea-coloured crack in the porcelain, which gave the basin its authenticity. In fact, the piece had been too perfectly restored when she bought it: she had been forced to whack it with the sharp end of an iron to give it what she called a 'lived-in' look.

Kendra folded her arms and surveyed the stack of thick cyclamen-pink bath sheets, the various bottles of bath salts and body lotions, the French soaps, each one hand-shaped to smooth stone, the recess of oils and unguents in simple packaging, belying their great cost, the row of a dozen candles in glass with handwritten labels: *chevrefeuille, tilleul, menthe, ambre, figuier.*

Luxury. It was all about simple luxury, she thought. A bottle of milk, a soft, thick towel, a mink bathrobe, a single South Sea pearl. This was the knowledge she dispensed to her clients at $1500-a-head seminars and $5000-a-day individual workshops. Your customers want passion and truth in the little things, she'd tell them. Authenticity. Real linen, glass instead of plastic, wool and cotton and sable instead of synthetics. They want to be soothed, balanced, surrounded by aromatic fragrances and sensual colours. They like new technology if it's simple to use but they crave old things with integrity. They are pragmatic, harassed, idea hungry. If you consider that most trends have a fifteen-month lifespan...

She had to stop herself. Her presentation was never out of her head, running through her brain like a subterranean stream. To think, fifteen years ago she'd been selling advertising space for a financial magazine, cooped up in a little cubicle, no one noticing the sharp cut of her yellow suit, the padded shoulders and tight little skirt. No one noticing the Chief Executive Officer stuff she had in her. It had only taken one good idea to get her out of there. A hiccup of the brain, as if it had turned ninety degrees in her skull.

People need to know what's next.

Her job was catching the waves before they came into shore. *Coolsurfing* she called it. She now had a team of five trend fore-casters, *coolsurfers,* working under her, combing the world for clues to the next fabric, the next shoe, the next kind of car people would want to drive. She was recruiting people all the time, East Village hipsters and Palm Beach old-timers, who polled their friends about attitudes and urges. Moods and feelings would be catalogued and collated for corporate presentations and the newsletter, *Prophesee*, that subscribed for two grand a year.

Sometimes it was exhausting being so ahead of everything. Kendra was forty-seven (and looked ten years younger, thanks to knowing ahead of time about miraculous anti-ageing products and treatments) but some days she felt like Methuselah.

She couldn't remember why she had gone into the bathroom. She took her tea into the sitting room and took a bottle of rum off the chrome cocktail cart. She poured a good dash of it into the glass. Ah, *that's* what she needed. She couldn't wait until people went back to drinking the hard stuff, but she knew the nature craze had a few years left in it yet. A good recession would get people back on the booze. It was coming. It would affect business, of course, because corporations that were in trouble today didn't have the resources to think about tomorrow. By then she would long be out of it. She was thinking of gardening, going back to the soil, to the roots—if not her roots, then someone else's. But she wasn't sure. Gardening was such a *today* kind of trend. Would it last? She didn't want to find herself stuck out in west Connecticut with twenty acres of rose bushes only to find the bottom had dropped out of the aromatherapy business.

The truth was, she didn't know. All those trend forecasters on staff, all the teenagers she recruited, the trips to fabric fairs and lifestyle expositions, the symposiums on style, the rattling around in Moroccan bazaars, the Spanish flea markets, the Hawaiian surfing carnivals, the forays into the former Czechoslovakia for communist artifacts, the massages and mud-packs, the fashion parades in Paris, Milan, London, New York, *Grozny*, wherever, the hanging out at malls observing fat slobs stuff their faces with fast food and scratch their Gap-clad backsides, all this investigation and documentation— it didn't tell her anything except that human beings were a capricious lot who sometimes, by sheer chance, formed themselves into groups that appeared to want the same thing.

She was somewhat relieved that her upstairs neighbour Simon Garten had gone to California. She had recruited Simon to clue her in on the gay point of view on different issues, but his responses had been predictable, boring. Everyone loves Martha Stewart. Clog dancing is the 'latest' thing. The gays were 'off' hydrangeas and into branches of dogwood. He was always calling her with dreary tidbits. She needed some younger blood. Perhaps the new neighbour upstairs might oblige.

She should have called out to him, asked him in for a drink. He had been moving fast but she caught a glimpse of his face. Strikingly handsome, if you liked that sort of thing, good-looking enough to be one of those young hustlers Simon sometimes brought home. But there was a swagger to him she'd never seen in any of Simon's furtive boys. He looked confident. He had posture. Good coat. Hip shoes. Hogan, if she wasn't mistaken.

A definite candidate for some coolsurfing.

'Hey, baby mine.'

Finley threw her satchel behind the counter and went over to where DJ BJ was spinning vinyl and gave him a high five. 'Hey, BJ. What's new?'

'Shit's new, that's what.' He took the LP off the turntable and threw it on a pile. He replaced it with another, spun it for ten seconds. 'Man, that's bad! It'll clear a dance floor in five seconds flat.'

It was 8.15 by the time Finley had taken Blossom home and walked back over to Sputnik on the Bowery. The record store was packed, even for a Saturday night. Kids drifted in and out until midnight, 1 a.m., when it was cool to go to the clubs. All the DJs dropped in, looking for new material. The store only sold vinyl. Techno House. Disco House. Tribal House. Hard House. French House. Domestic House. Deep House. Acid Trance. Progressive Trance. Euro Trance. Goa Trance. Vladivostok Trance. Whatever. Finley counted sixteen people bent intently over the stacks of LPs. There were three people looking at tee-shirts. Some goon was berating a staffer for not carrying The Goo Goo Dolls. Boy, had he come to the wrong place.

Finley hated working two jobs, but she needed both to make the rent. Three nights at Sputnik, four days at Wipeout. It was too much. Not that she had anything else to do. She had no ambition, one of the things that had driven Natalie mad.

A New Yorker with no ambition. She was a freak.

'Have you heard the new Turgid Felch?' Finley asked BJ.

'What?' The DJ frowned at her, lifted his headphones.

'Turgid Felch. It's around here somewhere. Hey, Blender,' she called out to a skinny teen in a Radiohead tee-shirt who was heading for the stock room. 'Can you find the Turgid Felch for BJ? It came in Thursday.'

'Sure thing.' Blender gave her a thumbs-up. He was a nice kid, obsessed by movies, music, computers and, she suspected, *her*—in that order.

Someone gangly and smelling of weed put his arms around her. 'Finley, Finley, Finley! Long time no see!' he exclaimed.

She elbowed him in the stomach. 'Shit happens, Rockwell, what can I say?'

It was her boss. He was a runt, a white boy with matted dreads, barely twenty-one. Daddy had bought him a record store and a little studio on East 9th Street because he couldn't decide whether he wanted to be a recording executive or a fashion photographer. Actually, Rockwell was OK. He never cared when she was late or if she didn't turn up at all, like last night, when she hadn't felt like it after a few hours dealing with the Barneys at Wipeout. He'd just rope in a customer to work the cash register. Most of the people in Sputnik as good as lived there anyway. Away from Sputnik, they just lived virtually, intravenously hooked to their computer games.

Finley went back up to the counter and kissed Esther on the cheek. She was spinning Acquaviva with one hand and swiping a credit card with the other. Some people got the two girls mixed up. Both were small and strong, short dark hair, fair complexion. But the similarity stopped there. Esther was sweet, compliant. You could never call Finley those things.

'Guess what? I'm spinning at Contaminated tonight after BJ,'

Esther shouted above the noise. 'Coming?'

'It's Blossom's birthday. I'm going home to watch a movie on TV with her.'

'You can bring her.'

'She doesn't like Acid Trance.'

Esther looked at Finley more closely. 'Is that a smile I see on your face?'

Finley shrugged.

'It's a guy! I knew it!'

'No way.' Finley took a stack of LPs from Darcy, a kid who DJ'd Tuesday nights at Aneurism on Crosby Street.

'I don't see you at the club anymore,' he teased as she took his cash. 'You're hurting my feelings.'

'Well, yeah,' she said, counting the twenties into the drawer, 'I've been sort of out of it.'

She handed back the albums and he put them in his backpack. She closed the register. When she looked up he was still standing there, leaning on his backpack and staring at her.

'Don't give me that look, Darcy,' she said. 'How old are you? Nineteen?'

'You don't like nineteen-year-old men?'

'Yeah, I don't like being homework.'

'*Wo!* I love a woman with a mean tongue! What else can you do with it?'

'Move it, Darcy, there's a line forming behind you.'

He hoisted his backpack and gave her a gummy smile. Then he raised his voice until it floated in a little pocket of air above the thudding bass of Neuro Sturgeon. 'So it's true what they say, Finley? You're a lesbian?'

A dozen curious faces, eleven sets of eyebrows (one was shaved), fifteen nose rings and one tattooed chin turned to look at Finley. Smirking.

'I'm not a fucking lesbian!' she hissed at Darcy.

'Whichever way you want it, baby,' he shrugged and saluted her.

'*What?*' she demanded of the room, angry.

The faces kept smirking. This was fine sport. Not that the word 'lesbian' meant anything to them. Who gave a fuck what you were? But denying you were a lesbian—vehemently—was offensive to certain powerful factions east-of-Broadway.

'I am not a fucking lesbian, OK?' Finley thumped her fist on the counter and sent a stand of Chinese fortune bracelets flying. She raised her voice. 'Did you all hear that?' She glared at the room. Only BJ, with his headphones on, was not listening.

'And you, Darcy, fuck off too!' Finley turned back towards him. But he had gone.

'Got any change?' Esther waved a twenty at Finley and pointed to the open cash register. 'I'm all out.'

Finley dug in her pocket. She pulled out some notes and swapped them for the twenty. Something dropped to the floor. She bent down and picked it up. It was the card Natalie had given her.

She studied it for clues.

LARA DINARDO.

Probably another dyke.

A small, round woman with a rockabilly haircut and a vintage copy of *Dusty in Memphis* in her chunky arms stood on the other side of the counter.

'*Breeder!*' she hissed.

Lara Dinardo lay in bed with her arms around her favourite teddy bear and the speakerphone on. It was a sunny Sunday morning, the yellow canaries were hopping about in their cage and the world's highest-paid TV star was on the line.

'I don't know what you're going to do about her, Brad. If she's returned your engagement ring…What did she say?…Oh, you only spoke to her press agent?…*He* returned the ring? Well, where is she?…I see…It's only a hotel for Christ's sake, it's not a fucking bordello…Look, I wouldn't worry about him. Like he fucks all his leading ladies, what's new? *Huge* cock…I'm not going to tell you how I know…What do you mean I'm trying to make you feel inadequate? So he's got a few inches on you? He only gets a measly five a picture…My advice is to get to Page Six before she does. You dumped *her*. No one would believe she dumped *you*…Tonight? Well, I have a date but you know I'm always here for you…I don't believe you can remember that! You're making me blush…Just a *talk*, OK? Your head in my lap like the old days?…No, I didn't mean *that*…Get Sergio to drop you round at eight. You still have Sergio, don't you? Well, whatever…'

Lara put the phone down. *Well.* Bradford Ford running back to her with his tail between his legs! This was going to be interesting.

She abandoned her bear and switched off the speakerphone. She slid into embroidered mules and scurried naked to the bathroom. After she'd had a pee she posed in front of the mirror. Eat shit, Bradford. I'm cuter than that fiancée of yours. Look at this bod! I could have cast *me* instead of her in that gladiator picture and I'd have been a damn sight more believable with an asp around my arm. She looked as if she had an asp up her *butt*.

If you read those showbiz magazines—and she did, religiously, it was her job—people were always writing in asking whatever happened to Biff, the cute little star of 'Mary Brown Is Coming to Breakfast', the long-running seventies CBS sit-com. American kids had grown up with Biff, lost their first molars with her, cried with her when her puppy died, cheered when she kicked the sour old school librarian in the shin. Golden-haired Biff was America's sweetheart but she disappeared from the television screens about the same time as she grew breasts. Biff was shipped off to the Netherlands to live with a Dutch family as an exchange student, and her TV family would read correspondence from her as they gathered around the faux log fire at night. Soon, however, she stopped writing. A cute Vietnamese child was fostered into the family as replacement. In a later episode, daringly topical, Biff was reported to have been kidnapped and murdered by the Baader-Meinhof gang on a school excursion to Germany. The viewers were not to know that the real-life Biff had gone on to make *Schoolgirl with a Whip* and other provocative titles in a hotel room in Las Vegas.

And here she was, still with a whip, but of a different kind.

I've got power over you, Bradford Ford, and all the others like you. One or two phone calls and I could turn America's favourite television doctor-hunk into an AIDS-blighted homeless person or a greedy stockbroker that no one will love. You are just roles, parts, and not even the sum of them. A serial identity crisis. I dish out who you are, like God giving out faces in Heaven.

It's a damn sight more fun than sitting in a cold room in white stockings and a gym slip waiting for your leading man to find his erection.

Lara pulled on a robe, trotted to the kitchen and made herself a decaf Costa Rica Organic, which she then took to her desk. She lit a cigarette and opened the file she had brought home from the office.

She smoothed out the crumpled poster it contained and laid it flat on the desk. WARNING: BREEDER.

She'd noticed it around the neighbourhood, thought the face looked interesting. And then it had appeared in the mail, sent to her by that caterer woman. Well, more unlikely things had happened. Lara had once been knocked into the gutter by a speeding messenger on a bike—now he was the one and only Bradford Ford, the star of 'Sutures', currently renegotiating for $1.5 million an episode.

She'd get the girl in. It was never a waste of time. If she had it, she had it. You could always send her off to a coach for a voice class. If she didn't have it, you billed the client anyway. It was the thrill of the chase. If you found 'em, your name was inextricably linked to theirs. Brad and Lara.

She turned to her desk and picked up the eight-by-ten glossy photograph of a male actor that Valerie Bone had sent her, then laid it out next to the 'breeder' and contemplated it. She liked the interrupted right eyebrow, the way the two halves didn't meet, as if they were slices of landscape skewed by an earthquake. It suggested a kind of recklessness she could work with.

Of course, the eyebrow could be an affectation, the slash created by a razor or a strip of wax and weekly maintained to give its wearer a rakish air. It wasn't unknown for actors to mutilate themselves to make their faces memorable. There was the guy with the half-chewed ear, got his friend's dog to do it because he thought it would give him a better shot at gangster roles. They'd do anything, these people whose grinning, pearly-teethed likenesses filled her filing cabinets and overflowed into boxes on her floor.

This one was interesting, though. Had already appeared in a television co-production with TNT, something about a Welsh wizard. The usual thing, shot in Australia, international cast. The script was lousy and his American accent was shaky. Still, you didn't come across one this good-looking every day, one who'd give Brendan Fraser a run for his money. Same bow-shaped mouth as Brendan, almost too pretty. Audiences wouldn't trust him unless he had a flaw.

She stretched out her arm and touched the photograph with a pink-tipped finger, traced the break in his eyebrow. *Hmmmm.* The eyebrow definitely saved him. She could work with it.

The Grimley brothers, Derek and Damian, had liked his picture when she'd shown it to them last night. Well, she thought so. Half the time she couldn't understand what they were saying, even if she understood every word. In the beginning, they had hated everyone she'd put in front of them to the point where she feared they would fire her.

'Don't worry, Ducky,' Damian had reassured her over burritos at Taco Bell. 'We *love* to hate actors. We get off on it, don't we, Derek? You should see our Y-fronts at the end of the day. They could walk out onto the street and hail a taxi all by themselves!'

She had no idea what they were talking about.

But this Burdekin guy—they'd admitted to 'going all shivery' when they saw his headshot.

'We like these big antipodean brutes,' Damian had said afterwards. 'I bet he's queer.'

'They always are,' said Derek. 'When they're from Sydney.'

'Who always are *what*?'

'Queer, Ducky. A nancy boy. A *poove.*'

'Maybe he's the sensitive type.'

'You call it that, dear, if you like.'

She put the photograph back on the pile. Those crazy Brits! But what if the Grimleys were right about his sexual orientation? These

Australians were usually macho types. There was something a bit suspicious about it. Look at *Priscilla, Queen of the Desert*. You couldn't be too sure. She didn't want to go down his road if it was going to turn into a dead end. Or a fucking roundabout like Brad, never quite making it into the driveway.

Well, there was only one way to find out.

Shane woke at midday on Sunday, rolled out of bed and stumbled down to one end of the loft to grab a carton of milk out of the Sub-zero. He took it with him to the bathroom, had a piss in the stainless steel cistern, grunted at the way his stream foamed like beer, didn't bother to flush, and then took the carton with him to the bed, on a platform smack in the centre of the room.

He threw himself on the bed and chugged on the milk. The loft was all glass facing south, a view over rooftops and water towers to the twin stacks of the World Trade Center. He liked the familiar sensation of being way above everything, and imagined himself standing on the peak of a tidal wave that was barrelling up the Hudson, taking with it everything in its path, the Statue of Liberty, the Twin Towers, that fucking building with the red neon umbrella. Mate, a few tokes, and he could ride that wave all the way to Nova Scotia.

He took some cigarette papers out of his pocket and rolled a joint along his left leg. The knee still creaked whenever he flexed it. His thighs had lost bulk, the muscles in his arms had atrophied from lack of paddling. If he did ever manage to catch a wave, he'd probably surf it like a girl.

He took a deep drag of the joint and looked around the room.

He had to get off his bum and raise some cash. The place was full of valuable lighting equipment and computers, and the guy collected old cameras, dozens of them, which he displayed on shelves along one big wall. Maybe he could rent a stall at the market and sell some of the stuff. He'd be gone before anyone ever knew.

But, nah. That was the kind of thing junkies did. Shane Dekker didn't need to stoop so low. Pity none of his mates back home had any spare cash. And he'd rather die than ask the old man. And he wasn't going to work in a bar, do shit stuff. It just wasn't going to happen.

Maybe there was another way. Everyone knew the story of the male model, handsome guy, who'd been riding his motorbike through a Manhattan pedestrian crossing, this woman steps out, he brushes her coat with his leg, maybe, but she fakes a fall, goes all hysterical. The next day, she recognises him from a Bloomingdales ad, claims psychological damage, takes him for everything he's worth. Fucking bitch.

You could do that here. Tear a fingernail on a doorknob, sue the fucking building for a million bucks. I could fucking well lie down in the middle of Sixth Avenue in the full light of day and a truck would back out right over me, that's how crappily they drive. I'd roll out of the way, get a little dusty maybe, pretend he'd ruined my leg. Call a lawyer. Make my fortune.

It was worth considering.

He took another toke of the joint. The sky outside the loft was fluffy as a puppy's belly. He could see the tarps on the scaffolding across the road flapping in the brisk breeze. Shit, it looked like the wind might come around.

He jumped off the bed, logged on to Dirk's Powermac and connected to the Internet. He tapped into his Bookmarks and pulled up the Interactive Marine Observations. A map of the northeast filled the screen and he clicked on point ALSN6. There it was, his little Ambrose, the buoy off Ambrose Lighthouse near Rockaway. The readings for wind direction, wind speed, gusts, air temperature and swell were listed hourly so that he could follow the ebb and tide of the waves.

Fuck. Not bad, considering how choppy it was yesterday morning. Ambrose was showing an onshore stream coming through. If the wind swung around offshore tonight and backed off, there might be a good wave by tomorrow morning. And it would be a good wave for a beginner. He thought of Finley.

He dug in his pants pocket and pulled out the scrap of paper she'd given him with the surf shop's number on it. He wondered if she'd really come with him. Most girls stayed on the beach, minding the towels.

She looked a bit small and frail.

Well, what the fuck, he could only try.

Finley was not in one of her better moods. It was midday and she barely had time to squeeze in a workout before checking in at Wipeout at two. Worse, the changing room was full of pink women chattering about diets and the latest devices for keeping you informed about the status of your on-line auctions wherever you were, even in the powder room of Henri Bendel.

O, brave new world that has such morons in it! She wished that extreme body contact was permitted in the Mo Bo class. Her toes tingled with the anticipation of a few well-placed kicks to the back of those perfectly coiffed heads.

She could feel the pink women looking at her as she undressed.

She tore apart the velcro on the ankle holster and threw it on the bench with her Timberland boots and socks. Hadn't they ever seen a box cutter before? She looked up and caught the eye of a blonde all decked out in shimmering spandex. 'What?' Finley asked her, fiercely.

The blonde looked away.

Scum, Finley thought. Swarming over the neighbourhood like vermin, throwing wads of cash at the realtors. Women in their twenties, looking like forty-five, with their shiny ponytails and expensive shoulder bags, all in pale pink, pale blue, white for fuck's sake, filling the air with the squeak of cell phone buttons being pressed and the latest stinking fragrance from Calvin Klein. Screwing the micro-economy below Houston Street with their profligate ways, the eight-dollar tubs of sorbet from Dean & Deluca, the $500 bed sheets, and three dollars for a tomato at the Korean Deli without even checking the change.

There were now dress shops where they used to sell cheese, Belgian restaurants where there were second-hand bookstores and cinema multiplexes where once neighbours tended gardens of hollyhocks and runner beans. And women in pink leotards where warriors should be.

She looked around the changing room, a few curtains drawn around a bench and an upright mirror. In the old days, when she was the only girl, she'd get changed with the men. But Mo Bo was no longer an obscure Burmese martial arts discipline practised since ancient times by the monks of Putao who dwelt among the finger mountains of the Himalayas. It was now a half-hour infomercial starring a beefy former professional wrestler who had discovered eastern spirituality, a set of four video tapes sold by street hawkers throughout the city for the special price of $29.99 and a collection of exercise clothes in karmic pinks, oranges and purples, sewn together by the children of Guatemala who earned a spiritual twenty-five cents a day.

The pink women admired each other, painted their toenails, applied mascara. It was like a high school reunion. Some women never got over high school, Finley reflected, as if gathering in twittering packs and sharing lipstick sealed some secret pact of girlhood. Finley had hated school, and had worn black lipstick and a scowl to set herself apart.

She pulled on loose white cotton pants and tied a frayed, sleeveless army shirt under her breasts. She contained the flip of her hair with a piece of fabric wrapped around her head Caribbean-style. One of the women stared at her bushy armpits, aghast.

Finley had been practising Mo Bo for four years, long before the current craze, when there were only four or five in a class and their teacher, Ra Ke Woon, barely spoke English. Now, he had written three books on eastern philosophy, gave lectures at the New School and welcomed everyone, even those who confused his strenuous classes with the Mo Bo franchise. Naturally, the franchise had tried to kill his business, claiming ownership of the name, but Ra Ke had fought them in court and was fighting them still. 'No one can own the name of your heart,' he protested.

But Finley thought they could. The bastards could buy anything. They could take a ritual that took centuries to perfect and turn it into a fad or a dirty joke with a hollow punch line. In her mind she could see the Burmese monks going through their exercises on stone floors, their feet cracked like parched earth from walking barefoot, their hands callused from scrubbing floors, their stomachs distended from fasting and their mouths dry from chanting. Every chop of the hand or twist of the leg was infused with meaning, piety, pain…and here was a fucking 300-pound wrestler in candy pink Mo Bo leggings with black dragons down the side punching the air and pumping his thighs to 'Eye of a Tiger' and exhorting America to get up off their butts and 'kick ass'. (*Mo Bo: Kick Ass* TM.)

Finley stuck by Ra Ke, even though her instinct was to flee once the pink women arrived. Her muscles had learned the fluid movements of the art; she had punched and kicked her way through a rainbow of belts to violet. And she was one of only three people attending classes whom Ra Ke had initiated with warrior names.

'Good afternoon, Sha Mu.' Ra Ke bowed low as Finley crouched in front of him, the tips of her fingers touching the dusty floor. The loft was used for ballet classes at other times and a barre ran along one mirrored wall.

'Good afternoon, Wei-Kei,' she responded, using his teaching name.

She stretched out a leg and flexed the ankle and then raised her foot so that all her weight was on one thigh. In the mirror, she watched the back of Ra Ke's smooth brown head, the veins like ridges on a walnut shell, the way the slender tail of the black-blue taipan tattooed down his spine began with a flick at the base of his skull and disappeared into the elastic of his cotton pants, emerging, she knew, with a fork of tongue at the bone of his coccyx. She had traced the snake with her own tongue, many times, in the early days when their cultural exchanges involved bodily fluids. It had been two years since she had practised the Insinuating Cobra and the Agile Orang-utan in his Elizabeth Street basement: now he owned the whole building and there was a shop underneath that sold handknits from Paris.

She had been sent off by him to a higher spiritual plane, one that did not involve sweaty copulations on stained futons, but she remembered his soft mouth with its sweet, fungussy breath and the fingers that kneaded her pressure points like cats' paws. For a while there, she had imagined taking Blossom with her to Burma, and living with Ra Ke on a mountain top under a pergola draped with saffron silk and lotus flowers, ministering to him with taro soup and yak oil and burning fragrant juniper branches to ward away malevolent spirits. But Ra Ke liked the espresso at Cafe Gitanes too much, and the stadium seating at Loew's Cineplex and the Staten Island Ferry, which he would take repeatedly, like a child.

In her experience, men were never what they should be. Carpenters carried around drafts of novels in their toolkits. Firemen wanted to be actors. Ra Ke should have been a peasant, but his mother was a lawyer.

But Shane, the surfer she'd met yesterday—he seemed so *authentic*. Salt of the earth. Salt of the *sea*. She couldn't imagine him suddenly developing the urge to write a novel or become an actor or direct a movie using digital video. That made him different from 100 per cent of the other men she knew. Just a man and his surfboard, pure and unadulterated.

She tried to make her mind go blank and not think about him. Did he really mean that he would take her surfing? Would he call? He was too distracting.

Kick. Lunge. Thrust. Punch. Crouch. Kick. Lunge. She was the mirror image of Ra Ke, standing in her usual place, directly in front of him. She reversed all his moves, rolling her hips in sway with his. Although his rhythm stayed smooth as silk, his breathing barely perceptible, she could feel a heightened intensity. She pushed him, put an aggressive edge on her movements, jerking and panting to let him know. He quickened the pace and took her through a crescendo of high kicks, until her legs tingled; her blood ran hot and effervescent. She knew the rest of the class had been left way behind.

Afterwards, one of the pink ladies was panting so hard she sounded like the soundtrack of a porn movie. The poor thing thought she was seeking enlightenment, when it was only *lightening* she needed. Finley didn't know why the pink women didn't just stay home and take diet pills. There was a new one on the market that any doctor would prescribe. You could lose 5 per cent of your body weight over one year if you combined the pill with a low-fat diet. The side effects were nausea, constipation, dizziness, night sweats and possible kidney failure. Finley had heard women in the street talking about how they couldn't wait to get hold of it. You could sell people anything if it was bad enough for them.

'God, Shelda, I feel five pounds lighter already,' Finley overheard one young woman say to another as they changed into their street clothes. 'Do you think I can lose another two by tomorrow?'

Finley couldn't help herself. 'The really great thing about Mo Bo,' she told the room as she crouched over the laces on her ochre yellow boots, 'is that you get a really big, strong butt in no time at all.'

Cheyne intended to spend Sunday afternoon watching the Grimleys' *All's Well That Ends Well,* but he was defeated by tiredness after a night of bar-hopping. Vaguely hungover, he had low tolerance for a play about misplaced affection and confused identity. During the scene where the corrupt cop Bertram (banished to a precinct in the South Bronx) is tricked into thinking he is seducing the pretty Latina ho Diana, when it's really his bitch, the Korean manicurist Helen, in disguise, he fell into a deep and untroubled sleep. Blue light filled the room. The video of *All's Well* ran its course and rewound itself.

The phone rang, a deep burr. He grunted. It stopped and then buzzed again, infiltrating his shapeless dreams. He reached for the receiver without opening his eyes. 'Hello. Hello…*Valerie?*'

Avalon could barely hear his voice.

'Cheyne, it's me,' she called down the wire.

'Valerie?'

'No, it's Avalon, you dickhead.'

'Valerie? Who *is* this?'

The line was thick with electronic noise. Avalon thumped the top of the phone box. The static got worse. She couldn't hear Cheyne at all now, just a loud *whooshing* sound. She clicked the receiver cradle a few times. The phone started beeping.

There appears to be a receiver off the hook. Please check…

'*Shit!*' She hung up. Now she had to punch in the elaborate code on her phone card again. It was Sunday morning in LA. Sunday afternoon in New York. Monday morning in Sydney. Fuck, it was confusing. There was a line of barely patient people behind her, most of them from her flight and, like her, anxious to contact friends and family waiting in New York who did not know that the 11 a.m. from LA had been delayed. After an enraged group of passengers had stormed the check-in desk and demanded to know how late the flight would be, the ground staff had announced it might be 'a few hours' and had distributed food vouchers. Avalon had gone to a kiosk and bought a phone card. Poor Cheyne, she couldn't have him standing at the luggage carousel for hours.

She pressed in Cheyne's number again. The line was busy. Was he still waiting for her to speak? *Shit* again. She clicked the receiver a few more times and then hung up.

It was only later, after her third unsuccessful attempt to reach Cheyne and her third Bass Ale in a departure lounge bar that she thought, *Who the fuck is Valerie?*

Shane stacked the two boards against the subway car window and pushed his backpack against them. He took Finley's bag and jammed it on top, between the seats. Then they sat together on a three-seat bench, one seat between them, facing a Chinese woman curled up asleep on the bench opposite.

'The whole fucking car's asleep,' said Shane over the thud of the train as it pulled out of West 4th Street. 'Mutants.'

Finley looked around. He was right. There were five other people in the car, all slumped into their puffy jackets, snoozing in rhythm to the train's sideward sway. 'It *is* 6 a.m.,' she reminded him. 'Maybe they've been working all Sunday night.'

'Work?' Shane pondered.

He seemed in a bad mood. When he met her on the platform his eyes were half-closed, his mouth sulky. He unzipped her board, borrowed from Wipeout, and shook his head in disapproval. 'Too long,' he said. Then he made her take out all her gear so he could check it. While she was stuffing the wetsuit back into her duffle, the train drew up and he left her on the platform, scrambling to catch up with him.

They rode a few stations together silently. At East New York station, a cop got on, his radio crackling, stared at Shane for two stops and then moved to another car.

The train suddenly emerged into daylight. Shane pulled his beanie off his head and shook his hair. 'Hate the fuckin' dark,' he mumbled. He studied the grey sky for a while. 'Wind's dropped.'

'Is that good?'

'Yeah, the swell's about four foot but I was worried about the chop. It should have gone around by now.'

'Gone around?'

'Offshore.'

'How do you know that?'

'Get the buoy report off the Internet. This place I'm staying at, the guy's got a fucking awesome Mac. There's a lighthouse out in the ocean transmits wave heights every few minutes. I can sit at the fucking thing all day and watch what the swell's doing. I can watch what the swell's doing anywhere in the fucking world. Not that it does me any good.'

'Why not?'

'I'm looking at a twenty foot at Maverick's, really *gouging*, you know and I'm stuck here with these tubes of piss.'

'Have you ever ridden, like, really *big* waves?'

'Rode a twenty-foot swell at Bell's one Easter. Un-fucking-believable. Once-in-a-lifetime stuff. It was like falling off a cliff, you know? I was, like, facing *death.* My feet were glued to the board by suction. And the monster was coming after me, like fucking Moby Dick. *Roaring.* Like I was an insect or something. But I fucking beat the bastard. I was *ripping.* Stayed on in the white water too. Then these guys came and beat me up.'

'Beat you up?'

'Yeah. Only had a short board, so I borrowed a ten-footer, right off the guy's roofrack when he'd gone to take a piss. His mates weren't too happy with me.'

'I bet.'

'Smashed an eye socket.'

'*Shit.*'

'Yeah, I was lucky they weren't *really* mad. They were just showing me what's what. I mean, twenty fucking feet! You'd trade in your grandmother for a board.'

'Does it get violent out there?'

'Shit yeah. You get some kook dropping in, it's like blood on the water. These tourists come and it's like, *get out or bleed.* I mean, there are traffic rules. If you steal another bloke's wave you've got to be prepared for the consequences. A while back, Nat Young got smashed up real bad on the north coast when he threw a punch at some grommet for dropping in. The kid's dad went at him like a kung-fu fighter. Fucking *Nat Young* of all people. Ended up in intensive care. It's fucking *vicious* out there.'

'Have you ever windsurfed?'

'Are you kidding? That's girls' stuff.'

'What about snowboarding.'

'Nah. Love to try though.'

'I've done it.'

'You have?'

'Where I come from, Oneonta, it's northwest of New York City. All the kids are doing it. It's, like, *fierce.* Three Christmases ago, I got my boyfriend to take me to some slopes in Vermont where it's'— she searched for one of Shane's words—'*ripping.* It was wild.'

'How was he?'

'Who?'

'Your boyfriend.'

'What do mean?'

'On the snowboard. Was he any good?'

'Average.'

Shane smiled as if he were pleased with her answer. 'How were you?'

'Well, I didn't disgrace myself. I went off an eight-foot peak and landed on my feet.'

'I'm impressed.'

'Beginner's luck.'

'Waves are different. They shift. It's not like a ski run. It's not like *static.* They've got a pulse. Like a heartbeat, they can go *dum dum dum* or *da dum da dum da dum*. You've got to know how they're beating. You can't know it first time.'

'You don't think I can handle it?'

'We'll see.'

'I've got great balance.'

'That helps.'

'I'm a violet belt in Mo Bo.'

'What's that?'

'It's an ancient Burmese form of martial arts.'

'Useless.'

'Why?'

'Didn't I just explain? You can't compare the earth to the sea. You do those kung fu exercises, you've got gravity working with you. But on a wave, it's fucking useless unless you know how to find your own energy curve and fast. You come off a wave and you get sucked down by the earth's gravity but you've got to resist, otherwise you're pulled under or smashed on the reef. You're riding the whole drift of the universe and you've got to fight it, if only for twenty seconds. What you want to do is fly across the face of it or through it or over it but not *down*. The wave is a being and you are a being and there's all kind of shit happening. You're just a fucking ant being siphoned into this awesome vortex of spinning water. But you are the being with willpower, it's you who makes the choice, it's you who has to find the moment when you and the wave are shooting in harmony through space. The wave can't do it. And you can't do it if you *think*. You have to *feel*. It's all sense, like you're a molecule of spray coming off the wall. Your nerves are more than tingling, they're *shredded*. But when you find that fucking moment, the balance of you and all existence on the planet's curve—man, it's the godhead. And you want to paddle straight back out and find it again.'

'Wow,' Finley said.

Shane's eyes were dewy under his drift of hair. 'I'd sit by a puddle in the middle of the road if there was the chance of a wave.'

'Do you think I could just…watch you today?'

'You're scared? I thought you were tough. All those martial arts and all.'

'I *am* tough. I'd beat the hell out of a grommet if he dropped in on *me*.'

'Well, then, you might have your uses after all.'

This time when the phone buzzed it *was* Valerie.

'Cheyne, darling, get yourself out of bed right now and go run around the block or whatever you do to wake up. You've got an audition today.'

Cheyne shot up in the bed. 'I have?'

'Lara Dinardo just called. The Grimleys want to see you at two. So find a pen and take down this address.'

He memorised it.

'Now, you'll be reading for Jack Worthing. Make sure you don't shave this morning. I want you to exude sexuality.'

'Maybe I should skip the shower too.'

'That's up to you, darling. It depends on what you were doing last night.'

'Not enough, unfortunately.'

'Well, the girls are going to be hanging off the chandeliers once you get this role. And you're going to get this role. So get going!'

At ten, an unwashed and unshaven Cheyne dashed up to Barnes & Noble on 8th Street to buy a copy of *The Importance of Being Earnest*, intending to scan it before he left for the audition. He stopped at a deli for the *Times* and two bagels. He didn't really like bagels but eating bagels for breakfast was such a New York thing to do, he couldn't resist. Besides, he could practise his American accent on the guy at the register.

Howya doin'? Wazzup?

It was bloody seductive, they way they said things. No wonder they'd been such a success at cultural imperialism. He'd sound like a native in no time.

'You too, buddy,' he responded when the deli guy mumbled *Haveaniceday*. See, he had already dropped the *mate*.

He clutched the *Times* and grasped the brown bag full of bagels and paper towel and plastic knives and packets of mayo and any other thing the deli man had tossed in there. He was astounded at the waste of paper. Whole Amazonian rainforests were doled out each day at New York deli registers. When he'd pointed this out one day to a Korean stuffing a bag with a handful of napkins, the guy just sneered at him and said, 'What's it to you, jerkoff?'

He stumbled down MacDougal Street towards Washington Square, wishing that he'd worn sunglasses and, conversely, a pair of gloves. He couldn't get used to the fact that blazing blue skies meant freezing weather. The glare gave him a headache.

At the corner of West 4th and MacDougal, Cheyne slowed down, his curiosity piqued by several white trailers that lined the street along Washington Square. Crews were loading and unloading tripods and cables from trucks half a block long. A rack of costumes sat on the sidewalk, unguarded. An old yellow cab, the kind you see in movies but never in real life, was parked at the intersection. Two cops on horseback conferred in the middle of the road.

As he passed them, Cheyne looked at the trailer doors to see if any actors' names were posted. Nothing. One door was wide open to the street, but all he could see was an empty chair. He moved on, not wanting to appear as curious as he was.

At the corner of Washington Place, a caterer was standing behind a trestle table tossing a salad, cigarette dangling from her dark-stained lips.

'Hi there,' she said.

Me? Cheyne looked behind him. There was no one. He smiled at her, encouraged, and stopped. 'Hmm. That looks *great*.' He reached over and picked up a meatball.

'Watch it,' she said. She tried to smack his hand with the back of her wooden spoon but he was too swift. 'Brunch'll be ready in five minutes. Do you think you'll be able to contain yourself?'

'Not if you keep standing there like that.' The woman was quite beautiful, in a curious kind of way he couldn't put his finger on.

She looked up and squinted at him. 'That's not going to get you anywhere, buster.'

'Not even a little nibble?'

'You'll have to wait your turn with the rest of the crew. I don't care how good-looking you are.'

Cheyne laughed. 'You think I'm crew?'

She put her spoon down and frowned. 'Not crew, cast. You're not?'

'No, just passing by.'

'Oh, you're GP. You're not supposed to be eating my meatballs.'

'Can't I have a little taste? I'm a neighbour, after all.'

She scowled at the innuendo. 'I see. When I got this job they forgot to tell me forty-five breakfasts and one extra for the *neighbour.*'

He realised what was unusual about her. She looked like she was dressed in costume. Rolled hair, dark lips, a blood-coloured jumpsuit with padded shoulders and a print apron over it. 'So what's shooting?'

'*Taxi Driver II.* A sequel, thirty years after the fact. Did you know there's a tree just over there in Washington Square where they used to hang petty thieves in the eighteenth century?' She pointed to a huge elm. 'That would make a more interesting picture, doncha think?'

'Who's starring in this one?'

'The usual. The new Robert De Niro. The new Jodie Foster.'

'Everyone has to be the new something.'

'Out of work actor, are you?'

Not for long, he thought but didn't say, bristling a bit. Why would she assume he was out of work? 'No, just a surf bum.'

'Everyone's a surf bum these days. A friend of mine works in a surf shop on Duane Street, can you believe it? In the heart of yuppiedom. Does a great business. She thinks all the dot-com people confuse surfing the web with surfing the waves.'

He was getting very hungry. Whether it was the meatballs or the wisecracking woman, he couldn't tell. 'You think I could have just one of those tomato things?'

She stubbed her cigarette out in a paper coffee cup. 'What's that accent of yours?'

'You think I've got one?'

'New Yorkers don't say *tomahto.*'

'Damn.'

'And they'd just grab the *tomahto* thing. If you want to pass as a New Yorker you better stop being so polite.' She stuck a fork into a stuffed tomato ball and handed it to him. 'I suppose you're one of those Australians.'

'Is it that obvious?'

'Don't look so crestfallen. The film business is full of 'em. What's left of the film business, that is. I'm catering *rock videos* now. Everyone's filming in Canada. Or Sydney, come to think of it. The last Aussie I worked with was a real *brute*.' She pronounced it *Ossie* not *Ozzy*. 'You're not a brute, are you?'

'I could be a brute if you want.'

'Are you always so amenable?'

'Only to beautiful women.'

There was a smile dancing behind her brown eyes. 'Boy, don't you have anything better to do than pick up women on the street?'

'Am I picking you up? What time do you finish?'

'If you knew me you'd know that I *never* finish.'

'You will with me.'

She kept her eyes on him and took a roll of tobacco from out of her apron pocket. She extracted a narrow paper with twisted ends. 'Well, that would be *swell*—'

'Cheyne.'

'Shane. I'm Natalie. But—'

She was interrupted by a rabble of people, some carrying lighting stands and boxes, which descended on the table.

'Is that coffee hot?'

'You only got Swiss cheese?'

'They got garlic in them? I'm allergic to garlic.'

Cheyne stepped back and shrugged his shoulders.

'Go to it, fellas,' she said and walked around to where Cheyne was standing.

'Want a toke?' She offered Cheyne her cigarette.

'*Swell,*' he smiled and took it off her, even though he didn't smoke.

He'd always wanted to use that word.

Afterwards, lying sprawled on the futon that was covered with black dog hairs and smoking a Camel, Shane said, 'You weren't bad.'

'You mean,' Finley said, placing a mug of tea on the floor beside him, 'I was really terrible.'

'No. You've got some style.'

She knelt down. 'I couldn't even stand up.'

'That won't take long. We could work on it.'

We could work on it? She liked that idea. He hadn't said much, but he'd been gentle, got her to practise on the sand first. When the first wave slapped her on the nose with the force of a frozen fish hurled by a running quarterback and threw her off the board, he scooped her up, put his weight on her board to steady it and hoisted her on it again. She was in his arms for only a few seconds, her nose and mouth filled with brine, the horizon slopping about like the contents of a washing machine, but she'd felt like a limpet prised off a rock when he'd let go.

'I could get time off Friday.'

'Depends on the waves.'

She sat down beside him and folded her legs. 'I suppose everything depends on *that.*'

He looked around for somewhere to butt his cigarette. She handed him the dish from under a pot plant. He rolled towards her and stubbed it out. The tangy smell of his hair so close to her face mingled with the smell of warm pastry from the cafe across the road. She wanted to reach out and smooth it behind his ears so she could see his face better.

He flopped back on the pillow, put his hands behind his head, like he was lying on the sand watching the sky. The pale midday sun shot fringes of light through the wooden blinds and across his body. She had entertained nothing this exotic in her bedroom since an East Village punk turned up with an iguana on his head one night.

Shane was like an iguana, long and sleepy, moving slowly. 'Life is about waves.'

'You mean it's up and down all the time?' Her life certainly was. She had to fight to keep it smooth.

'Nah. I mean you just drift with the tide. It's no use fighting it. It's going to take you there whether you like it or not.'

'If I did that I'd just end up where I didn't want to be.'

'And where would that be?' He propped his head in his hands and his hair looked at her. She wasn't sure what his eyes were doing.

'In the suburbs somewhere, trimming hedges.'

'That's not so bad. I used to mow lawns.'

'You know what I mean. The suburbs are so…false.'

'They're pretty fucking real where I come from.'

'You come from the *suburbs*?'

'Where else?'

'I thought—'

'We lived in tents or something?'

'No—but all those beaches.'

'We have suburbs on the beaches. And they're as fucking boring as suburbs anywhere else.'

She didn't believe him. She'd seen Australia on television. They had crocodiles in their yards. Snakes in their trees. In the suburbs of New York they had leaf-rot.

'So, you mowed lawns?'

'Well, I was a greenkeeper. You know about bowls?'

'Ten pin?'

'No, lawn bowls. It's a sort of game old-timers play back home. They dress in white uniforms and roll these little hard balls along the grass. You've got to keep the greens perfectly trimmed otherwise the ball could hit a bump and go off in the wrong direction. It's like cutting the weave of velvet when you make a dress.' He was sitting up now, making cutting gestures with his hands. 'My old lady makes wedding dresses. Real crap.'

'Tell me about her.'

'Nothing to tell.'

Blossom, who had been busy investigating Shane's backpack, sniffed her way along the floor until she arrived at the futon and began to slurp on Shane's feet.

'Hey, puppy.'

'She likes you,' Finley said.

'Nah, it's the salt. My dog loves to do it too.'

'You've got a dog here?'

'No, back home. Mavis. She's a red cattle dog. It's good to have a dog around.' He reached down and buried a hand in the folds of Blossom's thick neck. 'Isn't it, sweetie?'

Finley had a vision of Shane sitting in a sand dune with his red dog, both of them looking out to sea.

'You don't happen to have any bacon and eggs?' he asked, kneeling now and playfully giving Blossom his forearm to chew on. 'I'm getting peckish again.' He'd bolted down three hot dogs on the street.

'I'm a vegetarian,' she explained. 'But we could go to the diner.'

'You're a *vegetarian*?' He sounded disappointed.

'Mostly.' Except for Natalie's meatballs. 'What's wrong with that?'

'What is it with you New York sheilas?'

'What do you mean *sheilas*?' She liked the sound of it even though she suspected it was an insult.

'You never eat properly.'

'I'm extremely healthy.'

'Food isn't food unless it's bleeding.'

She grimaced. 'That's disgusting. I'm a vegetarian because I don't believe in farming and eating animals.'

He nodded. 'I should have known you'd be one of those. That picture up there sort of gave it away.' He pointed to a mandala pinned above the stereo.

'I'm not one of anything.'

'We're all one of something.'

'Well, what are you, then?' The old familiar sharp edge came back to her voice. It irritated her to think he saw her as one of the pack, something common.

'I'm Australian.'

'That's it?'

'More Australian than human.'

'People are more complicated than that.'

'You think so? Look at you, for instance. You're American. You're a girl who lives in New York. I can tell a lot about you from that.'

'Oh, yeah, what can you tell about me?' She folded her arms across her chest.

'You're neurotic. You're sentimental. You're spoiled. You can't cook. How am I doing?'

'I'm not neurotic.'

'Three out of four isn't bad.'

'What makes you such an expert on New York women? You've been here how long? Two months?'

'Wouldn't matter if I'd been here two days.'

'So you know all about me just by looking at me?'

'Of course not. You're different.'

'Well, I'm glad to hear it. I wouldn't want you to think I was *Karen* or someone.'

She thought he was smiling. It was almost a frown. 'No chance of that.'

'*How* am I different?'

'You really want to know?'

She put her hands on her hips. *Spill it, Buster.*

He pushed his hair behind his ears. *Finally.* There was a tiny shard of mother-of-pearl dangling from one ear. She hadn't noticed it before. He smiled with spume-coloured eyes, the palest yellow-green. 'Let me see. How are you different? Well, you're not the only girl I've known who's a slob, but you're the only one who's got dried dog turds by her bed.'

Finley jumped up, appalled. 'Where?'

Shane pointed in the direction of a stack of albums. She stepped on the futon to look.

'Shit! I never get out of bed on that side. *Blossom!*'

'Don't get mad at the dog. I sort of like it.'

'You do?'

'Yeah, everything in this country's so fucking *clean*.'

She dropped back down on her haunches, beside him. 'You're weird.'

'You might be right there. My old man always said there were two Shanes—one of them was a moron and the other was a fuckwit.'

'Which one am I talking to now?'

'Both of them.'

'Why?'

'We haven't kissed you yet.'

Cheyne took a seat in the dingy hallway outside the room where the readings for *The Importance of Being Earnest* were taking place. The three other men waiting their turn evaluated him. They looked openly hostile. He put his left foot on his right knee and hugged his boot. He looked at the ceiling. He worked on his breathing. Let them stare. He knew what they were thinking. *Damn, this guy's got the part for sure.*

Most actors were a miserable lot—stunted, mousy, unprepossessing at best and bitter about it. Fully aware that they wouldn't get a second look on the street. Whereas he *looked* like a star. He could sit quietly and still take up space. The focus of any room would always be him. The others resented it, but there was nothing he could do about it, even if he wanted to. It was how he was. If a terrorist entered this room right now and took a hostage—say that limp-looking guy with the goatee and the copy of *Backstage* by the door—everyone would look to Cheyne to be the negotiator. It was how things were. He was always the centre of attention. Even if he didn't like it, he couldn't change it.

What had any of these guys done? He recognised one of them from a cereal commercial—but the rest? He was vaguely offended to be included with this lot, not to be offered a private audition. But when the assistant called him in, she confirmed his thoughts.

'Mr Burdekin, come in.' She fluttered her eyelashes. 'We were leaving the best for last.'

The Grimley brothers didn't look like twins, at least from a distance. Damian was plump with a goatee; Derek, sporting square glasses, was concave and grey. They were sitting one behind the other, both with legs crossed, surrounded by the usual acolytes.

The girl he was to read with was pretty. Cheyne thought he recognised her. Maybe she was from television? But there were so many of them on television, pretty girls with flossy blonde hair and huge eyes. And they always had the same noses.

The brother in front, Derek, thin with watery eyes, did all the talking. 'Greetings, Mr…um…' He looked down at a clipboard. '*China* Burdekin.'

'Cheyne,' he corrected the Grimley over the coughing and scraping.

'*Shane* is it? Inventive spelling. I rather liked China.' There was an approving giggle from the fat twin behind him. 'Well, go ahead. Let's see if your performance is as creative as your name. What we're looking for in the character of Jack Worthing is a *lot* of raw sexuality.'

'Don't you mean *repressed* sexuality?'

'Mr Burdekin. Please. If you have the burning desire to perform in some high school interpretation of Wilde please leave now.'

'OK.' Cheyne gave him a full-wattage smile. 'I'll do it your way.'

'What a relief. Now this is the concept. When we first meet Jack and Gwendolen they are in the master bedroom of Algie's Park Avenue apartment, fucking each other senseless on a pile of mink coats deposited there by guests at the cocktail party raging in the drawing room. Algie and Jack both do something financial at

Morgan Stanley, although it's never very clear what. But then, it's never very clear in real life, is it? Algie is a lush and fond of the blow, Jack is a sex addict. Algie has created an alter ego, Bunbury, in order to escape recriminations at the office for the many occasions when he's too debauched to turn up at work. Gwendolen is the only child of a trillionaire media mogul, contributing a weekly column about sex and the single girl to one of daddy's newspapers. Jack is referred to frequently in her column, as her on-again-off-again boyfriend "Ernest". The wicked Ernest is a popular subject for discussion in women's magazine chat rooms. Cecily is Jack's niece. She lives in East Hampton and bottles perfume. That's all you need to know for now. Damian and I want the production to reek of money and power, of modern Manhattan with its gleaming towers of commerce, of black marble and gold Rolexes, cashmere coats, foot-long cigars and block-long limousines. All shot digitally, of course.' He clapped his hands. 'Now, what we need from you, Mr Burdekin, is frenzy, passion! You're a sex addict, remember. Think Michael Douglas. Miss Kinney, try to resist at first. But he's irresistible. Does he look irresistible to you?'

The girl pursed her lips at Cheyne. 'You can say that again.'

'He's your reward for being a good girl all day.'

She showed Cheyne the wet tip of her tongue.

'Very well. Now, Mr Burdekin, fuck her!'

Cheyne ran his hands through his hair. The actress stood with her hands on her hips, waiting. Eager, he thought. But it was all wrong. 'Look…I need some motivation here. It's not in the play. Why would Jack be so aggressive?'

Derek folded his arms and pushed back his chair. 'Do you really need any motivation for eating pussy?'

Someone snickered. The director turned around and scowled at the culprit, a fat little fag in silver sneakers. He said to Cheyne. 'Well, go on, Mr Burdekin. Or is all this new to you?'

'You OK?' Cheyne whispered to the girl. She gave him an odd look, like he was stupid for asking. So he put his arm around her. She arranged herself so that one breast peeped provocatively from her unbuttoned blouse.

He thought the occasion called for a line. 'Miss Fairfax, ever since I have met you...'

The actress screwed up her face. 'What?'

And then he couldn't help it, he could feel it coming. An itch and then the old familiar build up, like a sneeze. He started to giggle. He often giggled when he was asked to do something ridiculous. A few of the actors he knew did too. He had to choke it down.

'Now what, Mr Burdekin?' Derek pushed himself up off his seat.

'Sorry.'

The girl said something under her breath, grabbed a hank of Cheyne's hair.

'*Hey!*' It hurt.

'That's good, Miss Kinney,' said Damian. Cheyne turned and looked in surprise at the new voice. He was standing in his place, fiddling with his goatee.

Encouraged, the girl pulled at Cheyne's hair some more. He cursed those long strands that hung over his eyes. He grabbed her wrists and pulled her hands away.

'*Very* good!' said Derek. Cheyne imagined his lenses steaming up. That did it. The image made him snicker and he had to step away from the girl, clutching his sides. He couldn't control it. The laughter shook him like he was on a vibrating bed.

He could hear the director's chair scrape. 'This is *art*, Mr Burdekin! It's not a fucking sit-com. You're in *New York*, not some comedy club in Cape Town.'

'Sydney,' Cheyne said, holding his stomach, choking, trying to snap out of it.

'Well, good for you. Would you please continue or we'll call another couple. Miss Kinney?'

'I'm fine,' she said brightly, her voice ringing around the bare rehearsal space. 'I'm ready whenever *he* is.' She gave Cheyne a dazzling smile. Under her breath she said, 'You jerk. Just fucking do it. You're gonna ruin my chance, shithead.'

He recognised her now. She was quite famous. Slacker movies and a couple of costume dramas, playing a witch or something like it. Typecasting.

'Shall we start again, then?' the director closed his eyes. 'One last time, Mr Burdekin. I'd like to finish before the new year.'

It had been the girl he'd been worried about all along. He thought the directors were trying to humiliate her. Most of them hated women. He didn't want to be part of it. But with her breasts thrusting at him now, he realised that humiliation wasn't a word in any dictionary around here.

'Come on, you fairy,' she taunted.

The thin Grimley clapped his hands again. 'Just a moment.' He turned to his brother. 'I know what you're thinking, Damian,' he said. 'It would be better in the nude.'

'Yes, the nude, Derek. Very good.'

'The *nude*?' Cheyne groaned.

'You have an objection to taking your clothes off, Cheyne?'

'You want Jack to be a sex addict banker in the *nude*?'

'Precisely.'

'I just don't get it, that's all.'

'You don't have to get it. You just have to do it.'

'Well, fuck you,' said Cheyne. 'My agent said nothing about this. I'm leaving.'

'That's better, Cheyne,' said Derek in a tone of voice that showed no surprise. 'We like a bit of passion.'

'Absolutely,' said Damian.

'You don't want me to take my clothes off, do you?' They were just testing him. One of the amusing little tricks they liked to play on you in auditions.

'I wouldn't say we don't *want* you to take your clothes off, Cheyne. We find your reaction interesting. You were the only one today who said no. The only one who didn't start unbuckling right on the spot.'

'Then you want me to continue?'

'Please. You can keep your clothes on. For now.' Derek put his hands together. 'Miss Kinney?'

'*I'm* ready.'

Cheyne sighed and grasped the girl by the arm, a little tighter than was entirely necessary.

'Hey!' she hissed.

He dug his fingers in deeper. 'This is what you wanted, wasn't it?' he whispered.

She blew a pink bubble of gum at him.

'Excellent!' he heard a Grimley exclaim.

Afterwards, his chest was heaving. The girl adjusted her bra strap and smoothed down her skirt. She winked at him.

'Thank you, Mr Burdekin,' said Damian, still fiddling with his goatee. 'We'll be in touch.'

'Oh,' said Cheyne. Was this the brush off?

'Just one thing,' said Derek.

'Yes?'

'We'll be needing your credit card. You have to invest in the picture to be sure of getting a role.'

His credit card! It was a scam after all. How did Valerie get him into this?

Derek beamed at his bleak expression. 'Just joking!'

Damian started to guffaw.

'Aren't they *fun*?' said the girl who'd shown him to the room, as she closed the door behind them. The waiting room was empty and a janitor was vacuuming. 'They're the nicest people I've ever worked with!'

Cheyne didn't doubt it.

Blossom lay still on the floor at the end of the bed, her jowls slumped into her paws, her brow furrowed and her brown eyes lolling in the back of her head. Every now and again she would give a muffled snort, as if she were chasing pigeons in her dreams. In fact, she was wide awake and the rolled-back eyes were disgust in the guise of boredom.

It had been many sleeps since Girl had brought home a male Person to make strange shapes with her on the bed-on-the-floor. This Person tasted good and found the spot under her chin where the skin itched but Blossom knew that Girl would forget to walk her this afternoon and might even forget to feed her if the visiting Person kept going back and forth and up and down like that. Once, when the Person who smelt of burning sticks stayed, Blossom had missed two meals and three walks and even her best bark hadn't done any good.

By the look of it, the salty Person would be here a while.

She rolled on her side and crossed her paws over her nose. This Person was the same as the others—no fur when he took his blue covering off. But the place where he sat down was whiter than his legs. He was kneeling on the bed, with no covering on at all, the bottom of his feet on the floor, the undersides facing her, flat and white like those cold fish Girl sometimes brought home from the place where they sold food in tents. Girl's feet were stretched out too, folded across his, but her feet were black on the bottom from the dark stuff on the floor where the food was made. Her feet were always like this, even when she did the thing with bubbles and water.

Girl was making her howling noises. The first time she did this, when Blossom was a puppy, Blossom thought the Person was hurting her and took a nice tasty chunk from the place where he sat. Girl got angry and locked Blossom in the place with the basin that went *whoosh*. A few sleeps later another Person with a chain came but Girl cried so hard the Person went away. For many sleeps after that Blossom and Girl went to play with other puppies and a female Person who threw balls but hit her with a stick if she chased them. After this, Girl never made her Stay or Heel and even let her poop where she wanted but Blossom never again bit a place where anyone sat down.

The salty Person's rump looked too tough anyway. He was like the gristle on a bone without any meat. He had that thing between his legs that she would have liked to have snacked on, but she knew better. The way Girl had been chewing on it, it was a wonder there was any left. But it didn't seem to get any smaller, just larger and bouncier. It made Blossom drool all over her big paws.

The Person got up off the mattress and she could hear his tinkle in the basin that went *whoosh*. Except he didn't make it go *whoosh*. He came out with his bone straight in front of him, bobbing like a Dachshund on the trot. Girl got up off the floor and pushed him against the big thing that kept her chopped liver cold. Then they hid the bone and Blossom lost interest.

It was going to be a long wait until dinner.

What a waste of a day!

Cheyne flung himself on the sofa and untied his boots, which were soaked from the sudden downfall of rain between the West 4th Street subway station and home. Who did those Grimleys think they were? Little gods. They'd looked at him like he was a fucking *meatball*…

Meatballs. He thought about that sexy caterer, Natalie. There had been no sight of the film crew at the end of Washington Place a few minutes before when he'd dashed home. They'd packed up for the day and gone. He wondered if they'd be back. He hoped so. Next time he'd be less flat-footed and ask her for a drink when she was finished. The toke of pot she'd given him had made him so mellow he'd just drifted off home. He'd strike up a conversation and maybe she'd ask him to her place. This hardly looked like the apartment of a groovy bachelor. The bed would sway when you fucked on it. Not that he had the opportunity to try.

But entanglements with strangers on the street weren't his goal. He had to protect himself. *Save* himself. He'd been in enough disastrous relationships, ones he'd drifted into without thinking where they were going or even *if* he wanted them to go anywhere. Actresses, mostly, but none of them star material, a makeup artist, a producer, an entertainment lawyer…some of them cute, some of them smart, one of them certifiably insane, but none of them met his aspirations. There were other women, within arm's reach, he knew it, who were beautiful, smart, famous and available, who were between relationships with Matt or Ben or Josh and open to a handsome newcomer on the rise.

He'd meet the woman of his dreams at a film premiere or at a script conference or across a crowded VIP lounge. He'd be introduced by a director, or her publicist or their mutual business manager. Their first date would be at her place or his, not in public. He'd fly to Arizona to be with her on location. They would start going to parties together. They would be photographed cuddling at some nightclub. They would deny everything. They'd go shopping at Harry Winston for a ring. Her family, famous uncles and cousins and siblings, would welcome him into its bosom. Michael Jackson would lend them his ranch for their wedding...

Well, *that* was going too far. He smiled at the idea. That bit was the fantasy. But he knew the rest as if one of those fortune tellers who worked out of basements on Thompson Street had shown him his future in her crystal ball.

He would *not* meet the woman of his dreams on the street.

Still, she was beautiful. He hadn't stopped thinking about her all day, even when he was waiting for that ridiculous audition. She was so incredibly, adorably *feminine*...

He started to pull off a boot when the intercom buzzed.

He stumbled to his feet trailing untied shoelaces and pressed the button that released the downstairs door. He didn't bother to answer these days. It was rarely anyone for him, except the occasional messenger with scripts. On the other hand, the person in 2B had messengers coming and going all day and they never seemed to care what apartment buzzer they pressed.

He had the other boot off when there was a loud thudding on

the door. The messengers for 2B again, getting the floor wrong. It happened all the time.

He sighed and opened the door.

'Surprise!' Avalon held her arms out. 'Sorry I'm late.'

So he was dreaming again. He'd thought his morning bagel had been real, the audition real, the feel of his boot in his hand real. If he shut the door, he might wake up. *When I wake up there will be no one there.* He closed it.

This is one hell of a dream, he thought as he picked up both boots and put them under the coat rack. The pounding on the door became more frantic. He could hear a muffled voice, *Cheyne! Cheyne!* through the painted steel.

He went to the bathroom and got a towel to dry his hair. *If I pinch my hand I'll wake up.* He pinched it. The pounding stopped. *There.*

He mussed his hair with the towel and opened the front door expecting to see an empty hallway.

Avalon was still standing there, arms crossed. She was wearing a black padded vest over a shiny lycra top and black pants with red stripes down the side. Under her black baseball cap her face was tanned an artificial orange. Her cheeks glowed beet-red. All he could think of was that she looked like a Tropical Punch.

And punch him she did.

He stumbled against the wall, holding his jaw. 'Hey!'

'Why did you shut the door on me?'

'*Jesus*, Avalon!'

'Have you got a girl in there?' She pushed past him into the apartment. 'You can come out now!' she called.

He staggered inside after her, dropping the towel and rubbing his face. 'There's no one here.'

She turned to face him, her mascara-clogged lashes opening up like sea anemones. 'There better not be.'

'What the hell are you doing here, anyway?'

'What do you mean? You invited me.'

'*I* invited *you*?'

'Have you just got up, Cheyne? You look a mess.'

'That's because you hit me.'

'Well, I thought you were a hiding a girl in here.'

'And what if I was?'

'Cheyne, we've talked about this before. You can't be in a monogamous relationship and have other girlfriends.'

Cheyne groaned. 'Do you mind if I sit down?'

'Go ahead.'

He dropped onto the chintz sofa, spilling cushions on to the floor.

'Nice place you've got here.' She looked around the room. 'Phil said you'd lucked out. I don't know why you didn't phone me directly, Cheyne, instead of sending messages through Phil. Anyway, I got them and I'm here.'

What the fuck had Phil been telling her? Best friend Phil? The bastard had probably been teasing her and she was so thick she believed him. 'Look, Avalon—'

'I can share the rent. I'm fully prepared to do that, Cheyne. Even though you're a big star I don't expect you to pay for everything. I just got off one of those *Star Wars* things, so I'm loaded. Now, where can I put my bags?'

'Avalon, you can't stay here.'

'And I'll need to talk to your agent. She'll get me working soon enough.'

'She doesn't represent...stunt people.'

'I'm not a stunt person, Cheyne. I'm an action-adventure performer.

Anyway, your agent will know who I should talk to. Maybe you could call her now. I've been stuck at that fucking LA airport for almost twenty-four hours.' She bounced beside him on the sofa and linked her arm through his. 'I missed you, Cheyne. Did you miss me?'

It was better to pacify her than suffer another blow to the head. He was bigger, but she was faster, a graduate of Bruce Packer's Gold Coast Stunt Academy. He'd think of a way to get rid of her in a minute. 'It's just…I wasn't expecting you.'

'I wrote. I sent a letter.'

'I didn't get it. You must have had the wrong address.'

'Nup. It's the right address, all right. We all wondered why you hadn't written back. You should get email.'

'We *all*?'

'Yeah, you know. The girls from *Taliesin*. We meet every month, if we can.' She pulled her cap off her head and started to undo her vest. 'You know what I *really* feel like?'

'What?' he croaked, fearing the answer.

'Not *that*, silly. Not yet. I'm pooped. I feel like a cold beer. Got one?'

'Yes.' He stood up.

'No—I'll get it myself. Is that the kitchen? God, it's tinier than the one I had in Bondi.'

With dismay Cheyne surveyed the luggage Avalon had dragged into the apartment. Alongside two sizeable suitcases and her duffle bag were a set of skis, what looked like a snowboard in a padded bag, a tennis racquet and an enormous black case with stickers all over it. Noosa. Bali. Bugs Bunny. Planet Hollywood.

'You're wondering what that is?' she said as she came back into the room with two bottles of beer. 'It's my euphonium.'

'Your *what*?'

'My euphonium. I've played it since high school. I'm real good. They've got lots of brass bands in America. I thought I could join one.'

He took the beer even though he didn't want it. He remembered now that she was a serial drinker, one beer after the other. He'd have to go down to the deli and get in a supply…But what was he thinking? She wasn't staying. He'd let her drink her beer and then suggest a hotel. One in the South Bronx, preferably, as far away as possible.

He looked at Avalon standing there in that ridiculous sporting outfit. Her yellow hair was sticking out like a halo, making her look like a demented dahlia. God, how had he ever become involved with her in the first place? He vaguely remembered what happened on the set of *Taliesin* in Tasmania, a rainy night stuck in that pub in Franklin, the two of them left at the bar, Avalon playing footsies with him under the bar stool. She'd never gotten the hint that it was a location thing, the usual mating of star and starlet, meant to dissolve as soon as the First AD called 'It's a wrap!' She'd followed him to Sydney and it had taken months to get rid of her. He hadn't wanted to hurt her feelings, that was his mistake. It was when he decided she didn't have any feelings it became easier.

Now she was crying. Water gathered and pooled between those spiky black lashes and poured down her cheeks.

'Oh, Cheyne, I'd forgotten what a looker you are!'

She flung her arms wide and rushed at him. There was no time to duck. He took the full force of her hard body against his. Her mouth was all over his face, her tears mingling with the cold sweat he'd worked up the minute he opened the door. He grabbed her arms—pecs of *steel*, damn it—and pushed them down and away from him. The beer she was holding jerked out of her hand and bounced on the floor, emptying a fountain of foam down his left leg.

'Shit, Avalon! Look what you've done!'

She stepped back. 'Sorry.'

'You can't stay here!' he yelled at her, suddenly losing the last scrap of composure he possessed.

She blinked at him. 'I don't understand. You said—'

'I didn't say anything!'

'You told Phil—'

'I've hardly spoken to Phil!'

'That's because you're so busy. With the new film and everything.'

'What new film?'

'Haven't you just got a big part in something? Everyone's talking about it.'

'Oh, yeah…that,' he said, covering up quickly. He had led Phil to believe he was already working. But he was going to get the role in *Earnest*, wasn't he? He pushed the memory of the audition aside.

'It's OK, Cheyne. I know you were expecting me last night and when I didn't turn up you probably just thought I wasn't coming. You haven't had time to get ready for me or anything. You shouldn't be ashamed of this place. It's small. But *cute*. I like it, really I do. I could help you fix it up. We could get rid of those curtains in a tick— they make the place look smaller. And—'

If he didn't stop her, she'd be moving the furniture around any minute. 'You can't stay here,' he blurted, 'because…because the landlord's written it into the contract that only one person can live here. That's why the rent's so cheap.'

'That's stupid!'

'Well, it's the law. Only one person can occupy an apartment of this size.'

'Really? How would anyone know?'

'They come around and check. The real estate agents, I mean. They come every month.'

'Shit. It's not like Sydney, is it? You can get twenty fucking dole bludgers into a house at Tamarama no problem.'

'So you can't stay here. But I've been thinking about it.' Thinking about it for twenty seconds. 'I'm going to put you in a hostel. I'll pay for it. You can stay there for a few nights until you go.'

'I'm not going. I've got a six-month tourist visa. And, once I get working, I can stay as long as I like.'

'If you've got a tourist visa, aren't you going to tour? Miami's really great at this time of year. Or Arizona. Don't you want to go somewhere warm?'

'Nope. It's warm enough here with you. I'm looking forward to us sharing a white Christmas.'

He could see she was about to fling her arms around his neck again and he stepped back. The sofa stopped him. 'You'll have trouble with the unions. Getting stunt work. They don't hire foreigners. It's a closed shop.'

She tugged his ears playfully. It hurt. 'I know you're only thinking about me, Cheyne, but she'll be right. I met this Yank on a job in Sydney who said he knows someone. So just relax.'

'That's good, Avalon,' he appeased her. 'I'm glad to hear it. Let's go and find you a place to stay, then.'

'There's no hurry, Cheyne. It's only five in the afternoon. I changed my watch. Your landlord doesn't have rules about visitors, does he?'

'No, but you have to be out by 7 p.m.,' he said.

'If I didn't know you better, I'd think you were trying to get rid of me.' She took her hands out of his hair and pushed him down into the sofa. He knew it was useless to resist. She pinned him with her arms and straddled his thighs. 'I think you better tell me about this movie you're going to make,' she whispered in his ear. 'Are there any sexy bits in it? Who is your leading lady? Is she pretty?'

Cheyne at least knew the answer to this. 'Some may think so,' he told her calmly. 'But I don't find her attractive at all.'

'Good,' said Avalon, nuzzling her lips against his neck. 'Then I won't need to come on location *every* day.'

Picture Finley, age nine, in elementary school. Sitting at a desk by herself because she likes to pinch.

The teacher, Miss Forester, is conducting a spelling bee. 'Now, class, we're going to do things a little differently today. I'm going to ask one of you to give me a letter of the alphabet and then I want someone else to put up their hand when they think of a second letter. And then someone else can give me a third one, until we've finished the word. Do you all understand?'

Twenty-six little heads nod.

'Very well. Who can give me the first letter?'

Finley's hand shoots up.

'Yes, Finley?'

'F.'

'Very well, F it is. What will the next letter be? Can we all think of something swimming in the sea?'

Finley's hand stays up. The other hands stay down.

'Yes, Finley.' Miss Forester sounds weary.

'U,' Finley says.

'U?' Miss Forester asks. 'Are you sure, Finley?'

'Yes, Miss Forester.'

'Very well.' A sigh, realising what she's let herself in for. 'We have F and U, class. Does anyone have a third letter?'

Finley's hand shoots up again. Miss Forester ignores it. 'Well, class? Yes, Boris?'

Boris answers, 'Y.'

'No, Boris, I don't think there are any words that begin with F-U-Y. Anyone else?'

Finley's hand is straining for attention.

'Very well, Finley.'

'C,' Finley says.

The class starts giggling.

'That's enough, Finley. I will not have this kind of language in class.'

'No, Miss Forester. It's a real word.'

'It is not a real word, Finley.'

'But Miss Forester—'

'We don't tolerate curse words in this class. Anyone else?'

The class snickers. The other students look at Finley, willing her to complete the word. Finley's hand goes up.

'Finley, you can leave the room.'

'But I have the next letter, Miss Forester.'

'I don't want to hear it.'

'H,' says Finley.

'H?' frowns Miss Forester. 'There's no such word.' She doesn't want to spell out F-U-C-H in case it sets the class off.

'That's not the whole word,' Finley explains.

'Well, exactly *what* is the whole word, Finley? I'm going to have to get the principal in.'

'*Fuchsia*,' says Finley. 'F-U-C-H-S-I-A.'

Finley had trouble with *fuck*. Even tonight, at Sputnik, as she worked the cash register, she thought it didn't mean anything anymore. It wasn't a word, it was punctuation. Fuck you this. Fuck you that. Fuckin' get outta my way. Fuck off. People said it when they were angry or frustrated, which meant it got used a lot. If you sat on a park bench and listened to the rhythms of the city, you'd hear little explosions of *fuck* fill the air.

Listening to the crowd in Sputnik tonight, she heard the word over and over.

'What the fuck's up, Blender?'

'It's fucking shit, that's what it is.'

'Don't fuck with my mind, Esther baby.'

'Fucking stand in line like everyone else.'

'Fuck, man! That track's really weird.'

'Fuck that was good.' Finley smiled to herself as she took an album from a customer and scanned the price. She took his cash and counted it into the register. She gave him too much change without noticing. She was thinking of Shane.

'Fuck that was good.' Shane had rolled away from under Finley and found her tee-shirt where it had been discarded on the floor. Blossom was standing over it, quivering.

'You'd swear that pooch was watching us,' he said, scooping up the shirt and using it to wipe his genitals. Finley knelt on the mattress beside him, watching.

'You want it?' He clumped the sticky piece of navy blue cotton in his fist and offered it to her.

She shook her head.

He went back to rubbing his crotch. 'Do you always fuck like that?'

Finley wished that there were another word. You said 'Fuck me hard, baby' during sex and it sounded like a bad porno movie. It was better to say nothing. But the way Shane used *fuck*, it sounded different, like he'd invented the word. It seemed as natural to him as taking a breath.

Like everything else he did.

'What the fuck, Finley? Stop dreaming.' Her boss, Rockwell, snatched the album out of her hand and scanned it, nudging her aside. A line of about seven people had gathered in front of the counter. 'I'll scan, you wrap,' he instructed. 'What's the matter with you, anyway?'

The matter with her was that Shane had staggered out of her apartment with his board only three hours before. The salt was still on her. In her.

'She's in love,' Esther called out from the turntable, where she was changing records. 'Can't you tell?'

'*Oooooh*,' Rockwell vamped, coquettishly running a hand through his blond dreads.

'Get fucked.'

'Who is it *this* time?'

Finley shoved the album in a bag, snatched the receipt and pushed it at the customer. 'Have a nice day,' she snarled, ignoring Rockwell.

'It's a secret,' said Esther.

'Oh, a secret! Let me guess. One of those touring Shaolin monks? Some local junkhead with a whole fucking menagerie of rodents? Or am I assuming wrong? Is it *Rosie O'Donnell*?'

'Very funny.'

Finley kept tossing albums in bags until Rockwell got bored and went back to his usual occupation, smoking dope in the back room. She didn't want to talk about Shane and have them ridicule him.

Oh, he's a surfer is he? Bet he's got a big board.

She thought about him lifting her out of the ocean, the bright drops of water flying from them, the December sky so blue it hurt your eyes, the 747s flying low overhead into Kennedy airport like eagles poised to swoop.

'Come on,' said Esther. 'Give me his name at least. Do I know him?'

'No.'

'A clue?'

'No.'

'Well, make sure you invite me to the wedding.'

'Fuck off.'

'Get fucked.'

They smiled at each other.

'I intend to,' said Finley.

Tonight, the air pressure was 30.01. Normal. The wave height was 1.3 feet with a one-foot wind-wave height and a swell of one foot. The wind-wave period was eight seconds. A fucking lake with a bit of chop. He'd get more swell watching a porn movie.

Shane shut down and walked the length of the loft to the expanse of south-facing windows. He could see spires and towers that twinkled like Luna Park in the dark and intermittent stretches of blackness, the rooftops of low tenement buildings. The sky was so clear the water towers shot up like toy rockets about to be launched. Somewhere down there Finley was flogging records to a bunch of potheads. What was the name of the record store? He couldn't remember. He had the urge to turn up and surprise her but he hadn't been listening when she'd told him where it was. He'd been watching her mouth, the way it looked like someone had pushed their finger into her top lip and made a little dent. When God was giving out mouths, he must have liked this one and given it a poke of approval.

'When God was givin' out brains, you musta hidden behind the door, Shane,' the Old Fart always said.

Shane, Shane, shit for brains.

His stomach muscles clenched. He wouldn't think of any of them, he'd think of Finley, who had straight, fierce eyebrows and a tattoo of an 'F' on her hand. Finley who could stand on her head and put the soles of her feet together. Finley who didn't notice the dog turds on her bedroom floor. Finley who thought he was some kind of sex god and burnt incense while she kissed each of his toes.

'That's not how you do it, Shane. Are you a fuckwit or what?' That was Sharon, in the dunes at Gunnamatta, pushing him off her and hastily pulling up her bikini bottom.

Fourteen, his first time.

'Jesus, Shane, didn't you even get a poke in?' The mates, afterwards.

'Well, you know, Shane, you're nice and everything, but...' That was his girlfriend of three weeks, Melanie, giving him the brush-off at seventeen.

'Why can't we go to the pictures, Shane? You never want to go anywhere. You're really *boring*.' That was Danni, girlfriend of an unfortunate winter, standing in front of him, hands on hips, blocking his view of *Lancelot Link Secret Chimp*.

'You're an animal, Shane.' That was some girl he'd met at a party and who urged him to fuck her under the kitchen table in plain sight of everyone.

'Frankly, Mr Dekker, Shane's got the ability but he just won't do the work. He'll have to repeat fifth form if he doesn't try harder next term.' That was Old Limpdick, the maths teacher, at parent-teacher night.

'You're a no-hoper, Shane. The Lord only knows where we got you from. You've broken your mother's heart.' That was the Old Fart again, making a big deal of him dropping out of school. Sixth-grade educations, both of them, off to work at twelve, and they had the nerve to criticise *him*?

He didn't give a rat's arse about any of them. They all thought he'd never amount to anything. But he'd got off his bum and got out of there, unlike Darren and the rest. Even if this place was a dump, it was *different*. It had one or two good points, he could see that now. Since meeting Finley, he could definitely see it. Fucked waves, but no one thought he was a loser. The girls especially, they liked him. A lot. He only had to open his mouth and they'd fall at his feet. They called him 'cute' and 'a hunk'. He hated that, sort of, but it was better than 'fuckwit' and 'animal'. They respected him, even if he didn't respect them. He could see it in their eyes, a kind of calculating hunger.

And the men, they were impressed by him too. Those weeds arriving at the beach in limos, throwing him fifty-buck tips for an hour of waterlogged humiliation. They didn't know he was a dropout, that the old man, now retired on a disability pension, had worked on the railways, that the old woman made lavender polyester bridesmaid dresses and took in piecework from the local drycleaners. They heard his flat vowels and saw the way his muscles spooled down his strong arms and thought he was a prince among men.

'Are there more like you at home?' a rich bitch in a sarong and gold high heels had asked him at Brian Davenport's juice bar, stroking her glass of carrot beet with suggestive fingers.

Yes, there were more like him all right. Thousands of them. But here, there was only one. One Australian Shane. He had the territory all to himself.

No-hoper. He'd love to see his old man's face when he got to Spain. Shane in Spain with a board-shaping business and a shapely *señorita* minding his towel. Making fistfuls of pesos and sending photographs home. Paying for Darren to come over so that he could report back to all the mates.

The Shane in Spain falls mainly on the plane...

He grunted with satisfaction. He'd just fucking sell one of Dirk's big cameras and go there. Some of the cameras looked pretty valuable. He could bundle up a few of them and see what he could get...

And then he remembered Finley. If he went to Spain he'd be leaving her behind. The thought made him tremble. He looked at his hand in surprise. Well, she could come with him, couldn't she? What was she doing with her life but working in two dumb stores? She could teach yoga or whateveritwas on the beach. That big dog of hers might be a problem for Mavis but they'd work it out. The only thing was, she had such white skin. Would she refuse to go in the sun?

He was still thinking of her white skin half an hour later when he fell asleep in front of a repeat of 'Mary Brown Is Coming to Breakfast'.

He dreamt, not for the first time, of the break at Bell's, dropping down the face of a fifteen-footer, big bottom turn, and launching off the lip like a cork shot out of a champagne bottle, but this time he kept on going through the sky, hurtling high over the cliff and low over the car park, with the boards on roofracks like dolphins lined up for a water ballet. The ride kept on going, buffeted by warm currents of air, as he shot across the coastal scrubland and over the sheep farms of the Western District, above ribbons of rivers like golden syrup and red canyons freckled with the tops of black banksia trees. His feet seemed glued to the board as he swooped over broken-down pubs on dusty country corners, abandoned caravans, edges of billabongs and trees, like stubble, clinging to dry creek beds.

It was like...*wow*...the ride of his life. He took the gusts like a cowboy on a bronco, plunging, rising, shuddering along the corrugated ridges of air. He closed his eyes to feel the current and...*thud*...the board ploughed straight into a hill of red dirt, flinging him off onto the scorching ground.

He rubbed his head and knew he was dreaming but couldn't find the wherewithal to dredge himself out of it. He'd never been to the fucking Red Centre before. It wasn't something you did when you were young, unless you were one of those backpackers from Sweden. You saved it for when you were eighty and all you could do was ride in buses and look out the window.

He looked around. There was nothing to see except an arrangement of bleached kangaroo bones, a crow sitting on a dead tree. And then he noticed some movement. Slowly the land people emerged from caves, Aborigines with spears, sharp-eyed, bent at the knees like they were hunting, surrounding him.

There were dozens of them, men wearing little lap-laps and women with breasts drooping to their waists. The women carried bundles of twigs or piccaninnies on their hips. He'd seen them on old postcards or in the illustrations to childhood books like *We of the Never Never.*

Well, it's going to be Never Never for me, he thought, as a tribal elder danced forward with his spear aloft. Shane tried to crawl away in the dirt but was stopped by the sharp flint of a spear in his back.

The elder danced forward and then backward, making prancing steps. Shane imagined he was channelling a giant kangaroo or maybe a crocodile. He cringed as the elder stopped in front of him and touched his chest with the tip of his spear.

The women started chanting. *Wallawallawalla.* The elder's face folded into ridges of disapproval.

This is it, thought Shane. *Why can't I wake up?*

Wallawallawalla. They sounded like fucking red indians. The elder pressed his spear deeper into Shane's chest. And then, suddenly, he withdrew it. The chanting stopped. Shane scrabbled some dirt into his fist, ready to throw it.

The old man shuffled forward and bent over so that his grizzled face was close to Shane's. Shane lifted his arm to launch the dirt. The elder bent closer, his putrid mouth near Shane's ear. 'Shane,' he whispered, 'you're a *fuckwit.*'

They shot the cartilage right out of Cheyne's knee.

Bam! The knee exploded and fragments of flesh, bone and black leather splattered the road. His leg looked like a wasted firecracker, shredded, minced, a centre of red jelly erupting from a volcano of smashed bone. He felt no pain, only heat and fell hard to the ground.

The sky was so blue it hurt his eyes. He knew if he closed them he would die. His hip was bruised where he fell and his left elbow was braced against the bitumen. He could hear the rumble of motorbikes in the distance, coming closer. A crow flew overhead.

Out of the corner of his eye, he could see his gun glinting on the road. He shifted off his elbow, thudded onto his back, tried to stretch his right arm to reach the gun. His shoulder felt as if it had come out of its socket, every movement of his fingers sending fiery rockets up his arm. The Toecutter's gang smelt the kill. He could hear motorbikes on gravel, taste the red dust in his mouth. He needed that weapon, had to make it to his Interceptor. *Somehow*…He was Mad Max, after all.

When he opened his eyes there was a canopy of shimmering green above him, leaves fretted with sunlight. His head was nesting in something soft and fragrant, his brow pressed with a cool cloth. The crow had fled: now bellbirds tinkled. He smelt moss, not dust, and leaves burning somewhere far off.

Fingers stroked his cheek. Someone was singing. He knew the song; he reached in his mind for it. The singing was piercingly sweet. He floated on the melody, bodiless. A bird, the colour of tin, brushed his face with its wings.

He had to see his rescuer, the face that was married to the lovely voice. He discovered he had the power to raise his neck, turn his head a little.

She was smiling down at him, copper lips, green eyes. As he focused the freckles on her face began to teem like ants, her white hair started to twist behind her like a halo of serpents.

Avalon.

Cheyne sat up in bed, shaking.

He would have preferred to be in the arms of the Toecutter.

Cheyne hoped he'd be able to sneak out for a coffee before Avalon woke but she sprang up off the pillow the minute he put his feet on the floor. He averted his face from her good-morning kiss and excused himself to go and take a leak. It was the longest piss in history. He sat on the toilet seat for nearly half an hour. He must have been groaning because Avalon knocked on the door at one point and asked, 'Have you got the collywobbles, Cheyne?'

When he came out a slice of black toast and two rubbery fried eggs were sitting on a plate with an avalanche of something wheat-coloured and glutinous.

'What's that?' he croaked as he sat at the bench on a stool. Avalon had set a frilly place mat for him. She'd picked the last African violet flower and put it on the side of the plate.

'It's brown rice, Cheyne. I found some in the cupboard. You've got to eat up and get healthy. I don't know what you've been doing to yourself. It isn't drugs, is it? Do you like the flower?'

She stood on the opposite side of the counter and watched him eat. He thought about faking stomach cramps again but knowing Avalon she'd keep the food warm in the oven until he ate it. Even if that wasn't until midnight. He knew from experience how thrifty she was. She was the only girl he'd met who clipped supermarket coupons from the Sunday paper. And used them.

Last night she had succeeded, in a few hours, in completely re-arranging Simon's apartment. She pushed the glass coffee table against a wall so that she could roll out her exercise mat and do her daily sit-ups. She moved the 'idiot box' into another corner so that she could watch the motocross on cable while she exercised. She'd changed the towels in the bathroom. Even the cushions on the bed had been removed and shoved onto a closet shelf. Warily watching her do this, he suddenly found he was fond of the chintzy things. 'Leave the cushions, Avalon,' he had said. 'They're comfortable.'

'Cheyne, you've really got no taste! They're *daggy*.'

After breakfast she talked him into taking her out to see the sights. He resisted at first, claiming he had to wait for a script, but he relented when he realised that the sooner she knew how to use the subway the less dependent she'd be on him.

They rattled up to the top of the Empire State. They traipsed around Central Park Zoo. He bought her a Metrocard and showed her how to use it. He bought her a map and marked on it places of interest she might want to see. Alone.

'It's a bit iffy this place, isn't it, Cheyne?' she commented as they pushed through the crowds on Fifth Avenue. 'I mean, all these people give me the irrits!'

They stopped at a cafe on Bleecker on the way home. Cheyne ordered coffee despite her nagging that it was bad for him. Avalon ordered the local delicacy, bagel and cream cheese, to try it.

'Better with Vegemite, but,' she pronounced.

On the street outside, she waved three dollars at him.

'What's that?'

'You left it on the table.'

'Avalon, that's the tip.'

'We don't have to give them a tip.'

'Yes *we* do. Fifteen per cent, at least.'

'But he threw the bagel at me and sloshed your coffee.'

'You did call him "boy".'

'I meant *garcon*. That's what you say. Isn't it?'

'We still have to tip him. He doesn't get paid much otherwise.'

'Is that because he's black?'

'No, it's not because he's black. Put it back.'

'Rack off, Cheyne, it's too much!'

Cheyne snatched the money out of her hand and went back into the cafe.

'I think it's rude to tip people,' she grumbled when he came back.

'It's like they're our *servants* or something.'

'It's just the system, Avalon.'

'Well, you can do what you like. *I'm* never going to leave a tip.'

The phone was buzzing when they got home. Before Cheyne could stop her, Avalon had bounded over and picked it up.

'It's some *girl* for you,' she pouted as she handed over the receiver.

Lara Dinardo sounded young on the phone. 'Cheyne? Hi. This is Lara Dinardo. Valerie gave me your number. The Grimley brothers tell me you gave an interesting audition yesterday. Sorry I wasn't there. Why don't we meet?'

'That would be great.' Cheyne turned his back to Avalon, who was breathing into his collar.

'Yes? Good. Let me look at my agenda…Hmmm. Instead of meeting in this office, it's kind of hectic in here, why don't we have a drink? I'll be finished at—No, I won't. Damn. I have to go to the opening of *Foxy Brown*. Say, you're not free tonight, are you? It's a Miramax picture, remake of the old Blaxploitation thing. You know, you might make some useful connections and I could introduce you to Guy, it's his movie, he's a friend of mine. Sounds good? Great. My assistant will get back to you with the details in a few minutes…Oh, you *do* have a suit, don't you? It's kind of dressy. *Ciao.*'

'Who was that?' asked Avalon, predictably.

'A casting director,' said Cheyne.

'Why is she calling at this hour?'

'Avalon, it's only 4.30 in the afternoon. It's still business hours.'

'Well, you were smiling a lot.'

'I was smiling because she asked me to a film premiere tonight.'

'Wow that's beaut! What time are we going?'

'*We* are not going. She's asked *me* to be her date.' He added quickly, 'It's only business. I've never met her before.'

'Can't you tell her your Australian girlfriend is visiting—'

'No!'

'But Cheyne, maybe I should meet her. She might have a job for me.'

'It wouldn't work. I can't ask her favours. I don't know her.' He could see Avalon's expression growing darker, her hands starting to clench into fists. 'But, look, I'll mention you to her tonight. Informally. It will be better that way.'

'You're not shitting me, Cheyne? You're sure you've never met her?'

'Cross my heart.'

She folded her arms. 'OK. I'll believe you this time. You wouldn't tell fibs when you know I could so easily check up on you.'

'I better go and find a suit.'

'I'll iron it for you.'

'Don't you think you should phone that hotel? It's cheap and in a good location.' Cheyne had consulted a guide in a bookstore and taken note of a place on West Broadway. Far enough away. One hundred bucks a night. He offered to pay for the first week. 'If they've got a room for tonight I could take your stuff over there before I go out.'

Unexpectedly, she gave him a big smile. 'No fucking way! I'm going to stay up and wait for you to come home and tell me all about it.'

'But if the real estate agent comes round and finds you here—'

'Give it a break, Cheyne. I'll find something tomorrow. I couldn't sleep not knowing if you're home safe or not.'

Not knowing if you're home safe with Lara Dinardo or not, he thought.

The phone buzzed again. Avalon jumped on it. 'It's another *girl*,' she said crossly.

'That will be her assistant,' he said.

'It better fucking be,' Avalon said.

'So, how's our little Wahini?' Stewie took his board off Finley and unzipped the bag. 'Man, I'm surprised any of you girls even went into the water yesterday morning. The weather would have twisted your tits off.'

Finley scowled at him. She'd told him she was going surfing with some cousins from North Carolina.

'Anytime you want me to show you some moves, babe.' He leered at her and took the board to the back of Wipeout.

'Well, how *was* it?' Hiromi was arranging Roxy stickers under the glass counter.

'Cold.'

'I don't mean the water.'

'Hot.' Finley smiled. 'But don't say anything, will you? I don't want Stewie to give him a hard time if he ever comes in here.'

'What kind of guy is he anyway?'

'Well, you know, he's a surfer and they don't like to be tied down.' She knelt down behind the counter and started helping Hiromi arrange the stickers. 'Like, committed,' she whispered. 'He's got to go with the waves. I don't want him to think I like him that much.' She stopped what she was doing. 'But I do.'

Hiromi pushed the videos of *Biggest Wednesday* to the side. 'He sounds very romantic.'

'*God*, is he! He's got this way of talking…kind of long and slow. And he looks at you like he's never seen anything like you before. Like he's Adam, you know, and you've just sprung out of his rib.

And he's so fucking strong but really graceful in the water. I almost drowned and he just scooped me up. And he's funny too. That weird accent! I could lie there and listen to the way he talks for hours—'

'Uh-oh.' Hiromi raised her eyebrows and nudged Finley.

'What?'

'In front of you.'

Finley looked through the glass counter. Her view of a rack of a swimwear was obscured by something brown and furry pressing against the glass. Mink.

'*Excuse me.*' The sound of fibreglass nails tapping on the counter. 'Is *anyone* working today?'

Finley ignored the customer. 'We need something to prop up these watches.'

Hiromi looked around. 'What happened to that plastic lobster that was in the fishtank?'

'I took it out. It was frightening the fishes. They look much less stressed since it's gone.'

'I didn't know fish got stressed.'

'Didn't you tell me that uncle of yours who's a sushi chef massages the fish before he chops them up?'

'Oh, I forgot about that. But, like, it's only necessary with a certain kind of highly strung striped bass, I think.'

'This is *disgraceful.*' The mink did a 360-degree turn, looking for assistance.

'I didn't think striped bass were highly strung. I mean, they're so *big*.'

'Maybe it's sardines, then. They look neurotic.'

'Salmon are more neurotic. All that swimming upstream.'

'I'd like to speak to a manager!'

'Yes?' Finley shot to her feet. The mink glared at her. She was younger than she sounded, about twenty-five, her own age, she guessed. Tortoiseshell sunglasses pushed back on top of her tawny hair. One of those big expensive bowling bags sitting on the counter. Her mother's mink, probably. She looked like she was being swallowed by a grizzly.

'I've been standing here for ten minutes!'

'You don't have to get to work do you?'

'No. I don't—'

'Then what are you worried about?' Finley draped a fabric lei over the register. 'How can I help you?'

The mink was about to say something but checked herself. She tossed her head to show off the expensive highlights. 'Do you happen to sell jet skis?'

'Jet skis?'

'Yes, jet skis. I want to get my husband one for Christmas.'

'No you don't.'

'What do you mean?'

'I mean you don't want to get one. Don't you realise how noisy they are? How polluting?'

'If you knew what I was worth you wouldn't talk to me like that.'

'I know what you're worth. You're worth shit—'

'Finley!' Hiromi, still on her knees, tugged at the pocket on Finley's camouflage pants. She jumped to her feet. 'We don't sell jet skis. You could try Hammacher Schlemmer. But he's going to need a wetsuit and we have a few top of the line ones on sale…'

Shane heard the whole exchange. He lurked behind a display of Razor scooters and watched Finley make a disrespectful gesture to the back of the mink-clad woman, who was departing with several parcels of waterproof gear.

What a woman Finley was! A girl after his own heart.

He watched her scan the store, her eyes narrowed, as if she were checking for the presence of any other interlopers wearing dead animals. Her adorable mouth rounded in surprise at seeing him. He could see that she had actually blushed.

'Hi,' he said when he came forward.

'Hi.' She was making herself look busy, moving things around the counter.

The pretty Asian girl, a Jap maybe, was smiling at him. 'Can I help you?'

'It's OK, Hiromi, this is Shane,' Finley whispered.

'Oh, I see. Hey Shane. Pleased to meet you.'

'Why are you both whispering?'

'Stewie, our boss.' Finley jerked her chin in the direction of the back of the store.

'I want to ask you something,' Shane said.

'You do?'

'It's kinda private,' he said, smiling apologetically at Hiromi.

'What's the time?' Finley asked Hiromi.

'A quarter after five.'

'Close enough to quitting time,' Finley said.

'But you've just got here. Even for you, that's a record.'

'I'll get my bag. You OK, Hiromi?'

'Sure. What will I tell Stewie?'

'The usual.'

'Oh, the *usual*.'

Finley took Shane to a coffee shop with red vinyl booths and chrome bar stools.

The waiter brought two menus and two glasses of iced water.

'Hi, I'm Paulie. And I'm your waiter today.'

'I don't care what the fuck your name is,' Shane said.

When the waiter went away, Finley asked, 'What did he do to you?'

'I hate all that phony friendliness. Am I supposed to say, "I'm Shane, I'm your customer today"?'

'He's probably an out of work actor. He's been told to say that. He'll spit in our soup now.'

'Oh, yeah? Then I'll order pancakes.'

'Not safe.' She shook her head.

'How do you know?'

'I've waited tables.'

'You have?'

'Don't sound so surprised. Haven't you?'

'You won't catch me waiting on anyone. Be fucked if I'll do that.'

'It's just a job. You get used to it. People never look at your face, which is why I like it. You could be anyone and they wouldn't know.'

'Like an axe murderer?'

'Or a movie star.'

'You could be a movie star.'

'You think so?' Flattered, she reached for a salt shaker. 'I wanted to be an actor once but I got so tired of people looking at me.'

'I can see that would be a huge problem.'

'Have you ever wanted to be famous?'

'Famous? Why would I want to be that?'

'You see, you're the same as me. People always come to New York to be famous but the best thing about it is you can be so anonymous.' She shook some salt into a white pile onto the table and pushed at it with her finger. 'I don't like people knowing me.'

'I couldn't wait to get out of fucking Melbourne and all those people who think they know me.'

'I don't like labels. Like, you know, *dyke*.'

'Or *fuckwit*.'

'I like to confuse people.'

'I don't bother. Don't you ever get the feeling that you don't want people to call you anything? That when people ask you what you do you just want to say *"Nothing"*?'

'That doesn't go down too well around here. Everyone's so ambitious.'

'But they're ambitious because they're afraid to be fucking *un*ambitious.'

'You're pretty smart, aren't you?'

'Yeah, for a fuckwit.'

'Do you want to eat? You've scared the waiter away. Waiter!' She flung her arm in the air.

'Don't call him yet.'

'Why not?'

'I want to ask you something. It's about Spain.' He took a battered pack of cigarettes out of his jacket pocket and shook one into his hand.

'Spain?'

'Mundaka, where I'm going next.'

'You're going?'

'Of course I'm going. You don't think I'm staying here and waiting for the shitty one-foot waves to become two-foot, do you?'

'They'll get bigger.'

'Nah, I don't believe it.' He stuck the cigarette in his mouth and lit it with a Zippo.

'Exactly when are you going?'

'As soon as I can. When I come into some money.'

'I thought…'

'Don't you like Spain?'

'I haven't thought about it much. There are a whole lot of other places I'd like to go before I go to Spain.'

'Like where?'

'Tibet, for one.'

'There's no surf there.'

'I don't care.'

'But I do.'

'Well, that's apparently all you do care about. Look, I'm going over to Sputnik now.' She brushed the salt off the table.

'You're working tonight at the record place? I thought, you know, we could…'

'I'm not finished until one.'

'You can't smoke in here, sir.' It was Paulie.

'The fuck I can't,' said Shane.

'It's the law. You'll have to go outside.'

'I have to leave.' Finley started to slide out of the booth.

'Wait,' Shane said, pinching the end of his cigarette. 'I'll come with you.'

'You stay here and eat,' she said. 'You've got to save your strength for Spain.'

'Oh. OK. Will I see you later?'

She was out the door before he could answer.

He watched her go. He supposed she was excited about coming to Spain with him but she had a fucking funny way of showing it.

Lara was waiting downstairs for Cheyne in the car. The driver, a Sikh in a double-breasted wool suit, opened the kerbside door and he slid in. The car smelt unpleasantly of pine cleaner.

'Sorry about the smell,' she said as he stretched his legs. 'I'm going to report him to the car company.'

'Maybe someone was ill,' Cheyne suggested, not unreasonably.

'No, they spray it. They think *we're* unclean. It makes me sick to my stomach. Driver, could you *please* put down your window?'

The driver did nothing.

'You see!'

Cheyne didn't know what he was supposed to see. The driver pulled out onto the road. Lara leaned forward and tapped him on the shoulder. 'Take a right on Houston and then take Sixth all the way to 57th. Turn right and do a U-turn so you can drop us right outside the cinema.' She slumped back in her seat. 'He'll find a way to make us late. Traffic jam or something. They're very cunning. I'm Lara, if you hadn't guessed.'

She held out her hand. It felt like a collection of sparrow bones. 'Cheyne.'

'That photo Valerie sent me doesn't do you justice.'

'Thanks.'

'I can see why the Grimleys liked you.'

Cheyne was surprised by this. He thought the Grimleys had tried to make a fool out of him. He felt a little tug of pleasure in his groin. His mouth muscles relaxed into a smile.

'Good smile,' she said. She was tiny in the plush burgundy seat and wearing something black and skimpy that looked like she'd borrowed it from an older sister, a suede coat folded over her lap. Her dark blonde hair was arranged in that pinned up but falling down look he knew was fashionable. There was eyeliner on her eyes and glitter nailpolish on her long fingernails—peeling, he noticed—and sharp little heels on her shoes. When she smiled her creamy beige lipstick stretched over tiny pointed teeth. Cheyne felt that he was on a date with an extremely cunning predatory animal.

'So,' she said, watching him look at her slim knees.

'So,' he smiled. 'How long have you been in this business?'

'Oh, years and years.'

He didn't want to comment on her age, or seeming lack of it. 'How did you get into it?'

'Oh, well. I started as a kid actor. But let's not go there...' She shrugged. He could see the trough of her shoulder blade, dusted with metallic sparkle.

'But you got to the top fast?' He could tell she expected to be flattered. It was in the way she was looking at him sideways.

'I'm good at it. And my boyfriend at the time was an actor. I started managing him. He became successful.'

'Oh? Do I know him?'

'I'm sure you do,' she said and made a shape with her mouth: 'Brad.'

Cheyne was impressed but knew not to show it.

She reached over and stroked the lapel of his navy coat, played with the buttons on his taupe wool suit. 'Nice suit, by the way.'

'Thanks. Helmut Lang.'

'I'm surprised you didn't wear one of those Crocodile Dundee things.'

'You mean, a Drizabone.'

'*Loved* it, didn't you?' she went on. 'They've finished a new one.'

'We're not all from the bush, you know. We don't wear those hats and coats all the time.'

'Pity,' she said. 'I was kind of hoping you'd turn up like that.'

'Well, I'm sorry. I don't even own one of those things. Besides, you told me to wear a suit.' He was aware he sounded petulant.

'I just meant wear shoes or something, for God's sake. Not those flip-flops you wear on the beach.' She waved her hand to finish the conversation.

'These shoes are Commes des Garcons,' he persisted.

'So, you can do a great French accent. I'll remember that when the people at Canal Plus come by.'

They were silent for a while. The car bumped up Sixth Avenue. Cheyne looked out the window. He felt like he'd found himself inside someone else's movie. The neon. The streaming yellow cabs. The herds of people, travelling in packs. For a moment he felt disembodied, nothing more than a shimmering beam of light.

He could hear Lara rustling in her bag. There was a strange little noise, like a chime, and he turned to see what it was. She had a small video camera trained on him. She was staring at the flip-out screen.

'Look out the window again, would you?'

He *was* in someone else's movie.

'What's that for?'

'Great, isn't it? It's a mini DV. It fits in my purse. Makes Polaroids obsolete.'

'OK, but why are you filming me?'

'Oh, I film everyone, just for my records. I like to get actors in *action*, if you know what I mean. Just ignore me.'

'All right,' he said, but he felt uncomfortable. He hated his photo being taken by people who weren't professional. He always looked awkward in family shots, standing there between the Pie King and the Collagen Queen. Maybe he looked stiff because they weren't a family. Just a performance of one. There were his drama teachers, right there in the frame with him.

'Turn towards me now and start talking. Just naturally.'

He felt about as natural as if she'd asked him to dance the macarena. 'What do you want me to talk about?'

'Oh, anything. Yourself. Why you're here in New York. I don't know. Pretend it's an audition.' She fiddled with a button on the side of the camera.

'Now you've made me feel really relaxed.'

'You're not supposed to be relaxed. I want to see some *dynamism*. Beat your breast and swing from tree to tree, for instance.'

'Look,' he said lightly, trying to be good-humoured, but feeling irked. 'You've got the wrong idea about me. I only did one epic, OK? Well, two, if you count *Tribal Force IX*. I want to do theatre work here in New York and interesting pictures. Not *George of the Jungle II*.'

'Three,' she said. 'I think they're working on three.'

'Not that I have anything against loincloths,' he reassured her.

'I'm sure you've got a lot against your loincloth,' she said briskly. 'If you've got it, flaunt it, I say. Hold that smile while—Hey! Driver!' She swung the camera away from Cheyne to the driver. Then she leaned forward, rested her arms on the back of the driver's seat and put the video six inches away from his face. Cheyne could see the man's beard and sweaty nose fill the flip-out screen. 'Don't turn here! I said 57th Street!'

'Traffic, miss,' the driver said.

'Of course there's traffic! There's less traffic on 57th Street. Now, pull over!'

'I can't, miss. I have already completed my turn.'

'Then do a U-turn for Christ's sake!'

'It is illegal, miss.'

'Who the fuck cares? Do what I say or you won't get a tip.'

'I don't think—' Cheyne started to say, feeling sorry for the driver.

'Keep out of it, tourist!' she snapped at Cheyne, whirling the camera around.

'Hey,' Cheyne said. 'I'm not a tourist.'

'That's what you think.' Lara trained the camera back on the driver. 'Do a friggin' U-turn.'

'But, miss, I will lose my licence! I have six children to feed!'

'Haven't you heard of birth control? Turn now or I'll get out of the car.'

'Lara—'

She swung her camera back at Cheyne. 'Keep out of it! They don't like taking directions from a woman. It's in their culture.' She thrust the camera back in the driver's face. 'Turn now or I'll get out of the car.'

The driver shrugged (and, Cheyne thought, whispered a prayer) and suddenly swung into the oncoming traffic, turning the wheel hard. The other cars honked. The driver backed up, straightened, and crawled into a lane.

'Now, turn back into Sixth.'

About twenty minutes later, they drew up to the cinema, late, but exactly the right amount of late. Lara was in no hurry to get out of the car and made the driver wait at the kerb with the door open while she rewound her tape and showed Cheyne some selections.

All Cheyne saw of himself was a thick neck, a fleshy nose, limp hair obscuring sunken eyes and a look of general discomfort. 'Turn it off.'

'I like it. You've got a brooding quality I didn't see in your reel.'

'I do?' He brightened up.

'Brando,' she said.

'Really?'

'And puppyish like John Travolta. With a bit of someone intellectual thrown in. Like…let's see…Gabriel Byrne. But blonder.'

It's a wonder she didn't toss in Mel Gibson, he thought.

She snapped the screen shut. 'And Mel Gibson, of course. Say, you didn't go to school with Russell Crowe or anything, did you?'

'No, why?'

'It's an angle.'

'Do I need an angle?'

'Look,' she patted his knee. 'Take this as a bit of advice. You're *Australian*. You should flaunt it. I was thinking maybe a few barroom brawls. If you're too smooth, too sophisticated, you'll confuse people. They'll think you're British or something. You're not, are you? There are too many British actors. But there aren't too many macho Australians around. Not *this week* anyway. That's your window. I'd milk it for all it's worth. Get rid of that suit and buy a Bonedry. Now, let's get out of this stinking car.'

Cheyne was more than happy to comply. She'd given him an enormous headache. Avalon won't have to worry about me coming home with this one, he thought bitterly.

'Oh, and by the way,' she said. 'I'd change the spelling of your name to S-H-A-N-E if I were you. I can't do anything with Cheyne.'

Shane went home after Finley left him in the diner, smoked a few joints and fell asleep. He woke up a few hours later with a clearer head. Of course Finley didn't sound excited about Spain. What was he thinking? She didn't have any money! Working two jobs and living in that shithole, she probably didn't have any money to spare for the airfare. And she was too proud to tell him! That was it.

It was pretty funny, actually, because he didn't have the fare either. But he'd get it. And he'd get it for her too.

He sat on the edge of the bed and surveyed Dirk's collection of cameras. The time has come, boys, he thought. Time to sacrifice your creaky old selves for Shane.

He pulled on some jeans and sat at Dirk's Powermac. He booted up and went on-line. He found eBay and started scrolling through the lists of items for sale.

Shit, some of these old cameras were getting thousands of dollars! He could make a few handy bucks this way. And Dirk would never know. The things were just gathering dust. He could make enough bucks for Finley and he and Blossom and Mavis to live on the beach at Mundaka for months.

He clicked on *'How do I sell?'*

The remake of *Foxy Brown* was noisy and incoherent but at least Lara kept her video camera tucked away in her handbag.

There were several speeches afterwards and a few dutiful questions from the audience. Cheyne excused himself when they filed into the lobby and went to the bathroom to splash his face.

Standing next to him at a basin was the director of the film, Guy Mirren, a young man so pale he was almost albino. It seemed odd to Cheyne that someone so chalk-white was making a Blaxploitation movie. As far as he knew, no one else had noticed.

'Fun film,' Cheyne said to Guy's mirror-image. He tried to sound more enthusiastic. 'I'm Cheyne Burdekin. I'm here with Lara Dinardo.' He started to hold out his hand but withdrew it when he realised it was dripping wet.

Guy gave Cheyne a slow once over and said, 'That figures.'

Cheyne ran straight into Lara in the lobby. She dug her nails in his arm and whispered, 'Screw the party. A few of us are going to a club. Want to come?'

'Where are you going?'

'Oh, some dive downtown. Thalia knows it.' Lara waved in the direction of the star of the film, Thalia Heller, a pretty chestnut-skinned girl with a tangle of black braids. She was wearing a tight caramel leather skirt and scooped glitter top, from which her pillowy breasts puffed out. She had pillowy lips, too, and everything about her invited thoughts of soft, horizontal pleasures. Cheyne watched as Guy Mirren approached her and draped an arm around her shoulders. He noticed the way Thalia's body leaned into Guy's. 'Are they a couple?'

'On and off,' Lara shrugged. 'More on than off.'

'She was pretty good,' he said.

Lara waved a sparkling hand. 'Well, of course. She's going to be the black Julia Roberts.'

Cheyne imagined that a New York nightclub would be a vast, dimly lit cavern with disco balls and deep blue velvet sectional sofas, but Contaminated was two small rooms, one a bar, the other a dance floor with a dense pack of heads bobbing to the thumping bass produced by a female DJ in a skimpy halter top.

He followed Lara, Guy and Thalia to the bar and ordered a beer. The tab for everyone's drinks came to fifty-eight dollars and nobody made a move to pay it, so he put four twenties on the bar. He waited in vain for some change.

Lara had commandeered a table and an orange velvet sofa in a corner when he brought her cocktail to her. He went back and fetched three more drinks.

She patted the seat next to her. 'I can see you've been a waiter,' she said.

'You're wrong. I missed that rite of passage,' he said, sitting.

'Oh, a trustafarian, hey?'

Thalia and Guy went off to dance. Cheyne was sitting between Lara and a heavy-set bearded guy who had attached himself to their group.

'Joe. Cheyne,' Lara said, which Cheyne supposed was an introduction.

Joe nodded and sat on the edge of the sofa wringing his hands.

Cheyne stared at the dance floor and watched Thalia raise her arms in the air and roll her belly. Her shimmering top lifted to reveal a few inches of bronze skin. Guy stood sideways to her pumping his hands methodically as if he were winching a jack underneath a car. The other dancers pretended not to notice but the circle around them grew tighter.

He was inexplicably jealous of Guy as he watched Thalia rotate her body, her long black braids pasted with sweat to her shoulders. Guy looked all wrong for her, jagged where she was smooth, rigid where she was liquid. He watched Thalia throw her arms around Guy's neck. She seemed more aware of the crowd watching her than of Guy.

He felt as if he were just a forced smile and a body astral-travelling through. Lara's words in the hire car came back to him yet again. You're too smooth, too sophisticated. But what was he supposed to do? Get drunk and throw beer bottles onto the dance floor?

Probably.

He chugged on the beer, and slouched into the sofa, adopting a bored posture. Lara was now talking to a fortyish woman, slender and attractive in a black leather jacket, who had propped herself atop the rolled sofa arm. He decided to find the bathroom. Thank God for bathrooms. At least that would get him moving. As he tried to manoeuvre around the low coffee table, a skinny kid with his pants barely clinging to his hipbones came shuffling up.

'Hey, Cheyne!' the kid said and raised his hand.

Cheyne looked at him in surprise.

'C-H-E-Y-N-E,' grinned the kid. 'I'm Blender. Remember? From Blockbuster?'

'What?' Cheyne's mind flashed on the video of *All's Well*. 'Oh, yes. How are you going?'

'I worked out how to spell your name from your credit card. C. M. Burdekin. You know how I knew? This girl I work with at Sputnik, Finley, she's always going on about surfers. There's a surfer she's got a crush on whose name is spelt the same as yours. Cheyne Horan. Know him?'

Cheyne nodded.

'What's the M stand for anyhow?'

'My father's name.'

'Yeah? Like Melvin?'

'Yeah, like that.' The less said about his father the better.

'Cool.' Blender stared at him. His face was twice as long as it was wide, his eyes set right on the sides of his temples. 'It's weird you being here.'

'Why?'

'Well, I mean you're in the Village and then you're here...'

'So are you.'

'Yeah, I suppose if you look at it that way. You ever been to Sputnik Records near the Cooper Union?'

'No, I don't think so.'

'Anyhow, I work there too. My friend Esther, she works with me, she's spinning tonight.' She shrugged in the direction of the DJ. 'Do you want to meet her? She's going to have a break in a few minutes.'

'OK, why not?' Cheyne felt grateful for the excuse to do something.

'Great. She's cool.' Blender scratched his arm. 'You been here before?'

'No, it's my first time.'

'Great, huh? You can be yourself here. None of that posing stuff, you know?'

'Unfortunately I'm with a bunch of posers,' Cheyne admitted.

'Yeah? Oh, I see. Those indie movie types. The regulars don't like 'em. It's sort of a club, you know?'

'Who do you like?'

'People who kind of know who they are. Don't have to prove it.'

'And that guy over there—' Cheyne nodded in Guy's direction. 'He doesn't know who he is?'

'He thinks he does. But identity's a fragile thing, man. You don't, like, own who you are.'

'What do you mean?'

'I mean these days a complete stranger can take your identity away from you. You know? Like by having your credit card number and stuff. I know a hacker who catches passwords off the internet and sells them on to these crims. It's like a big racket. They charge all this stuff using the numbers and passwords, wreck the person's credit. Soon, the person can't even use his own name. He's like lost his identity.'

'I've heard of it.'

'It's cool.'

'You think so?'

'Sure, why not? The world's full of people who are nothing but names. You know, Donald Trump and shit. It's like power to them. No harm in bringing them down a few rungs. It's the disenfranchised getting their own back, you know?'

'But the hackers are ripping off ordinary people too.'

'So? My friend reckons people shouldn't care so much about their names. It's just a barcode Big Brother has given you. If the barcodes become meaningless, then there's no way the big guys can control you. Society will have to start all over again. And that rocks, my friend.'

'So you wouldn't mind if someone borrowed your name?'

'Why not? You think Blender's the name I was born with? Most of my friends, we're in this city because there's nowhere in the world as easy to be someone else...Hey, Esther's finishing up. Want to go meet her?'

Blender cut a path through the middle of the dance floor. Cheyne followed. Blender's path took him directly between Thalia and a girl who had moved in to dance with her. Cheyne tried to skirt them but Thalia suddenly stepped back and into him.

'Hey!' She turned around to accuse whoever she thought was fondling her.

He raised his hands. 'Sorry,' he yelled over the music.

A look that might have been a smile crossed her face. Her eyes flashed and she ran them up and down his torso. 'It's about time,' she said and touched his arm with her hand. 'C'mon. Let's get out of here.'

Blender found Esther sitting on the steps that descended to the bathrooms smoking a post-performance cigarette. 'I wanted you to meet someone,' he told her and turned around. 'I think he went off with this black chick, though. Thalia Heller, I recognised her.'

'Who?'

'This guy I met. Cheyne. He's Australian.'

'Oh?' She bit the black polish off one nail. 'What's he look like?'

'He's big and sort of blond. You'd like him.'

'I bet I would.'

'Let's get some air. Maybe he's outside.'

'It's fucking freezing out there, Blender. I'm going to sit here with my smoke and ruminate.'

'Well, I'll go find him then.'

'He's that cute, huh?'

Blender nodded.

'As cute as Russell Crowe?'

'Cuter.'

'God, he sounds like trouble.'

'Yes,' said Blender. 'I think he might be.'

Finley locked the door at Sputnik behind her at 1 a.m. Everyone had pissed off to clubs, including the customers. But she didn't feel like going to Contaminated to watch Esther spin. Her head had been spinning all by itself.

Fucking Shane.

She kicked trash cans all the way from the Bowery to Lafayette Street. The red-cheeked faces of plastic Santas beamed out at her from store windows. Well, you did get involved with a surfer, they smirked.

Yes, but one date and he's talking about leaving?

She hit a shop window with the flat of her hand and startled a window-dresser working late who was placing a red cap with a white pompom on the head of a dummy.

'Merry fucking Christmas!' Finley mouthed.

'That was fly,' Thalia purred, stretching her arms and grabbing hold of the drainpipe behind her. 'But we've gotta go.'

'We do?' Cheyne lifted his head from between her legs. It was freezing in the alley and the skip stank of bananas mushed with offal. She was still wearing a halter and one plum-sized nipple had forced its way out. She was naked from the waist down, her leather skirt crumpled around her belly, her pointy shoes kicked off onto the cobblestones. The skip was so cold he didn't know how her skin hadn't stuck to the metal. But her thighs were miraculously warm against his face.

OK, they were getting it off in an alley but he knew he'd been good, imaginative and graceful, forceful but considerate. Too considerate, perhaps. Now she was talking about going.

'Guy will wonder where I've gone, babe.'

'Let him wonder. Surely another ten minutes won't hurt?' He straightened his knees and kissed a scar on her inside thigh. 'What's this?'

'Oh, an old tattoo I had lasered off. Brad Forever, you know.'

'Brad?'

She shivered. 'I went out with him for a month. I'm kind of impulsive.'

She had the most fetching triangle of trimmed black pubic hair. 'Like it?' she asked. 'It's a Brazilian bikini wax.'

He grabbed her around the waist. The edge of the skip dug against his hipbone. He kissed her on the mouth. The skip swayed. So did his penis, which was hardening by the second. Pretty impressive even in the cold, he thought, as he unbuckled.

She looked down at him. 'I wouldn't mind trying that another time,' she said brightly, as if she were rejecting a pastry on a plate in favour of a tastier one. 'But Guy inspects every inch of me. Like a fucking forensic scientist.'

'I've got condoms in my pocket. Somewhere.' He patted his coat.

'Don't you think he knows the taste of rubber?'

'You could go home and take a quick shower.'

'How obvious is that? I'm away for an hour and I go back to the club smelling like pine needles?'

Cheyne hadn't had to debate the pros and cons of having sex with a girl since the fourth-form dance. 'He did see you leave with me.'

'Yeah, but he won't be suspicious.'

'Why not?'

'You're not my type.'

'Oh? I'm not?' He slid his hand between her thighs again. He found the place he was looking for, warm and gummy to the touch. She put her hands against his chest and gave him a little push. 'Didn't you hear me, big boy? Not now.' She slid off the skip and smoothed her skirt. 'Fuck, it's creased.'

Cheyne was sure that kind of expensive leather didn't crease.

'Help me find my shoes, will you, babe?' Thalia demanded.

'I don't understand why you care what he thinks.' Cheyne found her shoes and handed them over. 'I mean, it's obvious you aren't monogamous.'

'Are you from outer space? Of course I'm not mono—whatever.'

'Good, then give me your phone number.'

She gave him an amused little frown. 'I can't do that. I mean, who are you?'

He didn't have an answer to that.

They staggered back round the corner to Contaminated. They'd barely been gone for twenty minutes, he noted. No one seemed to notice.

Lara was on the couch in exactly the same position as when he left. He asked her if she wanted a drink.

She looked at him casually and said, 'My God, Cheyne,' she said, 'you look as if you've been in a brawl!'

He could see now that his taupe suit was smeared with something…Spaghetti-O's perhaps.

Lara beamed at him. 'I like a man who's quick to follow advice.'

Cheyne was more than a little drunk when he trudged upstairs to his apartment. God knew what time it was. Avalon would probably be standing at the door with a frying pan in her hand.

His feet felt like they were lifting cement blocks. As he passed apartment 2B, he could hear the predictable squeak of the door opening and his nervous Nellie of a neighbour checking to see if friend or foe was passing by.

'Cheyne!' Avalon's voice came from behind him.

He turned around, expecting to find her following him up the staircase. Instead, her head was sticking out from the door of apartment 2B. She was wearing short pyjamas with Jedi knights all over them.

A middle-aged woman in some kind of peculiar multicoloured caftan appeared behind her, smiling.

'Cheyne, isn't it wonderful? This is Kendra and I'm going to be living with her for a while!'

'You're what?'

'Well I came down to borrow a cup of sugar—'

He raked one hand through his long hair and addressed his neighbour. 'I'm sorry if she troubled you. She's new and—'

'No trouble I assure you. Kendra Spitz.' The woman held out her hand, revealing a bracelet of rock-sized mauve crystals.

'Cheyne Burdekin.'

'I was going to make a pavlova,' Avalon said. 'The sugar's bad for you I know, but I thought you'd like something from home.'

'We got to talking,' Kendra interrupted. 'And Avalon gave me that fascinating recipe for meringue. She explained your situation. It really is too bad. That Simon is too precious. It's not as if his place is a showcase, after all. I've told him the decor is too dowdy. I have a very good decorator. But he does love his chintz. Anyway, the upshot is I've offered Avalon a room.'

'But—'

'Oh, don't worry.' She waved white-tipped fingernails. 'Avalon can help me out in return. I'm fascinated by Australia. It really is the place at the moment. And I'm rather ignorant of it. Avalon can fill me in.'

'Kendra's going to Sydney in May. For the fashion shows.'

'I was really rather surprised that you have fashion in Australia,' Kendra explained.

'So was I!' giggled Avalon.

Cheyne looked at the two of them. 'Avalon, I don't think you can take advantage of Miss…er…Spitz like that.'

'Kendra, please.'

'It's only for a few weeks, Cheyne. Until you and me can find a place that's big enough for both of us.'

No place on earth would be big enough for the both of us, he thought. He said, weakly, 'That's nice.'

'I know it's late but you must have a nightcap. Why not a Caipharina? It's a Brazilian cocktail. I'm sure you're as bored as everyone else with Cosmopolitans.' Kendra clutched Cheyne's arm.

Brazilian bikini waxes and now Brazilian cocktails. 'No, thanks,' Cheyne said. 'I'm dead. I don't want to keep you up any longer.' He glowered at Avalon.

'Don't be silly,' Kendra said. 'This is New York.'

She led him into a white-painted room with red furniture. 'Avalon tells me you're Australian too. But your accent is different.'

'Oh, I can explain that,' said Avalon, bounding behind them. 'I'm from Brissie. But he's sophisticated.'

An Australian girl! What great luck, Kendra thought, as she tiptoed into the sleeping Avalon's room at 9 a.m. and left a fluffy white towel at the end of her bed. She'd be able to put together a report for the new year now. And an Australian issue of *Prophesee* was already in the works. She'd called her assistant editor at 4 a.m. and they'd tossed around a few ideas. They'd title it AUSTRALIA—STYLE CAPITAL OF THE WORLD. That would raise a few eyebrows. Maybe they could find one of those Aborigines to guest-edit. Or, failing that, Cate Blanchett.

Kendra stood for a few moments and observed the way Avalon slept with her arms bent and flung out to the side as if she were falling from a building and trying to protect herself. She was wearing Jedi knight boxer shorts, a sports bra and an airline eyemask to block out the morning light, which Kendra had artfully filtered through slimline venetians. Kendra admired the knotted muscles of her knees, the tight, long sinews of her thighs, the bulbous calves ending in slightly too-thick ankles, the way her pectoral muscles were taut even in repose. She had a remarkable tan, almost orange, and a rash of freckles under it, across her chest. For a minute Kendra considered reaching out and placing a hand on one globular breast to see if it were real.

What a specimen! How exotic! And to think Kendra had opened her door last night and there she was, holding out a china teacup and asking for sugar. Sweet, very sweet. Dressed head to toe in green and yellow. Tacky on a New Yorker, but on an Australian it was totally charming.

It was as clear as day to everyone, except her, poor girl, that that handsome boyfriend was trying to get rid of her. She'd run across these actor types before. They'd fuck anyone for a role. Judging by the alarm on his face when the girl had told him she was staying downstairs, he had a hot little pot on the boil already. She could smell it on him. It wouldn't be long before Avalon worked it out. But Kendra was very good at comforting the broken-hearted. She was almost looking forward to it.

Pity the girl was so clumsy, though. She'd already broken a decanter in the bathroom that Kendra had unearthed in the Paris *marché des puces* last October. She'd knocked over a stack of Marseilles soap and piled it up again with no sense of colour harmony. The primrose soap had to go on top of the almond and not the olive oil. Then she'd pulled the toilet lever up instead of down and blocked the cistern. She'd dragged her bizarre musical instrument across the parquetry floor and scraped the wood so badly the resurfacer would have to be called this morning. And she'd unrolled an exercise mat that was screaming blue and clashed horrendously with the lime and red sitting-room furniture.

When Avalon had gone to bed, Kendra cautiously picked up the Reeboks by the laces from where they had been left under the coffee table and placed them inside a Bergdorf Goodman bag. She placed this inside Avalon's room and spritzed Catherine Memmi White Flowers aerosol back and forth across the sitting room to get rid of the fungal smell. Then she went through Avalon's luggage methodically, professionally, to find out what products Australian girls used. Earlier, she'd watched in fascinated horror as Avalon pulled out of her duffle bag a huge jar of black gunk and proceeded to spread it on a hunk of stale Balthazar baguette. It was some kind of yeast paste, almost as bad-smelling as those rotten cabbages the Asians ate. She had to disinfect the kitchen later.

Thank God, the cleaning lady was coming this morning.

She was just reminding herself to leave Myriam a note when Avalon sat up and ripped off her eyemask. She blinked once and then was up on her knees, her hands rigid in front of her face in some kind of martial arts pose.

Kendra recoiled.

'Oh, shit,' Avalon said. 'Sorry, but. I was dreaming.' She dropped her hands. 'I was fighting Jackie Chan. I must have been the bad guy.'

'How could that ever be possible?' Kendra said.

'Funny isn't it?' She took in Kendra's Prada skirt and gold silk Yves Saint Laurent pussy-bow. 'Are you going to work?'

'I'm off to make a presentation. Will you be all right?'

'Yeah, I'll go up and make Cheyne brekkie. I don't think he's had a decent meal since he's been here. He's so thin he looks like he'd have to run around the shower to get wet.'

'Run around the shower?'

'Yeah, you know. Skinny and kind of sick-looking. And his hair's long. Like a derro.'

'Derro?' Kendra made a mental note to start carrying her Palm Pilot around the apartment to jot down Avalon's quaint little sayings. She'd memorised a few from last night. Mad as a cut snake. Built like a brick shithouse. Charging like a wounded bull.

Avalon bounced off the bed. 'I'm wrapped in that outfit of yours.'

'Thanks.'

'Do you think you could take me shopping? Show me where to buy stuff like that?'

'You have your own sense of style, Avalon.'

'You reckon? But I'm such a dag!' She started doing some vigorous jumping jacks on the floor. 'Shit, I need a workout. Is there a gym round here?'

'Everyone I know does Vikram yoga. It's very rigorous.'

'No. Yoga is for girls. I want some action. Kung fu. Boxing. I feel like kicking in a few heads!' She started punching holes in the air. 'Just kidding.'

'Thank God for that. Why don't you turn on the television? I have satellite. And a TiVo. Hundreds of channels. There's sure to be some exercise program on at this hour. Use the pay-for-view if you want. I won't be back until six or seven. Will you be all right?'

'No worries. Cheyne'll look after me.'

Kendra sighed.

Pow. Thwack. Grunt. Crash.

Avalon was having a lovely time. Pity about the glass-topped coffee table. And that weird pottery thing on top of it. She didn't know why people cluttered up their rooms with useless items. Oh, well, she'd get Cheyne to help her fix it later. Glass was cheap, wasn't it, and that pottery puppy dog looked like something you could find at the Salvos.

She'd pressed a button on the remote and the TV screen had filled with a group of tanned, pumped-up people punching the air and scissor-kicking. Some kind of martial art she'd never heard of before. Mo Bo. Stupid name. Sounded like a bunch of homeless poofs. It was a pretty ace workout, though. She had all the moves down after fifteen minutes.

She showered quickly and went to the refrigerator to find something for Cheyne's breakfast. The side doors were full of champagne and blue bottles of water. On a shelf were half a lemon and a jar of artichoke pesto. There was frozen Smoothie mix in the freezer. The cupboards above were stacked with Japanese crackers.

Oh well, she'd have to improvise.

The crash from downstairs woke Cheyne. His bedroom window was open and through it came the gut-upending thud of bass punctuated by loud grunts and cries. Then it stopped.

He pulled the corner of a patchwork quilt over his head. Now it was the phone.

'Congratulations, darling, you've got a call back.'

'Huh?' Cheyne pushed himself up into a sitting position and searched for a cushion for his back. Dozens of those wretched frilly things and not one when you needed it. 'Valerie?'

'A week from today. Next Wednesday, the 20th. That means you're short-listed. They don't know who the girl is yet.'

'The girl?'

'Gwendolen, you dullard. They're going to get you to read Jack with a different Gwendolen. Lara just called me.'

'Lara?'

'Cheyne, get out of bed and have a cold shower. Lara Dinardo who you dated last night.'

'I wouldn't call it a date.'

'No? Well, you must have done something she liked because she was on the phone to me first thing this morning with the call back all set up.'

'It's not what you think.'

'Darling, you could have tied her up and licked Miracle Whip off her belly for all I care. Just keep doing whatever you're doing to her. She said she is now convinced you have the qualities required for the part.'

All the qualities required for the part? Jack Worthing was a pompous ass. He wasn't the kind of guy who'd fuck a woman he'd just met in an alley and get Spaghetti-O's all over his pants. Then again the Grimleys said they saw the character as sexy, degenerate. Had Thalia been talking to Lara?

'And I have another thing for you,' Valerie was saying. 'A bit of a money-earner. Anonymous. The people at the Downunder Steakhouse need a voice-over for their new series of TV commercials. They just called. Seems their other Australian has come down with laryngitis.'

'I don't do commercials.'

'No? Harrison Ford does commercials. In Japan, anyway. I'm trying to help you out here. No one will know it's you. And the pay is off the meter for this sort of thing.'

'Sounds like crap. I don't need it.'

'All you have to do is roll out of bed and be at the studio tomorrow at five. How hard is that?'

'OK. If you think so.'

'I do. It will pay your rent for a year.' She hung up.

The small gilt alarm clock on the bedside table read 10.46. Early. He slumped down in bed again, closing his eyes and folding his mind around thoughts of dewy, moonlit thighs and Brazilian bikini waxes.

Thalia. He allowed himself to recall her coconut-scented skin, the taste of vinegar and peaches, the smell of rusted metal and rotting…broccoli. He tugged at his scrotum idly. Her plump nipple, red lips, the scent of meatballs in the morning air, the way she smacked his hand…

He had her on the trestle table with her apron around her hips. She wore flesh-coloured stockings with garters covered in white satin ribbons. She was paddling him with her wooden spoon as he rode her, the crew standing around them, watching idly, waiting for coffee. His right hand was in a bowl of guacamole, steadying himself.

'Natalie,' he whispered in her pearly ear.

'Keep that up, Pie Boy,' she commanded, rolling him over.

Pie Boy. Suddenly, he felt the urge go out of him. He tried to pull back, withdraw, but she had her strong thighs clamped over his, heavy as boulders. Her vagina felt like hot, wet sandpaper as she scraped up and down.

'Jesus, Cheyne, this is fucking amaaaaazing!'

He felt himself dissolve, a blancmange pudding tipped out of its bowl.

Avalon sprang off, dumping sticky fluids on his belly. She threw herself against his chest. 'Just like the old days,' she purred. 'Aren't you glad I stole your key?'

Finley punished herself with a double class of Mo Bo. On days like these she wished she'd taken up boxing. A punching bag with Shane's face on it would have been more therapeutic than punching the air.

She arrived at Sputnik at six.

'What's wrong with you this time?' Rockwell sighed, watching Finley fling her bag into the back room. 'In love yesterday and out of love today? Did he dump you or something?'

'Fuck off!'

'Finley alert!' Rockwell cupped his hands around his mouth and his voice boomed through the record store.

'What's the trouble?' Esther asked from behind the register.

Finley squeezed in next to her. 'Nothing, all right?'

'If you say so. You don't happen to know if we've got any Spiky Love Thang in stock?'

'Yeah, over in Detroit Techno.'

'Look in Detroit Techno, my fine young boy,' Esther told her customer.

'Hey, Finley, there's a call for you!' Rockwell was standing at the back of the room, holding out a receiver. 'It's your girlfriend.'

'Hang up!'

'She says it's an emergency.'

'Oh, Christ!' Finley pushed her way to Rockwell and snatched at the phone. 'She's not my girlfriend.'

Rockwell held the receiver behind his back. 'Hey, I'm not the one who called her that. She said, "This is Natalie, Finley's girlfriend." What am I supposed to think?'

'Give the phone to me!'

He handed her the receiver and she turned her back to him. 'What?' she spat at Natalie.

'That's a swell way to talk to someone bearing good news. Great news.'

'Stop playing games, Natalie. I'm hanging up.'

'No—don't. This is the thing. Lara Dinardo, that casting director I told you about, called me. About you. She wants you to come in tomorrow afternoon to read for her. *The Importance of Being Earnest!* Aren't you thrilled?'

'No. I told you—'

'Think about it, Finley. You don't want to work in that stupid record store forever, do you?'

Finley half-turned. Rockwell was right behind her, leering. 'No.'

'Everyone dreams of a break like this! To be discovered—and not have to struggle for it.'

'I haven't got the part yet.'

'But you will. I'll pick you up at Wipeout at four-thirty. Think you can manage that?'

'You're not coming with me!'

'Oh, yes I am. I'm the one who knows when and where it is, remember?' Natalie hung up.

Finley cursed. Natalie would be unbearable if she did get the role. But Natalie was already unbearable, so what was the difference? And she could do with the money. A movie role meant big bucks. If Shane went to Spain she would have the money to follow him. If he wanted her. Her mood darkened again.

'Lover's tiff?' Rockwell was leaning against the stock-room door, arms folded.

Finley pushed him in the chest and went back to the register.

An hour later, Rockwell again waved the phone in the air and called across the room. 'Attention Finley. Attention Finley. There's a Shane on the phone.'

Finley bolted to the back room and snatched the receiver off him.

'Finley?'

'I'm working.'

'Yeah, I know. The guy at the surf shop gave me your number.'

'Well what do you want?'

'I was thinking. There might be a wave at the end of the week. Want to come?'

Finley resisted. She wanted to say no. But then again, she didn't. 'I don't know.'

'But you've got talent.'

'I have?'

'I'll have you carving in no time.'

'All right. What day?'

'I reckon it will be barrelling on Saturday. Meet you at the station? Same time?'

'If I'm not there by 6.15, I'm not coming, OK?'

'It's a deal.'

He hung up. Finley looked at the phone.

'Funny accent,' said Rockwell, who was lurking.

'None of your business.'

Rockwell followed her back to the register. 'So this is the mystery boyfriend.'

'Who is?' said Esther, changing a disc.

'This Shane. He's Finley's boyfriend.'

'His name's Shane?' Esther asked.

'So what?' said Finley.

'Sounds like the Crocodile Hunter,' Rockwell said.

'Yeah, well he is Australian, if that's any of your business.'

'Australian?' This was Esther.

'So?'

'Well, Blender knows a Shane who's Australian, that's all.'

'He does?'

'Blender! Come over here!'

Blender shuffled up to the sales desk. He had a wad of credit card slips in his hand. 'You called?'

'Hey, Blender, don't you know a Shane who's Australian? The one who was at Contaminated last night?'

'You mean Cheyne?'

'Yeah, that Shane. He's Finley's boyfriend.'

'He is?' Blender was thinking of the blonde with Cheyne and the black actress Blender saw him leaving with.

'You know him?' Finley marvelled.

'Yeah, about this tall?' Blender raised his hand to about four inches over his head.

'That's right.'

'And he's got hair that's kind of blond and brown?'

'Yeah.'

'Good-looking?'

'That's him.'

'Sure, I know him. Met him at the video store. Nice guy.'

'You think so?'

'Yeah, gets around a bit, though. Anyone want anything at the deli?'

Before Finley could ask him what he meant, Blender was out the door.

Shit. Blender cursed on his way across Bleecker. Poor Finley. That Cheyne was a real playboy, he could tell. The way he arrived at the club with one girl and left with another in about ten minutes flat. Of course, the indie actress was a honey and given half a chance he would have left with her too. But, still…if Cheyne was hanging out with Finley it was a different matter.

He collected two Cokes from the deli refrigerator and ordered a meatloaf sandwich. Should he tell Finley about Cheyne's infidelities? Then again, did he really know they were infidelities? Maybe the actress was a cousin, or something. You had to give people the benefit.

Besides, he dreaded to think of the physical damage Finley would inflict on him as the bearer of bad tidings.

He'd keep the information to himself.

'If you say "It's going to be swell" one more time, I'll kick you,' Finley hissed at Natalie while they waited in the outside office for Lara Dinardo. 'And stop holding my hand!' She peeled Natalie's blood-red nails from her palm.

Shane said 'swell' a lot too. But it was a different kind. If the swell's big enough and the wind's offshore…And there was another kind of swell she thought about when she thought about Shane: it didn't have anything to do with the sea.

'Do you think they won't hire you for a sexy role if they know you're a lesbian?' Natalie adjusted her padded shoulders nonchalantly.

'I'm not a lesbian.'

'Well, dozens of movie stars are and by the look of that casting director when she came out to shake our hands she is one too.'

'You think everyone is lesbian!'

'Well, research shows that one in three women have dabbled in lesbian alliances. You can double that because no one ever tells the truth. And the rest are thinking about it. You shouldn't be ashamed of yourself.'

'I'm not ashamed. I'm heterosexual, that's all.'

'As far as I can see you haven't been having much success.'

'Actually, I've got a new boyfriend.' As soon as it was out, she regretted saying it. Natalie wouldn't stop until she wangled all the intimate details out of her.

'Oh?'

'And I'm not telling you a thing about him, so don't ask.'

'I suppose he's another one of those new-age phonies. Like that cowboy poet. Or that Zen capitalist you keep taking kick-boxing lessons from.'

'It's called Mo Bo. And Ra Ke isn't a phony.'

'Just a little short of what you expected, though. Only you would believe a guy with a name like that. Whereas I am 100 per cent pure authentic dyke. You have to respect that.'

'I respect you. I just don't want to sleep with you.'

'It wasn't sleeping that was the problem if I recall.'

'You know what I mean.'

'Why don't you whisper it in my ear?'

'Fuck off, pervert.'

Natalie snorted. She crossed her legs. She was wearing stockings with seams. 'What's so special about this boy, then?'

'He's different.'

'They've all been different. You have a talent for unearthing different. Does this different person have a name?'

'I'm not telling you.'

'What, do you think if his name's Rupert I'm going to call up all the Ruperts in New York and give them an earful?'

'Shane. His name's Shane. Now shut the fuck up.'

'You see, he is a cowboy!' Natalie took a compact out of her alligator bag and checked her lipstick.

'Actually, he's a surfer.'

'Finley, you little idiot. Everyone knows surfers are scum.' She clapped her compact shut for emphasis.

'This one's not.'

'Does he say "Dude" a lot?'

'Very funny. He's Australian.'

'Australian? You've really gone for a cave man this time.'

'He's not like that. Can we get off the subject, please?'

Natalie tapped her foot in the air. 'Shane? Hmmm.' She put a finger to her chin. 'You know, I met an Australian called Shane on the street the other day. A big, handsome brute. If you like that kind of thing.'

'You did?'

'Yes, we chit-chatted for a bit. That's your Shane, huh?'

'About six-two? Hair that's blond and brown, kind of long?'

'That's him all right. If I see him again I must question him more closely.'

'You will not.'

Natalie smiled at her. 'Don't worry. I won't spoil anything. Judging by the look of him you've got your hands full anyway.'

'What do you mean?'

Lara Dinardo's assistant came out of the inner office and beamed at Finley. 'Lara's ready when you are, Finley.'

'I'm ready,' Finley sighed. 'I suppose.'

'For God's sake, Finley, show some enthusiasm!' Natalie whispered sharply. 'And take that army jacket off. You look too butch.'

'Do you want to bring your mother in with you?' the assistant asked pleasantly.

'I'm not—' Natalie started to say, indignantly.

'No, my mother will be just fine out here,' Finley replied, deadpan. 'Especially if you could find her a copy of *Hustler*.'

'OK, Cheyne,' the muffled voice of the female producer said through the headphones. 'We're ready when you are. Just give me a sound level.'

Cheyne bent slightly towards the microphone. 'But you don't really mean to say that you couldn't love me if my name wasn't Ernest? But your name is Ernest. Yes, I know it is. But supposing it was something else? Do you mean to say you couldn't love me then?'

There was a sound through the headphones like paper being crumpled. He heard a male voice chip in, 'What the fuck he say?'

'Don't know,' the female voice said. 'Maybe it's an Australian folk song or something. Level's OK, though.'

The male producer's voice boomed back at him. 'Let's do it. You OK, Cheyne? Give me a moment…And…recording!'

The script was affixed to a lectern with a bulldog clip. Cheyne had been bundled into the studio with barely time to glance at it. Through a glass window he could see the two producers at a console looking at him.

'Down Under we're overachievers,' he read. 'We like everything big. Big country, big outback, big rocks, big critters. We like our steaks with big flavour too. Over here at the Downunder Steakhouse we're not cooking kangaroo. Just the biggest and best steaks this side of the Black Stump. Why not come on down and crack a tinnie with us? Experience some good old Australian hospitality. "How are you going, mate?" Bonza! At the Downunder Steakhouse.'

God, what codswallop. It sounded like it had been written by a copywriter who hadn't been closer to Australia than sitting next to a bottle of Fosters at some midtown bar.

'Cheyne? Cheyne?' The female producer was fiddling with a switch. 'Can you hear me?'

'Yes, I can.'

'Could we take it again? This time, could you make it a little more Australian? A little more rugged?'

'Rugged?'

'You know, like the Crocodile Hunter. A bit…cowboy. So, can we try it again?'

The Crocodile Hunter! What was this American obsession with Australian men who liked to frolic with large reptiles? He didn't argue, though. Just get through it and get out of here, he told himself.

He began to read again, slower this time, dragging out his vowels, hardening his consonants, adding a rising inflection to the end of every sentence.

'How was that?' he asked when he had finished. 'I mean,' he flattened his voice, 'howzat?'

There was a short silence. The woman spoke. 'Not really, Cheyne. It still doesn't sound Australian enough.'

'It sounded Australian to me,' he said. 'And I'm Australian.'

'Are you sure?'

What kind of idiot was this woman? 'The problem is the script,' he explained patiently. 'That's what sounds American.'

'We had an Australian write it, Cheyne. He's a very famous Australian novelist, in fact.'

'Well, for a start "critters" sounds American, no matter what kind of accent you have. And "come on down" sounds like a quiz show.'

'I'm sure you have quiz shows in Australia too, Cheyne. We have complete faith in our writer. Lord knows, he cost enough. Now could we just try it again? Maybe if you could do some visualisation for a moment. Imagine yourself in the outback doing whatever you used to do there. Shearing sheep perhaps?'

He bit his tongue. It was good money. 'OK, let's see what I can do.'

He did the worst Australian accent of his life, so broad he could feel his jaw muscles twitching in protest throughout. God, he'd be the laughing stock of Sydney if they ever found out. But they wouldn't. No one could possibly recognise this voice. Kangaaaroooo! Bonzaaaaa! Owayagoinmade?

They loved it.

Lara Dinardo assessed the hostile girl across the desk from her. In her camouflage pants and khaki jacket she looked like she was ready to take up arms against some Central American dictatorship rather than drink tea in a nineteenth-century English drawing room. But then, the Grimleys might like that. They'd rejected about every other female actor in town.

'I'm going to read Jack Worthing,' Lara explained. 'And you read Gwendolen. We'll start here.' She pointed to a place on the page. 'OK?'

Finley shrugged.

Lara began. 'Personally, darling, to speak quite candidly, I don't much care for the name of Ernest…I don't think the name suits me at all.'

Finley frowned as she read. 'It suits you perfectly. It is a…a divine name. It has music of its own. It produces vibrations.'

'Well, really, Gwendolen, I must say that I think there are lots of other much nicer names. I think Jack, for instance, a charming name.'

'Jack?…No, there is very little music in the name Jack, if any at all, indeed. It does not thrill. It produces absolutely no vibrations…I have known several Jacks, and they all, without exception, were more than usually plain…um…Besides Jack is a notorious domestisy...domesticity for John! And I pity any woman who is married to a man named John! Oh, shit, this sounds stupid!' Finley dropped the script to her lap.

'Go on,' Lara said.

'I can't. It's a waste of time.'

'Maybe if you tried to be a bit more feminine.'

'I am being feminine!' Finley stood abruptly, the script tumbling to the ground. 'How fucking more feminine can I fucking be?'

'I didn't mean to suggest—'

'This is not working for me,' she said, knocking over the chair in her rush to get out of the room. 'Sorry.'

She slammed the door behind her.

Lara watched her go.

Interesting. In her experience, this is how all the truly talented actors reacted under scrutiny. They were sullen, awkward, resentful. They'd all squirm like children getting a lecture from a grade-school principal. The squirming was almost the best way she knew to tell the really good ones. Look at De Niro! Look at Mel Gibson! Now, those boys were agitated. You couldn't give them direction. They knew all about the character from the lines on the page. A few vowels and consonants were all they needed. The word made flesh. The good ones were fucking gods, that's what they were.

OK. The little minx could have her chance. The Grimleys might respond to her ferocity. God knows, they hadn't responded to anyone else. Besides, the girl was clearly a dyke, judging by the girlfriend. They'd been holding hands in the outside office. Lesbian actors were doing better than straights these days. Commanding bigger paychecks. Look at you-know-who, a raving rug-muncher if ever there was one, playing a doe-eyed hetero in hit after hit. She didn't understand it. But, hey, if it worked for the producers...

She emailed her assistant in the next room to let the Rule girl know about next week's audition.

'You see,' Natalie said as they stood in the elevator, descending. 'You were good.'

'I was terrible. She must be a nut.'

'She saw some quality in you.'

'Well, I wish she hadn't. I hate this shit.'

'I don't understand why.'

'Because what's the point? Either I say those lines or someone else does. It doesn't matter. The lines stay the same. Where am I in all that?'

'Don't tell me you're having an identity crisis.'

'Can't this elevator go any faster?'

'You see. Always trying to control things. I wouldn't think that surfer boyfriend of yours likes being pushed around.'

'Leave him out of it. If you see him on the street again, I forbid you to talk to him.'

'What if he talks to me? I must say, he seemed kind of interested.'

'In you? Please!'

'I'm an attractive woman.'

'So was Leni Riefenstahl.'

The elevator doors opened and Finley stalked out. Natalie made quick little steps to catch up, but Finley was too fast, disappearing onto the street and the rush-hour crowd on Lexington.

Ungrateful little wretch. Natalie changed direction and headed for the subway. Forbidding me to talk to her boyfriend, as if I'd—

Then again, she smiled as she perused a newsstand for a copy of *Girlfriends*, I just might.

After the Downunder debacle, Cheyne sat in the bar without the 'R', killing a few hours and thinking that he would have to stay there until Avalon was safely asleep in Kendra's apartment.

He hadn't been to bed with her in, what, nine months and she'd still followed him to the other side of the world. Now that she was all cosy with Kendra she could stay in the apartment below him indefinitely, lying in wait for him every time he crept past the wretched door, flinging her arms around him and telling him she would wait forever if necessary. It was beyond her comprehension that he didn't want her. The part of no she didn't understand was all of it. She didn't understand his hints and she wouldn't understand a sledgehammer either. The only way he was going to get rid of her was to hack her in little pieces and bury the parts in different states.

Now that would make him appealing to Lara Dinardo.

He emptied his beer glass. The bar was crowded, people standing behind his stool, every table taken. In a corner near the door, a pale, blonde woman was sitting with a stroller. She'd entered the place thirty minutes before, looking dazed, found a table, jammed the stroller in a corner so that the baby faced a wall, and nursed a bottle of Corona sullenly. She'd been over to the pay phone a few times and gone back to the table chewing her nails. The baby had not made a sound. He wondered what drugs she'd been feeding it.

One of the cocktail waitresses put down her empty tray and leaned across the bar, resting her freckled cleavage on her folded arms. Fine, curly hair frizzed around her small face. She had too much pink on her cheeks and the blue shadow on her eyes had melted into the creases. She looked like a bit-part player in an old Jack Nicholson movie. She might have been—her age was indeterminate.

'How's it going, Mel. Want another?' She pointed to his empty glass.

'Mel?'

'Yeah, Mel. Mel Gibson. You look just like him. Different colour hair, taller but yeah. Same sexy eyes. You should get yourself an agent.'

'Oh, really?' he asked, pleased.

'Sure. A lot of worse-looking guys than you are up on that screen. I mean, Ethan Hawke, give me a break.'

'Maybe I'll think about it.'

'Well, don't take too long. You think about something too long—poof! You wake up one day and you've missed your chance.'

'Sounds like you're talking from experience.'

'Story of my life. Bad timing with everything. Boyfriends, career, lottery numbers, you name it.' She edged closer to him across the bar. 'Maybe my luck just changed. You married?'

'No.'

'Divorced?'

'Afraid not.'

'Girlfriend?'

He hesitated. 'Maybe.'

'Maybe? I bet she'd like that. What's her name?'

'Avalon.' She had her uses after all. But inwardly he cringed. He was superstitious.

'Weird name.'

'She's named after a beach in Sydney.'

'I've got a cousin called Venice. Named after the beach.'

'Not after the city?'

'What city?'

The bartender gestured to the cocktail waitress. 'You've got some disgruntled customers.' He pointed to a couple at a table calling for the check.

'OK, OK,' she shrugged. 'You stay here, Mel.' She placed her hand on his, let it linger.

He watched her flounce off, apron tied tight around her tight little backside. The baby by the door started wailing. Everyone turned, then turned away. The mother didn't move, sat staring into the room as if the baby didn't exist. She was beautiful in a raggy, flower-child way. She had on a long silk skirt, far too light for the weather, and suede clogs like gardening shoes. She was wrapped in a thick cardigan with a hood, cream with brown llamas across the chest, the sleeves rolled up several times to expose fine brown wrists tangled in woven bracelets. She was very tanned, fine white hair, pale eyes when she blinked up from her beer. Scandinavian, he guessed. Beach girl or snow bunny.

The baby kept howling. He got off his stool and went over to the mother. 'Is the baby OK?'

The woman stared blankly at him.

'Do you need some help? I'm good with babies.'

Her mouth started moving but no sound came out.

Cheyne bent down and made a funny face at the baby. It kept on screaming. 'Boy or girl?'

'Don't touch him!' The woman gave Cheyne's arm a push and jumped up from the table. She scrambled through a bag on the floor and came up with a handful of crumpled notes, which she scattered on the table as if she was anxious to get rid of them.

'Wait!' Cheyne said, but the woman was already manoeuvring the stroller away from the wall. She pulled her cardigan tightly around her and exited.

'What was that all about?' Cheyne shrugged as the waitress

walked over and cleared the table.

'Not used to a woman running out on you?'

'No, actually.' It was true. 'She looked like she didn't have anywhere to go.'

'I wouldn't worry about that. Look.'

She held out her hand. In it were three crumpled twenties.

'Drugs?'

'Broken heart, more like. I bet the daddy dumped her and the kid and she's come in from the burbs to beg him to come home. Looks like she was sniffling. Tears not coke.'

Cheyne wondered. He didn't like the thought of a distraught woman out in the cold with a child in this weather. 'Maybe I should go after her.'

The waitress narrowed her eyes. 'You men. Don't know why we bother to dress up for you. All it takes is tears.'

He could see he'd hurt her feelings. 'OK. I'll have another one of those.' He gestured at his empty bottle over on the bar.

She put her hands on her hips and beamed. 'Anything you want, Mel.'

Coming along nicely, Shane thought, coming along nicely.

He was checking the status of his eBay auction. The big camera that had 'Toyo View' written on it had already passed $300. The small silver one that said 'Contax' had reached $215. The elephant-dick-sized lens was currently $155.50. The enormous case with all the lighting in it was a whopping $465. And there were six days to go.

He'd already had a few emails from interested bidders asking for details of the equipment. To all he sent back this message: 'i know fuckall about cameras these are my uncles who has died. He was a profesional photographer. Everything is in a-one condition no scratches or anything. Take advantage of me and find yourself a bargain.' In later emails he added, to give it a ring of truth: 'my uncle who has died young of a heart attack'.

Fuck, I should go out and celebrate, he thought, looking at the time. It was after eight. I could shout Finley a meal. Work out what was wrong with her. She was acting as if he'd pissed in her slippers. He felt a dark shadow pass over him like a monster wave breaking before he paddled up to it. Could it be another bloke? Maybe it was that wanker she took martial arts lessons from. She'd raved on about him enough, like he was some sort of fucking god or something.

Well, fuck her. He'd go and have a good nosh-up by himself. He knew what he wanted: lamb chops, a big pile of greasy, sweet ones, with mashed potatoes and stewed peas on the side. And some of that gluggy gravy the old chook made. He hadn't had a chop for months. In his mind he could see the pink Noritake plate (the old bag's best china) glistening with pools of animal fat and watery minted peas. He could feel the saliva fill his mouth.

There was a restaurant up in the meat district he'd passed last week on the way back from a bar, a fancy place, looked like a complete dump but he could tell it was pricy from the limos lined up outside. Every time he'd walked by he could smell lamb on the sizzle. Well, he'd go there now and fuck the cost. He'd be in the money soon anyway. When his stomach called he had to answer.

Thank Christ he'd remembered to take his beanie. It was brass monkeys outside. The wind rattled up Greenwich Street and he fought off a Doritos wrapper that blew on to his face. He had to step over a puddle of blood to get to the restaurant door.

Inside, it looked like a crummy cafe with a big, old bar that you could barely see for people. Under the noise of people yelling, glasses clinking and chairs being scraped across a tile floor, some French chick was singing on a tape.

There was a girl with cleavage standing inside the door with a clipboard and headset.

'Who do I have to fuck to get a meal around here?' He was joking but the girl looked alarmed.

'Do you have a reservation, sir?'

'No. Do I need one?'

'It is the Christmas season, sir. I'll give you our number,' the girl said efficiently, handing him a card. 'You need to call the restaurant at least six weeks in advance. But don't call earlier than six weeks or later than six weeks and one day because we change the number.'

The odour of lamb chops stewing in their own delicious juices was overwhelming. 'Can't I just wait at the bar?'

'There's a waiting list for the bar, sir.'

'Fuck this,' he said, but the girl was already talking to the couple behind him, a scrawny blonde clinging to a short guy with a baseball cap pulled down over his face. The doorbitch was creaming herself, because he was some kind of movie-star faggot. 'Mr Ford, what a pleasure!'

Shane felt like a shag on a rock, standing there, ignored. He moved to the side a little, reluctant to leave. There were at least two empty tables, obviously reserved. What if he just sat down at one of them? The girl had her back to the room. She wouldn't spot him.

While he was contemplating his move, the table behind him shifted with the sound of fingernails on a blackboard and five men stood to put on coats and knot scarves. Shane slid beside the table to get out of the way and watched as the group blocked the aisle.

They stood facing away from the table shaking hands and thumping each other on the back.

Shane looked at the debris on the table—a couple of dozen glasses of different sizes, crumpled napkins and a bottle of Armagnac emptied and on its side. In the middle of the table was a dish with a credit card receipt and a fanned-out bunch of twenty-dollar bills. Eighty dollars, he calculated.

Fuck it, he thought, no one's looking. The five men were still blocking the waiters' view of the table. He scanned the room quickly and reached over and pocketed the money. He put his head down and pushed through the throng.

He was on Ninth Avenue before they would have even noticed. He felt good about it. Pack of snobs, refusing to serve a starving man. He noticed that his triumph had dulled his appetite. Maybe he could wait a bit and pick up Finley from work. As long as she didn't want to eat that vegetarian crap.

He felt the crisp notes in his pocket. Serve them right for tipping, he smiled. He didn't believe in it.

Lara Dinardo tapped Bradford Ford on the arm and said, 'Did you see that?'

'Uh?' he grunted. He was slumped in his seat, goatee in his chest, baseball cap on his head, signalling to the room that he was a movie star trying not to be recognised.

'That guy in the plaid jacket. He came in off the street and stole the tip off that table.'

'Yeah, so?'

'Well, he looked interesting, that's all. I should go and find him and give him my card. I'm like fascinated by the criminal element.' She pushed her chair back.

'Keep your ass on that chair,' Ford growled. 'The moment you get up a dozen fuckin' fans'll come over for my autograph. I want to eat my burger in peace.'

'And you were doing such a good job of disguising yourself,' she said, eyeballing the two bodyguards standing behind his chair muttering into headsets.

Shane's grin disappeared very quickly as he took his key out to open the door to his building. A spectre stared back at him from the other side of the filthy glass porthole in the door, a thing with big eyes, frayed hair and pale fingertips pressed against the glass.

He opened the door. She stood there, shivering, dressed in a long skirt and a hooded cardigan with llamas around the chest, with the kid in a stroller that looked like it belonged to a doll. She was the kind of woman who, stripped of her bikini, didn't have a clue how to dress.

'Brian's gone south,' she said.

'Shit. Cassie. Why the fuck are you here?'

'Don't be like that. I had a reunion with some of the girls from modelling days. I missed the bus. I've been trying to call you from a bar.'

'Fucking hell, you shouldn't have a baby out in the cold at this time of night. You're not a fit mother.'

'I don't see what that's to you. You don't care what kind of mother I am. All you want—'

'Well, I'm going out. I just came home for a minute. I'll take you to a subway and you can go to the station. It's only nine. There's got to be a Montauk train.'

'Can't I come up first? I think I'm cold.'

He now noticed that her sarong was silk under her cardigan and that she had felt clogs with no socks on her feet. 'You think you're cold? Shit, Cassie. What are you on?'

'Nothing…much.'

'Yeah, and pigs can fly.'

'I could do with some socks, Shane.'

He relented. 'All right. Socks. That's all.'

She followed him into the elevator. 'Where are you going?'

'To a party,' he lied.

'Can I come?'

'No, you can't.'

'Do you have another girlfriend?'

'I have a girlfriend.'

'Well, that's all right. I don't mind.'

Shane ignored that. 'How's Brian?' As if he gave a shit.

She shrugged. 'Don't know. He's surfing in Costa Rica I think.'

Lucky prick, Shane thought.

'Did I tell you he rode a forty-foot wave in Hawaii last month? Won a prize or something. They're making a documentary about him. *Even Bigger Wednesday* it's going to be called. He's stoked.'

I really didn't want to hear that, Shane fumed as he opened the elevator doors on his floor. The bastard. He's got the boards, the waves and the dough. And a beautiful girlfriend, tragic as she is, who once appeared naked on a surfboard in *Maxim*.

He watched Cassie drift towards the bed and kick off her clogs. Well, I do have her. Serves Brian right if she runs to me the way he's treated her. Serves Finley right, too, the left side of his brain calculated.

Cassie dropped onto the bed. She sat on the edge, her fingers fiddling with the hem of her sarong.

'I'll get you some socks,' he told her. 'I think I've got a clean pair.'

She looked up at him with wide limpid eyes. 'I'd rather have the sock you keep down your pants, Shane.'

In that instant he was transported back to the sand dunes at Gunnamatta. Show me your pork sword, Shane. Come on, Shane, where's that beef bayonet?

'Are you sure you're not Australian, Cass?' he asked her, unbuttoning his jacket.

It had never been a good idea. With the baby on the bed it was even worse. 'Look, Cassie, aren't you worried what the baby might think?'

'Babies don't think.'

She lay back, nipples pointing at the pressed-tin ceiling, knees open, the kid on its back beside her, both of them staring up at him. He felt self-conscious kneeling above them like that, his erection bobbing with the movement of the bedsprings. The baby had a gleam in its eye, he was sure of it, a young poofter in the making. One wet, pudgy hand stretched out towards him as if his penis were some kind of dangling nursery mobile. His erection began to trickle away.

'I can't do it with the kid here.'

She pushed herself into a sitting position. 'Brian doesn't have any problems.'

'Brian's a pervert.'

'Well, where are we going to put him, then?'

'In the bath?'

'He'll cry.' The nipples now pointed at him accusingly. Child abuser. He remembered how the firm sacks felt under his hands. His penis began to lurch again.

The baby clapped, he could swear it.

A pale dawn was breaking as Shane watched Cassie take a taxi east along Houston Street.

He pulled down his woollen cap and shoved his hands in his jacket pockets, feeling the roll of notes he'd extricated from her. Must be two hundred bucks at least. He didn't see why she couldn't wait at the station for the morning train, it was cheaper. Fucking waste of money a taxi to Montauk. Almost as much as a ticket to Madrid. But she'd promised to send him some more money. He'd spun some story about needing his teeth fixed. She didn't know about Mundaka.

He watched the back of her head lurch away. The baby was over her shoulder looking blearily back at him. He looked more alert than his mother.

The kid's name was Auster or Austin, Shane never knew which.

Cheyne skipped his morning shower. The minute Avalon heard the water gushing down the pipes she'd be upstairs offering to dry him off. It wasn't much use taking back the key she'd stolen off him. He knew she'd climb up the drainpipe to get to him if she could.

He had found himself a job. Not a real job. But in order to get away from Avalon every morning he'd found it necessary to invent one. In fact, he didn't have to wholly invent it.

'It's *The Importance of Being Earnest*,' he told her last night after she'd pushed her way into his apartment when he came home from the bar. Well, it wasn't quite a lie. He had a call back. He was just being a few months premature with the shooting schedule.

'What's that?'

'Don't you know?'

'Nup.'

Good, he thought.

'So who do you play in it, Cheyne? A man called Ernest?'

'Yes and no. It's a very important role so I have to be on the set practically all the time. For the next six weeks.'

'All day?'

'Sorry, but we can't afford to upset Mr Grimley can we?'

'Could you ask him if there's a job on it for me?'

'You don't have your working permit yet.'

'Shit. You're right. I better get off my bum and do something about it. It's just you're so distracting, Cheyne.'

And that set off another frenzy of sucking, biting and bouncing him around the apartment as if she were some crazed rooting wallaby.

The problem with this scheme was that he had to keep movie-making hours. That meant getting up at dawn. He had sent Avalon downstairs to sleep but he stomped loudly around the bedroom and slammed the front door when he left just in case she was listening. Unfortunately, she took this as a sign to dash out of Kendra's apartment and meet him at the bottom of the stairs in her Jedi knight pyjamas. It was another ten minutes before he could make his crumpled exit.

He had another motive. Somewhere out there the *Taxi Driver II* people would be setting up. They hadn't been in the neighbourhood since Monday. Every day he'd gone out and hoped to see her. Natalie.

He wandered around the West Village following the scent of food. This led him to street carts, Korean delis and a soup kitchen but not a trestle table laden with juicy meatballs. Eventually he went to a screening at the Waverly Twin cinema and slept through three sessions.

Avalon was waiting when he got home. 'Why don't we go out and get a video? I feel like snuggling up in front of the telly tonight. We could get some of that take-away food Kendra gets delivered. I'm craving sweet-and-sour. And I love having some chink on a bike bring it to me.'

'I think Valerie wants to take me to a play.'

'That's unlikely, Cheyne. It's 6.15 now. I've checked your answering machine. There weren't any messages today.'

'I've told you not to do that.'

'I'm only helping, Cheyne. I'm like your personal assistant.'

Too fucking personal, he sighed.

Behind the counter at Blockbuster, Blender said hi and asked if he had been to any nightclubs lately.

Avalon went straight to the Action section. 'What about *Chop Chop, You're Dead*?' she called out to Cheyne. 'Or *Kung-fu Krime Wave*? Sounds like a beauty.'

Cheyne ignored her and pretended to be considering a Julia Roberts movie. One day he'd probably be considering Julia Roberts, going over their lines together in an anonymous little diner.

Blender was strangely terse when Avalon bounded up to the checkout, but maybe that had something to do with her choice of video. *Fight Club*, for Christ's sake.

Holy shit, thought Blender. This time Finley's boyfriend is with another woman. Another honey, too. What a body, although a little underdressed for December. It's like freezing point outside and she's not wearing a jacket?

Maybe she's his sister. She sounds Australian. More Australian than he does. Next to her he sounds like *Star Trek*'s Captain Picard. A sister would make sense, just on a visit. She's got a suntan like she's been in the Australian outback. But it doesn't explain why she's got her arms around his waist and looking at him like that. And now she's got her hand right on his butt.

No, not a sister.

'Hey, Esther.' Blender tapped her on the shoulder.

Esther was scrutinising an album with a sour look on her face. 'Damn! How did this get scratched? Hey, Blender. What's up?' She rubbed at the scratch with her sleeve.

'I've got to talk to you.'

'Yeah?' She looked up from the record. 'Say, you look sick.'

'I feel sick. Can we talk?'

'OK.'

She followed him to the back room.

'It's Finley,' he said.

'Shit! What's happened?'

'No, nothing like that. It's her boyfriend, Cheyne.'

'The Australian you met at Contaminated? She's kind of hung up on him, don't you think?'

'Right. So the problem is this. I told you he went off with another woman that night.'

'So?'

'So he musta been seeing Finley already. I mean, she was hooked by then. And now he keeps calling her at work.'

'Well, maybe he broke up with the other girl.'

'No, but, you see, I just saw him at Blockbuster…with another woman. They were taking out videos…and she was all over him. Two different babes and neither of them Finley.'

'Wow.'

'Is that all you can say, Esther? Wow?'

'Well, you've got a problem.'

'We've got a problem,' said Blender. 'You know about it too.'

'But I'm not the eyewitness. You're the one who's got to tell her.'

'Do you think I should, Esther? I don't know.'

'You've got to tell her because this dick is toying with her affections.'

'But we don't know that. Maybe they've got an arrangement. It might be none of our business.'

'You are your brother's keeper, Blender. Finley's clueless in these matters. Look at all her other doofus boyfriends. Did you notice the way she jumped on the phone when this Shane called the other day? So, you've got to tell her.'

'OK, but not today.'

'Why not today?'

'I need to take a few of those Mo Bo classes before I do. She'll fucking wipe the floor with me.'

'Well, don't take too long about it, Mr Concerned Citizen. It's only going to get worse.'

Finley was waiting for Shane at West 4th Street at 6.15 on Saturday morning.

He couldn't believe his eyes. He was sure she wouldn't come, the way she'd been so bad-tempered with him on the phone on Wednesday night. He threw his arms around her neck and hugged her head to his chest.

'Shane, I can't breathe,' she said after a while.

The waves were so bumpy they kept losing their boards. For once, Shane didn't care. When they scrambled out of the water he took Finley to shelter behind a shed at the back of the boardwalk and undid his wetsuit using a long ribbon tied to the zipper. He pulled the wetsuit down to his hips and struggled out of the long-sleeved spandex top he wore underneath. Then he wiped his chest and underarms with a towel.

'Here, I'll help you,' he said. She was standing with her arms around her chest, the warm water inside her wetsuit insulating her but her cheeks and fingers turning bright pink from the cold.

He unzipped the back of her wetsuit and handed her a towel. She pulled the neoprene over her head and quickly wrapped her torso in the towel. It had pink flamingos on it, absurd in a northeast gale. She shuddered and started patting herself dry through the cloth.

Shane leaned against the low building and pulled his wetsuit over one foot, then the other. He stood there naked, except for the towel over his shoulders, shaking out his suit.

'Aren't you cold?' she asked, shivering. 'There are people looking.' She made a gesture towards the road behind them, where an old couple in white anoraks were throwing sticks to a dog.

'Let them perve,' Shane said, giving his genitals a good frisking with the towel. 'You always get a few sickos at the beach. You should see them lined up at the car park at Bell's. You can always pick a pervert. They're the ones fiddling with the roofracks of their cars for hours. There was a guy who secretly used to videotape the surfers changing. Years later the cops raided his house looking for dope and found hundreds of tapes of bums and dicks. Don't know if one of them was mine.' He wrapped the towel around his waist and found a tee-shirt, which he pulled on, and then a sweater. 'I'll hold the towel up if you're shy. But you weren't shy last time.'

'That's because you went around the other side of the hut.'

'I've got a better idea,' he said. 'Come on.'

He threw his wetsuit over a shoulder, bundled up his clothes, hoisted his surfboard under his arm and then slid everything under the boardwalk. She followed, squeezing with him under the supports and into a low crawl space. She found that she could sit, but not stand, although Shane had to bend at the shoulders when he kneeled. The shed acted as protection on one side. On the beach side, Shane got busy, laying the padded surfboard covers against the timber as windbreaks. He spread his jacket on the cold sand and lay Finley's army coat next to that.

'Cosy?' he asked. 'No one will know we're here.'

'I'm still fucking freezing,' she said, pulling her towel around her more tightly.

'Here.' He gently unwrapped the towel and eased her into a tee-shirt. Then he pulled her sweater over her head and smoothed it down. 'Now let's get you out of that wetsuit.'

She lay back on her elbows while he unpeeled the neoprene slowly, patting dry her hips, inner thighs, knees and ankles with her towel. The wetsuit discarded, he rubbed her feet briskly and then found her socks, making warm little parcels of her toes with them. She was still naked from the waist down and he was crouched between her knees in a cream sweater the size of a ram, but with his thin towel still wrapped around his hips.

'I hope no fucker's videotaping us now,' he smiled.

'If they are, they're not getting much of a show,' she giggled.

'We should do something about that,' he said.

'Quickly,' she agreed. 'Before you have to use an ice-pick to get at me.'

He dropped his towel.

She looked at his half-erection. 'You should put a sock on that too.'

'There are better ways to keep him warm.'

'Shit, Cheyne, look at this!' The ten people standing in front of him at the Balducci's check-out and, for all he knew, the ten people behind, turned to look at Avalon where she stood near the fruit display. 'One fucking little passionfruit for two dollars! What a rip off!'

He looked away and smiled apologetically at the elegant woman in front of him. She clicked her tongue.

'And look at this!' Avalon came over to him with something round in the palm of her hand. 'I found a Christmas pudding in the grocery. It's about the size of a dingo's ball and guess what it costs?'

It was no use pretending she wasn't with him. 'What?' he hissed, holding a parcel of lamb chops up against his face as partial conceal-ment.

'Guess!'

'I'm not guessing.' He gave her his filthiest look.

'Spoilsport. Twenty-nine dollars! I should get my granny to send me a few and go into business. Couldn't find any custard powder but.'

That would be a good thing, he thought, if the lumpy mix of egg and milk she'd cooked for him last night was any indication of her custard-making skill.

'And did you see the size of those prawns? No wonder they call them shrimp! Oh, hang on a minute, I forgot the kiwifruit.'

She came back with two kiwifruit and put them in the cart. She snaked her arm around his waist and inside his coat. 'How's the old fella? Missing me?' Her other hand dug inside her handbag and emerged with a little tin of mints. 'Look at these. They're Altoids. Just like Minties. If I suck on them—' She grasped his dick and squeezed it.

Cheyne could feel himself blush. He grabbed her wrist and moved it away. He'd have to concoct a date with Valerie. Quickly. There'd have to be a message on his machine when he got back.

Dear old Valerie, his own personal Bunbury.

Natalie, who had been waiting at the back of the line with an armful of blood oranges, pricked up her ears at the girl's accent. When she saw Finley's Shane she shrank back but not before she saw the blonde put her arm around Shane's waist and down his pants. It was quite clear, even from a distance, what she was doing.

Finley could pick 'em. Beneath those angry eyebrows and shredded Deep Purple tee-shirts beat the heart of a wilting idiot when it came to men. It was easy for Natalie to sort the wheat from the chaff because in her opinion all men were chaff. But Finley's men were always prime specimens of chaffiness—self-absorbed, unfaithful and adept at justifying their lack of moral fibre. Finley would never listen until it was too late and when it was too late she would go too far. Only a few months ago, there was the incident of the bike messenger and the box cutter—slashed tyres, smashed videos and the offending philanderer laid out on Sixth

Avenue South with his dreads caught under a taxi's front tyre. God knows what she would do to Shane if she ever found out he was fooling around.

Naturally, it was Natalie's responsibility as a friend to fill her in.

'Look at her nails!' Avalon declared at the front of the line in a voice that could be heard back in the pasta section. 'How does she push the bloody keys?'

'That will be $109.98,' said the girl at the check-out, flashing curved, inch-long talons painted with palm trees.

Cheyne, blushing, handed the girl his Mastercard.

'I'm sorry, sir,' she said after the machine gave a loud bleep. 'It's been declined.'

'Declined?' Cheyne had been living off his Mastercard. His mother had been transferring funds to it each month without fail from his Sydney bank account. 'The machine must be wrong. Try again.'

'Sorry,' she said after a moment. 'Do you have another card?'

He handed her his emergency Visa card. Twenty-three per cent interest and near its limit but it would do.

The beep again. 'Sorry, sir.'

What the hell was happening?

'Oh, for Christ's sake, Cheyne, I'm loaded.' Avalon said impatiently. 'What's the damage?' She unzipped the bag wrapped around her waist.

'How did we spend a hundred bucks?' she exclaimed, pulling out some notes. 'Have a squiz at this, Cheyne. Is it right? The money's all the same colour.'

Cheyne took a handful of bills and passed them to the cashier. She counted out his change. He handed it to Avalon. 'Thanks.'

'Ta. Aren't you glad I'm here?' Before she pocketed the change, she looked at it thoughtfully and then passed a dollar bill back to the girl at the check-out.

'That's your tip,' she told her.

She grabbed Cheyne's arm as he picked up the bags. 'See, I'm getting the hang of it at last.'

Blender sat back at his computer and admired his handiwork.

It was the bomb. He'd never gone this far before. He knew it could be done. He vaguely knew how. But he'd never done it. There wasn't any reason before. The other hackers said you didn't need a reason, it was all part of bringing down the system, man. But he didn't want to mess with strangers' lives. What if you wiped off someone's social security number and there was an emergency, a child involved maybe, and the hospital didn't recognise the insurance? Or you took down someone's bank account and they didn't have money for medication and they died? He didn't believe, like the others did, that people were just numbers. It was wrong to destroy a person's identity just because, say, their social security ended in 666.

But it was different if you knew the person. If you knew the person deserved a little inconvenience in his life. If you wanted to fuck with his head a little. Nothing long-term harmful—just screw up everything for a while. And screw Cheyne was what he had wanted to do.

It was dead simple. The video store had a record of his Mastercard number and expiry date. That was all he needed. Two credit cards cancelled. Non-immigrant visa changed to 'expired'. One digit altered in the number of a bank account in Sydney. Small stuff, really.

He could have been cleverer, done more. Given him a police record, blown his passport away. But he didn't want to obliterate him, just teach him a lesson.

Don't go fucking around with my friend Finley.

Blossom was a big fan of 'The Undertaker'. If Finley didn't switch the television on and tune into MTV by 7 p.m. on Sunday nights, Blossom was in front of the box barking, whining and peeing on the matting. Finley knew to leave the television on when she was going out if she didn't want her pillows chewed up and the plastic casing of the TV set scoured by Blossom's hoary claws.

Tonight, the Undertaker was being ambushed by Triple H and a bunch of beefy cronies in spandex tights and dark glasses. Blossom whimpered each time the fallen wrestler took another kick in the crotch. Finley had tried to explain to Blossom that the kicks and punches never connected but, like every thirteen-year-old boy in America, Blossom believed she was witnessing a tribal war, complete with strangulations, broken bones and head injuries. More than once, Finley had found Blossom lying in front of the television with her paws over her head. She growled at the villains and yapped at the heroes and rolled over every time Shane MacMahon, the pudgy son of the World Wrestling Foundation's owner, appeared on the screen. Finley suspected Blossom had a crush on him.

Finley lay on the floor with one arm around the dog's scruffy neck. 'Look at us, baby,' she sighed and ruffled Blossom's collar. 'Both of us besotted by Shanes. Two of them.'

Blossom grunted assent.

'At least you know where yours is.' Shane MacMahon had Triple

H in a headlock on the mat. But where was her Shane? It was stupid, but she had never been to his place, even though he had said it was somewhere around here. She didn't know where he hung out or who his friends were. He'd worked for the famous Brian Davenport at Montauk, but that was months ago. Besides, Brian was probably on the big wave circuit right now not sitting round with Shane having a beer in his loft.

What did Shane do when he wasn't with her? She'd never asked. She hadn't, until now, thought of him doing anything except waxing his board and smoking a few joints. He'd come to her out of the sea like Botticelli's Venus, tangle-haired and salty, more Australian than human he had said. He was a loner with a mysterious past, like Shane in the old Alan Ladd movie. He was drifting, a creature of the tides. Riding into town on a surfboard, not a horse. He had scooped her up out of the water with firm hands, unpeeled her wetsuit and dried her tenderly. He will save me from the bad guys, she thought, the novel-writers and the actors and the ones in button-down shirts who smoke cigars.

She had to stay calm about this talk of Spain. The two Shanes, Alan Ladd and her surfer, were their own men. You couldn't tie them down, with lasso or leg rope. They'd ride off into the sunset but they'd be back. Because everyone knew what they needed most was the love of a good woman.

And she was that woman. Trusty, strong and loyal, like a horse. She felt reassured.

She was making chocolate milk for herself and Blossom when the phone rang.

Shane!

'I'm glad you're home.'

No, Natalie.

'What do you want?'

'Why do you always think I want something? I might be calling to wish you Happy Hanukkah.'

'It's a week until Hanukkah.'

'Maybe I want to get in first.'

'Go to bed, it's eleven p.m.'

'Is that surfer with you?'

'None of your business.'

'Is he there?'

'No. Why?'

'Because I've got to tell you something about him. It's been on my conscience all last night. I couldn't sleep.'

'Natalie, hang up. I don't want to hear any shit about surfers being the scum of the earth. You don't know him—'

'But I do, remember?'

'You met him on the street for five seconds. Big deal. He's allowed to walk around the Village by himself. He's a grown-up.'

'Yes, but is he allowed, as you say, to fuck strange blonde women?'

'What are you talking about?'

'Interested now, are we?'

'Shane doesn't fuck strange blonde women.'

'Well, how do you explain, then, the one I saw with her hand on his dick yesterday?'

'What do you mean?'

'I was standing in line at Balducci's and I heard this girl talking in an Australian accent. Who should I see ahead of me but that big, handsome brute of yours with a blonde all over him? Of course, it could be perfectly innocent. An overly affectionate sister, perhaps?'

'He doesn't have—'

'Well, then. Who could she be? The way she was rubbing herself all over him I doubt whether she was his landlord. Unless he has an interesting way of paying rent.'

'What did she look like?'

'Standard surfer chick. Blonde. Tan. Big tits. Appalling taste in clothes.'

'I don't believe you, Natalie. You're just trying to cause trouble.'

'How's that for thanks! I call you as a pal to clue you in and you insult me. Why should I lie? Only a fool would want to be the bringer of bad tidings. The problem with riding those big waves, sweetheart, is that sooner or later you're going to get dumped. I'm just warning you.' She hung up.

Finley threw the phone at the refrigerator. It bounced off and landed in Blossom's bowl.

'She needs new glasses, Blossom,' Finley explained, crouching down and extracting the phone from the soup of chopped liver. 'Shane doesn't even know about Balducci's.'

When he called, five minutes later, Shane thought Finley sounded kind of pissed.

There was some problem he couldn't understand about a food market. 'What the fuck is Balducci's?' he asked.

'I knew you didn't know it,' she said triumphantly. 'Good night.'

It was almost midnight. Cheyne sat on park bench in Washington Square, under the tree where the sexy caterer had told him they'd once executed thieves. Sitting in the grainy light of a street lamp in the icy drizzle, circled by assorted drug-dealing, pocket-slashing lowlife, he was waiting for a safe time to return home. He had to make up this ridiculous story of going out with Valerie to get a few hours to himself.

He rose to his feet. He'd be taking up residence on this park bench if he didn't do something about Avalon soon. Or sort out his cash-flow situation. The cafe he'd lingered at until ten had refused his Mastercard and Visa and he'd had to empty his wallet and search the bottom of his trouser pockets for the last fifteen cents. Then the bloody ATM on LaGuardia Place had rejected his Bankcard and so had another on Sixth Avenue. He'd have to call his mother when he got back and remind her to pay his bills.

Big fucking hero, I am, he thought as he trudged down the path to the street, shrugging off a shadowy figure trying to sell him some weed. Can slay animated dragons in *Taliesin* but too weak to fight off an amorous blonde with a bad spandex habit.

He tiptoed past the door of Kendra's apartment, expecting Avalon to leap out and crush him with an embrace. But as he ascended the staircase to the third floor he realised he was going to get a reprieve. No dreaded creaking door, no wet sucking sound as she ran towards him smacking her lips, no crow-like cawing of Cheyne! Cheyne! as she threw her legs around him and knocked him against the banister. His lower back twinged in a memory spasm as he reached the top of the stairs. He was careful to step over the loose floorboard that heralded his arrival or departure. He took his keys out of his pocket gingerly, making sure they didn't rattle. He put the silver key in the Medeco—and he was in!

It was past midnight. He checked each room. No naked Avalon doing headstands on the bed. Thank Christ for that. He'd pour himself a celebratory drink and flop on the sofa in front of the television. But first he had to phone his mother about his bank account.

She wasn't there.

'Pissed off to Bali, son,' said the Pie King.

'Well, can you transfer some money into my Mastercard for me?'

'Can't do that.'

'Why not?'

'You're on your own, my boy. You know I don't approve of you farting around over there with a bunch of Yanks after what they've done to our beef exports. Now you come home and we'll see about some allowance.'

'I'm twenty-seven. I don't need any allowance. I just want you to move some of my money from one account into another.'

'Your mother will be back next week. Or so she said. Wish she'd stay out of the sun, she looks like a prune. And it's hurting my wallet, all that fucking surgery. "It's only a nip, Murray," she says. I'm in the wrong business I can tell you.'

'What about the money?'

'Sorry, son. I'm off to Coolum in a tick for a spot of golf with the Japs and then I'm in the Kimberley checking out the cattle. You can't make a decent pie unless you get the smell of live steer up your nose.'

'So you've said before.'

'That bird of yours said you had a part in a film.'

Cheyne cringed at the way he said *fillum*. 'What bird?'

'The one who rang your mother a couple of weeks ago.'

'Avalon?' The name caught in his throat.

'Yeah, that's her. She asked if we had anything that she could take over to you. Your mother thought you might of had something to tell us. Like you're getting married? Shacked up with her are you, son?' He chuckled.

'No, I'm not.'

'We're all broad-minded over here, Cheyne. Look at your mother. Up there slurping on some darky's prick. Not that I give a rat's arse.

There's Bruce with the Jag now. Taking me to the airport. You'll be right, son. Give your mother a ring next week. She's missing you.'

Yeah, sounds like it, Cheyne thought, hearing the line go dead. He crept over to Simon's liquor cabinet and got out the Stoli that Avalon had paid for when his Mastercard had been refused at the liquor store.

'It'll rot your gut, Cheyne,' she had scolded him. 'You drink too much.'

Yeah, well maybe he did. He'd come here to get away from people like her. And here he was cowering in his apartment afraid to confront her. And, on top of that, having to ask Murray the Pie King for money like he was twelve years old again. They were two of a kind, Avalon and Murray. Thick as bricks when it came to other people. And cunning as sewer rats. He didn't doubt that under that look of sunstruck devotion Avalon had some kind of sinister plan to wear him down. She was cunning enough to steal his spare key, after all.

He downed the Stoli and picked up the TV remote. He flicked through an old episode of 'Bewitched', a John Wayne war epic, Ricky Lake, a basketball game, the English soccer, the inevitable screening of *Jaws*, a Japanese cooking program, an infomercial for Mo Bo, a kind of kick-boxing exercise routine, Cary Grant pointing an angry finger at Rosalind Russell, 'Scooby Do', a meeting of the New York City Board of Education, a surfing competition in Hawaii, a flaccid penis jiggling in time to 'I Feel Love', a demonstration on how to load an assault rifle and the gospel-singing congregation of the Righteous Church of Alabama. The damn Crocodile Hunter was on two channels.

Stuff this crap, he thought. He went to the bedroom and pulled a Samsonite case from a cupboard. He took from it the envelope that contained his NTSC copy of *Taliesin*. Shaking the tapes onto the bed, he picked out one at random and then went back to the sitting room and pressed it into the video player. It was the second episode, where Taliesin comes upon a pig-dance celebrating the Goddess Ceridwen and discovers she is his mother. Good. He liked this episode the best because he got to show off some emotional highs and lows. Even now, with the sound right down, he almost made himself cry.

The Stoli kicked in. He felt much better. Mellow, in fact. Avalon took a pig and slit its throat. He couldn't really hate her, she was just a scrubber, a girl from the bush looking for a husband. Six kids and three extensions to the house later she'd still be as cheery as ever, driving the boys to football practice on Saturday mornings and the girls to ballet classes in the Rotary hall. She'd have a green thumb and know one hundred things to do with mince and be studying web design part-time at the local TAFE to improve herself and maybe get a small business going, making embroidered ug boots out of sheepskin. She'd assist the local charity with clothes drives, bake cakes for the school tuckshop and dispense earthy wisdom to anyone who sought her out with a broken heart. And she'd always have new ideas about what to do in bed, one hundred things to do with a dick that she'd found in a manual at the library. And she'd be so good and so smug and…

He could really hate Avalon.

On the small screen she was anointing him with pig's blood. He looked away. He never did like the sound of squealing pigs. The drumbeat in the background was giving him a headache. Thump…rat tat…thump…rat tat tat. But the last noise wasn't the television. It was a sound at the door, more a tapping than a knock. He jumped up, alarmed at first and then darkly furious.

Avalon again. Well, fuck her. He flopped back on the couch and ignored the tapping. After a while, the phone rang. He let it ring until the answering machine picked up.

'I know what you did and I'm going to do it to you.'

Shit!

He grabbed the receiver. 'Thalia?'

'I'm outside your fucking door. I'll leave in ten seconds if you don't let me in.'

He bolted to the door, raking a hand through his hair to neaten it. She was standing there with a cell phone pressed against her ear, wearing a tight white cotton dress with a cherry pattern and needle-thin stiletto heels. The very large expanse of bronze skin across her chest glowed at him.

'Aren't you cold like that?'

'Limo, babe. I never wear coats.'

She brushed past him and stood in the middle of the room. She put her phone in a small jewelled case hanging off her shoulder. 'Did you see *I Know What You Did IV*? I was the killer. I love playing the bad guy, don't you?'

He stared at her. 'How do you know where I live?'

'Give me some credit, babe.'

'How did you get in?' All he could think of was logistics.

'Does it matter? Two dykes let me in. What are you watching? Is that you?' She pointed a pearly fingernail at the TV.

Something in what she said bothered him, but he was distracted by her gesture. Despite his surprise, he was pleased she'd arrived just now. It was a pity his screen face was greasy with pig's blood. But there was a scene at the end, where the forest maidens strip him of his clothes and wash him. He thought it might come across as very erotic, even though having his semi-naked body sponged with cold water in a damp Tasmanian forest was hardly arousing at the time.

'Oh, it's just a thing I did with TNT earlier in the year.' He tried to be casual.

'Is that Brenda Thurber?'

'Yes. She played my mother.'

'I'm impressed, babe. And here I was, thinking you were just some dumb stud. Well, aren't you going to offer me a drink?' She flung her bag across the room and it bounced off a chair, hitting the floor with a thump. Thank God they weren't precisely above Avalon's bedroom, he thought as he poured her a vodka. If they were going to indulge in any carnal activities, it had better be in this room. That at least, didn't appear to be an issue—Thalia had arranged herself on the sofa like an odalisque, arms wrapped around her head, burnished legs stretched along the cushions and crossed at the ankles. Her skirt had ridden up her thighs and the lacy edges of her turquoise bra were peeking out from the place where her dress had scooped too low.

'You can sit between my legs if you like.'

He lowered himself and she scissored him between her thighs. 'Watch this bit,' he told her, stroking her knee, getting comfortable. 'It's my favourite part.'

'This is my favourite part, babe,' she said. He felt her fingers tug at his hair and slide under his tee-shirt, down over his belly.

They sat through a sword fight and a confrontation with a witch who was trying to take his powers away from him. And then Taliesin sang and played the lute. Cheyne was now so aroused that if his dick were a rocket it would lift him off the sofa.

But Thalia had stopped stroking his navel. 'I'm beginning to think you find yourself sexier than you find me.' Her voice sounded whiny. She lifted a leg off his lap.

'No, don't move!' He put a heavy hand on her thigh and looked over his shoulder at her. 'It's almost over. You'll love the end.'

'I'm almost over, baby. Didn't I tell you I only had five minutes?'

'You're not staying?'

'I can't. I'm between parties. You can only invent so many traffic jams.'

She disentangled herself and stood up, smoothed down her dress. 'Anyway, I expected more action from you. That guy up on the screen seems to be able to fuck and fight at the same time.'

He jumped off the sofa and took one of her hands. 'Hey, don't go. I thought you'd want to know me better.'

'That would be nice but I have three minutes. And I don't like to be rushed.'

'So you're still worried about Guy.'

'You seem more worried about him than I do.'

Cheyne threw up his hands in frustration. 'I don't give a fuck about Guy. I just want to take my time and enjoy you.'

'Look, babe, do you know how much I'm worth an hour?'

'Well, fuck you.'

'You've got two minutes.'

'Did you hear that?' Avalon looked at the ceiling and clenched her fists. 'It sounds like she's throwing her shoes off now. I'm going to go up there and fucking beat her so bad she won't know her arse from her elbow.'

'Calm down,' said Kendra, scrambling across the vintage Marimekko rug in her lizard-skin mules, trying to keep up with

Avalon's pacing. 'That wouldn't be smart. You don't want the police involved.'

'I don't fucking care.'

'Yes, you do. The police will arrest you for anything these days. Jaywalking. Turnstile-jumping. You'll be deported. You don't want that.'

'Jesus. Really? Just for chucking a wobbly? What am I going to do then?'

'You're going to go to bed.'

'With them playing hide the sausage up there? No way. I've got to stop it before it happens.'

'I think you might be too late.' There was no sound from above and Kendra took this to mean horizontal activities had commenced.

Avalon read her mind. 'They'll be in the bedroom. You can hear the bed creak. That's why I can't sleep. His bed creaks and I wonder what he's doing. I'm going to spit the dummy if it's creaking now.'

It wasn't. Avalon and Kendra stood in the middle of Avalon's bedroom and stared at the silent ceiling.

'I don't think—' Kendra began.

'Shoosh! I hear something!'

'It's a branch scraping against the window.'

'Yeah, you're right.' Avalon relaxed her shoulders. 'They must be in another room. To think we let her in. I should've known when I saw her. She's just his type. He likes darkies. In Tassie there was this Abo, before he and me got together. The crew all joked, trust Cheyne to find the last Tasmanian Aborigine.'

Kendra was appalled. 'I thought you were his type.'

'Yeah, but he doesn't realise it yet.'

'Look, I'll give you a sleeping pill. You should sleep.'

'Not with that going on upstairs I won't. I'll pitch a tent outside

his door and wait for her to come out, then I'll give them too-what.'
She started towards the front door, knocking over a vase of peonies
as she did so.

'Shit. Sorry.' She stared at the broken glass. 'Put it on my tab.
How much do I owe you now?'

Thousands, thought Kendra. Oh well, the vase was slightly out-
of-date, anyway. And I can charge tens of thousands of dollars for
the inside information she's giving me. She stepped over the scattered
petals. 'Look. Why don't you phone first?'

'He won't answer and it's just putting off the inevitable. You've
got to show them you love them, Kendra. It's the only way. Even if
it means beating the shit out of them.'

Hiromi loved the feel of Fifth Avenue in her white hair. She always
rode without a hat at night. The downtown air was heavy with grit
and fumes but up here it was like cool silk, fragrant with the scent
of stone and gold and the spritzing of expensive perfumes that fell
like dew from the open windows above the trees. The lights of the
boulevard were like fairy lights and the deep forest of Central Park
breathed like a sleeping dragon beside her as she balanced both
purple glitter platform shoes on her tiny silver Razor and wove
between the taxis.

Six other riders swooped down the avenue with her and soon
they would be joined by more at 57th Street and more again at 51st
and so forth, all the way to Chinatown, by which time there would
be more than one hundred Japanese kids speeding towards
Battery Park, their multicoloured heads bobbing up and down as
they kicked their child-size scooters along the potholed streets.

Occasionally one of them would lead some of the others in song and there would be whoops and war cries and a universal finger given as they passed City Hall. At Battery Park they would stop and flirt and there would be some pairing-off before the troupe kicked back up South Street to dismount at Mothra, a Ludlow Street bar.

Tonight, Hiromi was riding alongside Benji Miyabe to whom she was dimly related. Benji, who was a sword-and-sorcery fanatic, was wearing a silver plastic breastplate over his red tartan pants and yellow sweater. Hiromi had fancied Benji ever since that time, as eleven-year-olds, they'd been sent off to 'play' in Benji's father's limo and had taken the car to an adventure park in New Jersey where they'd ridden the Viper for hours, after throwing up the contents of the limo's wet bar on the Batman and Robin ride. Benji and she had locked spumy braces on the trip back to Manhattan.

Now Benji had spiky canary-yellow hair and thick glasses like Harry Potter. He was a student at NYU but Hiromi couldn't imagine what he did there. He rode his scooter with daredevil grace, letting go of the handlebars every now and again, manoeuvring it backwards, even flipping off walls like a skateboarder. Hiromi would stop to giggle at his clownish performances and then they'd both scoot like crazy to catch up with the others.

Before Union Square, Benji veered off.

'Hey!' Hiromi shouted. 'Where are you going?'

'Come and see!' he called over his shoulder.

She stopped on the corner of the park. There, on the bitumen where the Greenmarket stood during the day, a group of men in medieval armour heaved heavy swords and spiky balls on chains in battle with each other. The air was filled with grunting and clashing.

'Cool, isn't it?' Benji scooted up to her. 'Want to watch for a while?'

They sat on a low wall. Benji took a crumpled packet of Skittles out of his pocket and passed it to her.

'They do this for fun?' she asked as she took a piece of candy.

'Yeah and I'm going to join, as soon as the rest of my armour arrives from Prague.'

She poked at his breastplate. 'You mean that's not plastic?'

'No way. I got it off a dealer in Lyon. It's fourteenth-century Sarazin.'

'Wow.' She stroked it admiringly.

'Say, do you want to give the Razor Club a miss and come over to my place? I've rented a few tapes of my, like, favourite ever TV show. It's the second part, but I'll fill you in.'

'Great.'

He fingered the tangled plastic cord around her neck. 'What's this?'

'Oh, just a surfboard leash.' She fluttered her pink and silver lurex lashes.

'You wear the weirdest things.'

Benji's father had bought him a building on Avenue D.

'I'm a landlord. Isn't that cool?' he said, showing her his tenants' names on the downstairs intercom.

They folded up their scooters and climbed the four grimy flights to Benji's apartment. There were bicycles stacked in all the hallways. The smell of weed pervaded the atmosphere. Each doorway gave out a different sound—an argument, a crashing drum solo, the distinctive wha-wha of a DMX song. Hiromi almost tripped on a stray skateboard.

'I only let cool dudes live here,' Benji explained.

Benji opened the door on to a room full of boxes. 'Don't mind those. My dad's got a temporary storage problem in one of his shops. The basement's full of them too.'

'What's in them?'

'Dried peas. Want some?' he put his hand into an open box and pulled out a packet. 'I live off 'em. Do you want the wasabi kind?'

'Thanks.'

They sat on the bed, crunching. It was the only place to sit. Under the boxes she could see some beaten-up furniture and a coffee table patterned with glued-down matchsticks.

'Do you want to do some other stuff before we watch the video?'

'Sure,' she said and struggled out of her koala backpack.

The other stuff kept them occupied for an hour.

The videotape whirred into action. They lay back against the pillows, naked, tousled-haired, munching peas, enveloped in the blue glow of the big flat-screen television and the soaring sound emanating from Benji's elaborate speaker system. The pink glitter on Hiromi's toes sparkled violet in the cool light.

'Watch this, this is really great,' Benji exclaimed at three-minute intervals.

It was a sword-and-sorcery epic about a Welsh poet with magic powers. Hiromi didn't share Benji's enthusiasm. There were not enough dragons for her taste and too much reciting of incomprehensible poetry. She was more interested in the costumes the wood nymphs wore. Easy to appropriate, too, from bits of leaves and debris lying around Tompkins Square Park. If she lashed some bark to her clothes she might come up with a new look. A kind of eco-terrorist/cyberpunk/comic strip chic.

'The really neat thing is that it's made in Tasmania,' Benji was saying as the credits began to roll.

'Tanzania?'

'No, Tasmania. The little island at the bottom of Australia.'

'Oh, yeah, Aunt Murasaki went to Australia for her honeymoon, remember?'

'They have those devils in Tasmania. Like in the cartoon.'

'Oh, cute. I want one as a pet.'

'Maybe you want the lead actor for a pet.'

'I've got my own pet.' She ran her foot along his leg.

He giggled. 'He's pretty cool though, isn't he? He's my second favourite Australian actor behind Russell Crowe. I mean that Gladiator! Man!'

'He's Australian? He doesn't sound it. Finley who works in the shop has an Australian boyfriend and he doesn't sound like that.'

'Well. I think he's mean. See, his name is Chayanne Burdekin.' He pointed to the credits as they rolled. 'I'm going to build a website about him. He's really great.'

'His name's not Chay-anne, stupid.'

'What do you mean?'

'It's Cheyne. See? That's pronounced Shane. Like the surfer. Cheyne Horan. Finley's got a shrine to him.'

'That's what I like about you Hiromi. You know lots of stuff.'

'It's funny, you know,' she pondered. 'Finley's boyfriend is called Shane too.'

'Maybe all Australian men are called Shane.'

'Could be.'

'Except Mel Gibson. He's called Mel.'

'Duh,' said Hiromi, making a face. 'Anyway, he's not Australian. He was born in New York state.'

'No kidding? You see. You do know all kinds of stuff.'

'I wonder if Finley's seen this TV show,' Hiromi thought out loud. 'I should tell her about it.'

But then Benji fed her another wasabi pea and she forgot all about Finley.

Esther lay on her back in the darkened room, sticky with green mud from forehead to toe and wrapped in strips of wet gauze like a soon-to-be-buried-alive handmaiden of Ramses III. Her hands were tightly bound by her side and her eyes were covered with cold compresses. She could feel the warmth of a lamp on her body and see the red on the inside of her eyelids but she had no other sensory perception, except for the birdcalls being piped through the sound system.

She panicked about panicking. Shit, she thought, what if I panic and can't get out of this fucking wrap? What if I started screaming? Would anyone hear me? Like there was a fire or something? Would they forget me and leave me to burn? She knew instinctively you couldn't trust beauticians. They'd drop their tweezers and be out the door at the first whiff of smoke, leaving you for toast.

Esther was starting to regret that her sister Rachel had given her the certificate to the day spa as a birthday present. Rachel worked for a handbag designer and, for some reason never entirely apparent to Esther, had to get her eyebrows plucked and skin oxidised every week to stay beautiful enough to keep her job. Esther worked at both Sputnik and Contaminated, spent all her spare cash on records and couldn't afford—didn't want—sixty-dollar bikini waxes. But Rachel was adamant. 'No wonder you don't have a boyfriend. You're so toxic.'

Actually, a lot of the boys she knew were pretty toxic too, but she didn't argue. She thought it would be pleasurable to lie on a table and have a stranger anoint you with oils. And she was still waiting. She'd been scrubbed, pummelled and steamed—and now mummified—but the promised caress with soothing potions had yet to materialise. Instead she felt like a medical experiment on a slab in the Nazi horror camp where her Great-aunt Amalie had sorted teeth.

She tried to move her hands and could only wiggle her middle two fingers. She tried to jerk her head so that the compress fell off her eyes—it stuck like cold glue. She badly wanted to call out, to shriek in fact, but she resisted. You need to focus, she told herself. Count to a million. Recite the lyrics of the new Turgid Felch song. The girl said she'd be back in twenty minutes. There must be only, what, fifteen to go…

With relief she heard a door open. 'Um, could you—' Esther sounded like one of the recorded birds was being strangled.

The door closed and she heard voices. Damn, it was the cubicle next door.

'Just pop yourself on that table with your forehead on the towel.'

'Ta. Like this?'

The two female voices floated over the top of the partition.

'Is this your first time?'

'Yeah. My flatmate sent me here.'

'Flatmate?'

'The woman I share with.'

'Oh, room-mate.'

'No, we each have our own rooms. There's no funny buggers going on. Anyway, she said what I needed was a massage. To get the knots out.'

'I like your accent. Where are you from? England?'

'You think I sound like a Pom? I'm Australian.'

'Stralian?'

'Yeah.'

'Oh, how wonderful. I've always wanted to go there.'

'You'd love it. Best country in the world.'

'But it's a long way isn't it? How long is the flight?'

'About twenty-four hours. Doesn't seem like that, but.'

'I couldn't do it.'

'You should. It's worth it. I fucking miss it already.'

'You haven't been here long?'

'More than a week.'

'Oh, really? Hmmm. You must have a very connected friend. We have a waiting list of four months. Monday mornings are really busy.'

'Shit, yeah? I just walked in the door.'

'We must have had a cancellation.'

'I've always said I've got Sagittarian luck.'

'Now I'm just going to apply some warm oil to your shoulders. I've mixed in some neroli and lavender to help you relax.'

'Smells yummy.'

'I'm going to start on your shoulders first. You are tense.'

'Yeah. I had a fight with my boyfriend last night.'

'Oh, I'm sorry.'

'I'm pretty bummed myself. I caught him with another woman.'

'Oh, dear…Just keep your arms to the side. That's right.'

'Cheyne, that's his name, he's Australian like me, he said he works with her. Well, he can pull the other leg.'

Shane? Esther wriggled in her wrappings.

'I've come all the way from Australia to be with him. Then he says I can't live with him because the landlord won't let him share. And he's out all the time. I mean, I wasn't suspicious, 'cos I trust him, you know?'

'Uh-huh.'

'But there they were, in his flat, looking all flustered. I have to knock on the door a few times and then she opens it. All bright and bushy-tailed. She pisses off before I can say, "Who the fuck are you?" And there he is, coming out of the kitchen with a glass in his hand, all innocent as if they've been talking about the weather…Ouch!'

'That hurt?'

'More like tickled. Keep going, I'm pretty tough.'

'Sorry.'

'It's OK. And I say to him, "Cheyne, you ratbag! You've been deceiving me." Or something like that. And he says, "It's not what you think." And I point to his pants, which are all sticky-looking and say, "What, did you pay to go all the way but got out at Redfern?" And he says—get this—"No, I've been cooking." As if. He can't even boil water! And I say "Who is that girl?" and he says "She's on the film." And I say, "Pull the other one, Cheyne. I knew you had another girl. Stop fucking pretending." And then he had the nerve to say to me, "OK, so what? So what if I have another girl?"'

'That's terrible. I'm going to work on your legs now. Just relax. That's a good girl.'

'And that's when I punched him.'

'You did?'

'I hit him right in the smacker. And he's screaming and holding his mouth, so I have another go and get him right in the eye. He's going to have a fucking beautiful shiner this morning.'

Shit, thought Esther, lying under her coating of volcanic mud. She's probably the girl Blender saw at Blockbuster. And she's talking about that other girl who was at Contaminated. An actress or something. There's no way out of it, we have got to tell Finley. But not at Sputnik, in case she goes ballistic. I better get out of here and have a look at this girl before she goes. The guy must be a real jerk. Now, if I can push my fingers through the wrapping I could maybe unravel the rest…

She heard a door open again. The rustle of crisp cotton and the squeak of nurse's shoes. A voice boomed overhead. 'Panicking are we?'

We sure are, Esther said to herself.

However Cheyne looked at it, it didn't look like an eye. It looked like a pool of oil streaked with petrol yellow, a black-bean dip swirled with guacamole, a spiralling supernova spitting debris. Somewhere in there was an iris but the lid had swelled the size of a toad sitting in a pond. His left eye was undamaged and therefore doomed to gaze in the mirror at what a mess his right eye had become.

His head felt like a log that had been split through the top and left in the forest to gather moss and lichen. In the fuzzy recesses of the part of his brain that continued to function this image reminded him of *Taliesin* and he shuddered. A spasm ran from his right shoulder to his kidney, where Avalon had kicked him when he was down. He twisted to ease it and his right knee locked painfully.

He had the *Earnest* call back in two days. *Miss Fairfax, ever since I met you*…Fuck, what was it? He'd slept with a quilt over his head, a chair and a bookcase wedged against the front door to keep Avalon out. He hadn't heard any thumping nor were there any messages from her on the answering machine when he at last dragged himself out of bed this morning. Even the sound of his shower hadn't conjured her up.

Oh, God, please let it be that she's packed up and left.

He touched his left cheekbone and withdrew his finger sharply. It stung. He found a facecloth and wet it and then went to the kitchen for some ice.

The blue plastic ice tray was empty. He vaguely remembered the vodka bottle and lots of ice. There was a Rite Aid pharmacy around on Sixth Avenue. With the number of bondage shops in the neighbourhood they probably did a brisk trade in ice packs.

He pulled on some clothes, moved the furniture away from the door and locked it behind him. If Avalon appeared he'd bloody well thump her back. Failing that, he'd fall to his knees and beg for mercy. But he limped to the bottom of the stairs without incident.

The door opened on to intense sunshine and bitter cold. He covered his bruised eye with his hand and staggered along the street. He'd only taken a few steps when he stumbled over something. He looked down. It was a twisted mass of cables, running to a generator on the road.

A girl with a headset and a clipboard came up to him. 'Do you mind, waiting, sir?' She blinked when she saw his black eye. 'Say, are you all right?'

'Yeah, I'm fine,' he croaked.

'They won't be long. They're almost finished with this take.'

Another film shoot. An old taxi had stopped in the middle of the road and its door was flung open. Behind it, a big white bank light was illuminated.

He suddenly realised what he was staring at. 'Is this *Taxi Driver II*?' he asked the girl.

'Yeah. Weird isn't it? All these sequels.'

He looked around. 'Can you tell me where the girl who does the food is?'

'Natalie? She's around the corner on Houston. Why, do you know her?'

He turned without answering and was already halfway back down the block. There she was! He could see she was wearing some kind of red print dress with a white apron wrapped tightly around her body. She had her head down and her hair was caught in a net at the back. His heart was thumping so violently it felt like it might break a rib.

She didn't sense he was there.

'Found you,' he said.

She looked up from squeezing orange juice, frowned. 'Was I lost?' Then she cocked an eyebrow. 'Well, look who's here. Shane, I believe.'

'You remembered my name. I'm touched.'

'I'm not likely to forget a big handsome Australian like you, am I? Especially when he's called Shane.' She dropped the orange. 'Say, what happened to your eye? A jealous boyfriend?'

'Something like that.'

Natalie wiped her hands on her apron. 'Let me give you some ice.' She took some cubes from a bucket behind her and wrapped them in a dishtowel. 'Here.'

She came around to him and held it out. She had clear plastic gloves over her hand and Cheyne could see the blood-red nails underneath. He took her hand between his and raised it up to his eye.

She pulled her hand away. 'So what did you do to make the boyfriend jealous?'

'It wasn't a boyfriend. I'm ashamed to say it was a girl.'

'Oh, really. What happened?'

'She found out about another woman I was seeing.'

'Did she just? You're a busy boy. Just how many girlfriends do you have?'

He gave a mock sigh. 'Looks like none now.'

'You don't seem too unhappy about it.'

'Not when I'm looking at you. What are you doing after work?'

'You mean when I feed the ten thousand with Danish pastries? I'm going home to have a nap. I've been up since four.'

'You don't need a nap. Have coffee with me.'

'You don't mean coffee, do you?'

He smiled. 'Not really. What if I help you get your things home? You could show me around.'

'I've got my own van.'

'But you don't look—'

'Butch enough? I've heard that before. I've got baker's arms. See?'

Natalie held out an arm and flexed a bicep. He took advantage of the offer and circled it with a hand. The print fabric felt far too thin for the cold weather.

He didn't let go of her arm. She didn't shake him off.

'So, are you going to show me how you drive?'

She raised an eyebrow. He noticed how perfectly arched it was. 'I might go too fast for you.'

'I don't think so.'

'You should see me around hairpin bends.'

'I'd love to.'

'There could be some nasty surprises.'

'I'm prepared.'

She prised his fingers from her arm and smirked. 'Well, let's see about that.'

Cheyne leaned against a stainless steel bench and watched Natalie put away trays. Her apartment was a loft on a deserted street near the Hudson River. The kitchen was vast, with all its surfaces stainless steel and glowing cookware hanging from racks suspended from the tin ceiling. Rows of cookies in cellophane bags sat on the counter. He picked up one and looked at the little printed tag tied to the bag. Sappho's Kitchen. Curious name for a business.

He opened the bag and munched on a peanut butter cookie while she worked. He had offered to help but she told him to just stand and look pretty. But it was she who looked pretty, crouched on slender ankles, rearranging a low cupboard, her sleeves pushed up and strands of dark hair tumbling out of the pins that had held it in rolls. He thought of his mother, how he'd never seen her do anything in the kitchen, except maybe get some tonic out of the refrigerator to splash in her midday gin.

'Don't you have any assistants?' he asked, watching her shoulder the cupboard door closed.

'One. But I gave her the day off.'

'I'm glad you did.'

She stood and picked up a pack of cigarettes from the bench. 'Judging by that black eye, you don't mind having more than one woman around.'

'I do if the one woman is you.'

She held the matches out. He took them and lit her cigarette. She puffed on it and stepped back a few paces. 'Tell me about your other girlfriends.'

'They're in the past.'

'Not too far in the past by the sound of it. What about the girl who punched you?'

'Let's not spoil a beautiful day.'

Why did he say that? He was talking like a bad movie. It was something about her, the way she talked. They weren't having a conversation, they were speaking lines and he couldn't stop himself.

And she was standing there, at least six feet away, with a cigarette in her hand, looking at him like he was an amusing toddler struggling with his first words. He needed to break the distance, get closer. She'd wrapped herself in a cocoon of cool bemusement.

She should wrap herself in him.

'If it's such a beautiful day, why aren't you surfing?' she asked.

'What?' Then he remembered he'd told her he was a surf bum. 'There isn't any surf in New York City.'

'That's not what I heard.' She looked at him quizzically.

He held her gaze for a while. He was confused. Then his head remembered that it was aching. 'You don't have a Coke, do you? I'm feeling a bit rough.'

'Coming up.' She shoved her cigarette in her mouth and opened the big refrigerator, handed him a bottle. A spark flew in her eye and she fluttered her lashes.

'Here,' he said. 'I'll get it out.'

'The old eyelash trick,' she smirked, holding her cigarette away from her face.

'You're so pretty,' he said, tilting her chin with one hand. 'And so feminine. I've never met a woman like you.' He held the back of her neck and bent down, covering her lips with his. She didn't push him away, but neither did she really respond.

He came up for air. 'Am I going too fast?'

She crossed her arms and took a step back. 'Let's get this straight. You don't have any girlfriends at the moment?'

So that was it. 'If that's what's worrying you—'

'Do you or don't you?'

'I don't. Promise.'

'Then get out.'

He smiled at her. She really was very sexy, standing there with her red lipstick blurred. He liked the way she played verbal games with him. The mental effort of keeping up with her banter was strangely arousing. It was her movie and she was calling all the shots. He liked that.

He stepped towards her again. 'Don't you mean come in?'

She stood her ground and put out a hand to stop his approach. 'Look, you two-timing jerk, I mean it.'

She looked awfully serious for someone who was flirting with him. 'Who am I two-timing?'

'Your other girlfriend.'

'I've just told you I don't have any other girlfriend.'

'Well, you're two-timing the girlfriend you don't have.'

'Is this a joke?'

'You think it's a joke to fool around with me behind your girlfriend's back?'

'But I've just told you—'

'Why don't you tell her?'

'There isn't any her to tell!'

'She'll be pleased to hear that.'

He looked at her in exasperation. Why didn't she believe him? 'Look, I know we've only met twice, but I really…feel something for you. You shouldn't think just because I'm…well, I look like I do…that I'm a playboy. I've known a lot of women but I'd give every single one of them up for you.' He stepped closer and slid his arms around her waist.

'Boy, you really take the cake!' She twisted out of his grasp. 'I can't believe how vain you are. Anyone who gets mixed up with you is a silly little fool.'

'Wait a minute,' he insisted. 'You asked me to come here. I'd already explained to you down on the street that I'd had a fight with a girl. You seemed to think it was funny.'

'It's the other girl I'm thinking about. She happens to be a friend of mine.'

God, she was still going on about this other girl! What had he said? He studied her face. She had stubbed out one cigarette and was lighting another. Her hand was slightly trembling. What other woman did he know that she could possibly know too? Lara? That condescending dyke Avalon was living with? Could it be Thalia? Natalie did work on movie sets. Maybe she and Thalia were best friends. It could be.

'I can explain about that,' he said cautiously.

'Now you admit it!'

But what was he admitting? Thalia didn't care about him. 'She came on to me,' he said. 'Anyway, she has Guy.'

'She doesn't have a guy! She doesn't need a guy! You just got her confused. And you've got the nerve to practically rape her best friend!'

'A kiss is rape? Look, I was only—'

But Natalie wasn't listening. She had turned to the counter behind her and was lifting something.

When she faced him again he could see it was a metal tray of little pastries. She glared at him, the inch-long tube of ash on the end of the cigarette in her mouth dangling precariously.

'If you don't get out of here right now, I'm going to throw this tray of pigs-in-blankets at you,' she mumbled through a mouth full of tobacco. The ash tumbled onto her breast.

'Wait a minute—'

She hoisted the tray above her shoulder. Some of the pastries slid on the floor. 'And one thing you should know—I never miss!'

He wasn't fast enough. The tray gave the edge of his temple a glancing blow.

He held up an arm. 'Look, you don't understand. I've been thinking about you ever since I first met you.'

Natalie had her hands on her hips, glaring. 'You'd say anything, wouldn't you? Surfer scum.'

'I love you isn't just anything.' He took a step towards her.

She looked around her, picked up a thick chopping board and held it out like a shield. 'Now, are we going for a matching black eye?'

'Well, what?' Finley frowned across the formica table at Esther and Blender. It was Tuesday lunchtime and Katz's deli was buzzing. They were sitting under a photograph of former President Clinton, who was chowing down on a pastrami sandwich. Finley had taken a bite of a pickle and put it back on the plate. 'I can't sit around here all day. I'm late for Wipeout.'

'We're all friends,' Esther began.

'I know that,' Finley said impatiently. 'Why are you looking at me like that?'

'You tell her, Blender.'

'I think it's better coming from you.'

'You found out first.'

'Found out what?' She looked back and forth between them. 'Shit, Rockwell hasn't found out about those records I borrowed, has he? I can sneak them back in tomorrow.'

'You'd need a forklift for that,' Esther scoffed. 'It's half the store.'

'It's nothing to do with Rockwell,' Blender interrupted. 'It's to do with Cheyne.'

'My Shane?'

'Well, what other Shane would it be?' Esther asked.

Blender gave her a sharp look. He fidgeted. 'I saw him with another woman.'

Finley sighed. 'Is that all? That wasn't another woman. He doesn't even know where Balducci's is.'

'What has this got to do with Balducci's?' Esther interrupted. 'Blender saw him with another woman at Blockbuster.'

'Well, two other women.'

'What do you mean?'

'This blonde beach babe, he was renting videos with her.' Blender gulped, reluctant to go on. 'And then there's the indie actress he was with at Contaminated. Esther was there too.'

'But I didn't see her.'

'Actually there were two women at Contaminated. A snotty blonde and the sista.' He slumped down in his chair, hand over his face, waiting to be hit.

Instead, Finley smacked the table. 'Wait a minute! You saw my Shane at Blockbuster with a blonde? And then you saw him again at Contaminated with a different blonde and a black girl?'

'It was the other way around. I saw him at Contaminated first.'

'Yeah, but Esther was there and didn't see them? Shit, Blender, you're imagining things.'

'I didn't see her but I heard her,' said Esther.

'This is stupid! How do you know it's her if you only heard her? How do you know it's anything to do with Shane?'

'Because she spoke about him. Listen.' Esther reached out and tried to take Finley's hand. Finley shook it off and folded her arms. 'Remember I went to have that detoxifying massage at Touchy Feely yesterday? The one Rachel gave me? Well, I was lying all wrapped up and this girl came into the next cubicle. You can hear because it's only curtains between you. And she started talking to the masseuse about her boyfriend Shane and how she discovered him the night before with another woman.'

'You see,' said Blender. 'It has to be the same blonde I saw in Blockbuster. Only she's found out about the Afro babe I saw at Contaminated. The indie actress.'

'I still don't see why you think it's my Shane.'

'But it has to be because she says he's Australian!' Esther grabbed a fork and pointed. 'How many Australian Shanes can there be in this city? Anyway, this girl's hopping mad. She lives downstairs, you see, and goes up to visit him, only to find him at it with this other woman. So she punches him right in the face and knocks him out!'

'You're making this up!'

'Finley, why would we make it up? We're risking life and limb telling you,' Blender said reasonably.

'Face it, the guy's a scumbag.'

'I don't believe you.'

'Well, there's only one way to find out.' Esther stirred her coffee.

'What's that?'

'Check out whether he's got a black eye or not.'

Finley stomped into Wipeout, flung her backpack at the counter, knocking over a pyramid of Mrs Palmer's wax, picked up the bottle of Windex and started squirting it at the fish tank.

'What happened?' Hiromi looked up from where she was crouched on the floor, arranging bikinis on a low rack.

Finley said nothing but kept pressing the trigger of the Windex until ripples of chemical covered the glass.

Hiromi stood up, making an effort to be cheerful. 'Hey, I went to Benji Miyabe's place Sunday night and he was showing me this like pretty cool video. And the star of it was a guy—'

'Fucking Esther and Blender,' Finley muttered, not listening.

'Why? What did they do?' Hiromi took the bottle of Windex out of her hand. Finley flopped down limply on the seat. Hiromi sat beside her.

'What has everyone got against Shane? Everything was fucking great until now. Even that bitch Natalie is trying to agitate. I knew he hadn't been to Balducci's. And now Blender says he's seen him with two blondes and a black chick!'

'At the same time?' Hiromi asked.

'At the same time what?' Finley said blankly.

'Was he with the two blondes and the black chick at the same time?'

'I can't understand who he was with when. It's all so fucking confusing! And now Esther says he has a black eye. One of the blondes got jealous and smacked him in the face. When I see him I'm going to smack him in the other eye.'

'But they might be wrong.'

Finley looked at her. 'You think?'

'All you need to do is like find out if he has a black eye.'

'That's what they said.'

'Well, go on.'

'I don't know if I want to know. If I didn't know then we could just go on like this. Smooth waters. I'm sick of being tossed around.'

'I sort of thought you were the one doing the tossing. I mean, all those boyfriends of yours. You always left first.'

'Yeah, before I was dumped.'

'Who says Shane's going to dump you?'

'Because he's going to Spain. He's like a fucking tidal wave. It's only been, what, ten days and I already I feel like I'm drowning over here.'

'You don't need a tidal wave for that,' Hiromi said. 'You can drown in an inch of water.'

'Is Finley there?' Shane asked when someone picked up the phone at Sputnik.

'No, she's not,' said Blender curtly. 'By the way, how's your bank balance?'

Shane looked at the receiver and hung up. He dialled again. Wipeout this time.

'Is Finley there?'

'Yeah, just a minute.' It was a male voice, probably that manager, Stewie, who loaned Finley his board. He could hear the bloke call out. 'Hey Finley, call for you. I think it's your surfer dude.' He hadn't put his hand over the receiver. He heard Finley say, 'I'm not here.'

'She's not here.'

'I know she's there. Tell her it's Shane.'

'He knows you're there. It's someone called Shane.'

'I'm still not here,' he heard her call back.

He was puzzled. Why didn't she want to speak to him? 'I'm not hanging up.'

'Get your ass over here, Finley. He's not hanging up until you come.'

'Well, hang up on him, doofus.'

But after a few moments there was a crackle and Finley's voice came on the line, ferocious. 'What?'

'What have I done?' he asked, confused. She was like a fucking roller-coaster. Talk about moody. Almost not worth the effort. Almost. 'Is there some other Shane?'

'Of course there's no other Shane.'

'Then why didn't you want to speak to me?'

She didn't answer. Then, after a silence, she asked, 'Do you have a black eye?'

'Of course I don't have a fucking black eye! What makes you think that?'

'You don't?' She sounded surprised.

'Cross my heart and hope to die.'

More silence. Then a smaller voice. 'Oh.'

'Want to come for a surf?'

'Tomorrow?'

'Same time, same place?'

'I don't know.'

'Come on. It's my mission to get you standing on that board…or on your back under the boardwalk.'

She smiled. 'OK.'

'Great. See ya then.'

Finley hung up the phone.

'Is that a smile I see on your lips?' Hiromi asked.

'A half-smile,' Finley conceded. 'He says he doesn't have a black eye.'

'See?'

'And he can't be lying because he wants to take me for a surf tomorrow. If he had a black eye it wouldn't go away by tomorrow. I feel like a dope for doubting him.'

'You should, like, go with the flow, Finley.'

'Yeah, I know. But sometimes I don't know which flow to go with.'

Shane held the phone to his ear long after Finley had hung up.

Have you ever been to Bald-whatsit? Do you have a black eye? Jesus. Sometimes he didn't know why he had included her in his plans. She was a load of fucking trouble and probably a slice short of a ham sandwich on top of it. What did he know about her anyway? He'd met her less than two weeks ago. She was acting like one of those split personalities, all sexy and enthusiastic one minute, snaky and suspicious the next. What had he done? Nothing. She had no right to be suspicious of him. But did he have a right to be suspicious about her? The way she hadn't wanted to come to the phone when that bloke Stewie had said it was Shane. There couldn't be another Shane, could there? That might explain it. Another fucking boyfriend called Shane and she was getting them mixed up!

But, nah. That was far-fetched. This New Hampshire pot must be mixed with Angel Dust or something. He was tripping. Finley was going to come with him to Spain, wasn't she?

He ambled across to Dirk's computer and connected to eBay. The auction would be over tomorrow. There were about fifteen emails requesting further information on the equipment. The Toyo View camera had now reached $1820.50. The Contax was $1125. The lens $790. The lighting—shit, almost $2500! Each time he pressed 'Refresh' the numbers jumped higher.

His mood lifted. He was a genius. He'd be off to Spain in no time. And there'd be plenty of money for Finley and Blossom as well. He could send for Mavis. He could even buy a new board. One for

Finley too. It was stupid thinking of her not going with him. He had visualised her sitting on that beach minding his towel so often, he couldn't imagine Mundaka without her scowling face.

Then again, maybe he could. He'd been to Bali once, with Darren, sleeping on the beach with their boards stuck in the sand like spears, the girls wandering up like stray dogs. Scrubbers, all of them, hair braided with seashells by little native women at Kuta who squatted in the sand, heavy bosoms pimply under too much oil and vinegar, eighteen-year-old skin already tough and wrinkled in the baking sun. There to fuck surfers, the whole point of the exercise. And the rich women too, sitting in cane chairs on hotel patios, perving on the boys through binoculars. One of them, bag from Sydney, covered in so much gold she clanged, good body though, invites him for a drink in her house. He goes—why fucking not? Free booze, a meal. Servants. The woman's got some mouth on her. Lobster, champagne. All in all a good experience. Except then she goes and tells him she's the Pie King's wife. Bloody Burdekin's Homestead Pies! I love those pies, he says, and now you've gone and ruined it. From then on in, when he munches into a pie, he thinks of munching her…

There'd be bags like her in Mundaka, brown and scrawny, on the prowl. He could set himself up quite nicely. None of them would think of him as a fuckwit. He could say whatever he liked, they wouldn't understand it…

Finley didn't think he was a fuckwit. He was a hero in her eyes. Except when she was in a mood, like tonight. But tomorrow she'd come to the beach with him and the waves would be piddling again and it would be cold enough to freeze your balls off but it wouldn't matter because she was there. Even when she went all pouty it was better when she was there.

The sound of a buzzer suddenly cut the air. Shane jumped up from his chair. 'Fuck!' The unrolled joint on his leg wafted into the gap between two industrial floorboards. 'Fuck. Fuck. Fuck.'

Someone had their thumb on the buzzer.

Cassie. Who else did he know? Finley had never been here.

With a sigh he went to the intercom and released the door. He heard the grinding noise of the elevator going down. He meant to tell her last time not to come again. But it seemed a bit rough. He didn't want a weeping woman on his hands. Christ knew what she would do. She'd left him with a roll of cash, enough to spring for an ounce of weed and a good meal. He felt a bit guilty about it—her being there, not the cash—but what could he do if she kept on coming after him like this? It wasn't as if he started it.

He pulled the iron gate aside and waited for her, hoping she hadn't brought Austin or Auster with her. No sound of a baby, though. He could see the bleached blonde of the top of her hair rising...

'Cassie.'

But it wasn't Cassie.

'G'day, mate.'

An American trying to sound Australian. *Might* not *mayt*.

Brian.

The elevator wobbled to a standstill. Brian Davenport in his Costa Rican tan with his big wave muscles and his tough, scabby, board-shaping fists stood there with his arms crossed. 'Expecting someone else, mate?'

'No,' Shane croaked. 'No one at all.'

'Cassie was sorry she couldn't come but I've got a message from her.'

'What?' Shane was frozen on the spot, caught in the glare of Brian's white Californian smile and crinkled Baja blue eyes.

'This,' said Brian and punched him in the face.

'I heard him go out this morning and he still hasn't come home!' Avalon wailed. 'It's tea time. I did what you said and stayed away. Sat on my bum all day. Now he's fucking done a runner.'

'He'll be back,' Kendra said from the bar, getting out the cocktail glasses. 'Now, what did you say that "shandy" thing was made from? Beer and what?'

'Beer and lemonade.'

'Equal parts?'

'I reckon.'

'Heineken do?'

'I dunno. It's better with Four X.'

'With condoms? How do I do that?'

'Don't be a duffer.'

'Duffer?'

'Four X is beer.'

Kendra put two bottles of beer on the tray with the glasses and brought it to where Avalon was flopped on the sofa in her boxer shorts and cut-off Bruce Packer Stunt Academy tee-shirt. She sat next to her and put the tray down on the coffee table.

God, this Australian stuff is hard to keep up with, Kendra thought, as she went to the refrigerator and dug out a bottle of Sprite. She suspected it had gone flat but it would have to do. Keep plying Avalon with alcohol and anything might happen tonight.

'Do you think he's mad at me for punching him out?' Avalon asked when she returned.

'For the hundredth time, you did the right thing.' Kendra tried to keep the irritation out of her voice but knew she wasn't succeeding. Cheyne deserved everything he got and now Avalon was feeling sorry for him?

'I mean he invited me over here and everything. I should have come sooner. He probably didn't think I cared, so he found this other girlfriend. But we were almost engaged.'

Kendra poured the beer into a martini glass, topped it up with Sprite and handed it to Avalon. 'Drink this. It'll make you feel better.'

'Ta. I feel like getting plastered.'

'You do that. Cheers.' Kendra held up her glass.

'Cheers.' Avalon clinked Kendra's glass so hard the pale amber liquid sloshed all over the section of red sofa between them. 'Shit, I'm sorry.'

'Don't say sorry all the time.' Kendra pounced on the cloth she'd hidden under a cushion since Avalon arrived for these very occasions and pressed it on the stain. 'See, no harm done.' Avalon rubbed at a wet patch on her thigh. 'Let me get that for you.'

God, it was a firm thigh! Kendra dabbed at the wet patch a little longer than was necessary. She even managed to slip a couple of fingers up under Avalon's boxer shorts without any noticeable reaction. The Australian seemed more intent on drowning her drink in one gulp. The thigh was hard as a rock and slightly sheeny with perspiration. Divine.

Avalon handed Kendra the empty glass. 'You don't have any rum do you? I feel like a rum and Coke. You can't get pissed on shandies but.'

Kendra brought her a bottle of Mount Gay and can of Diet Coke.

'Pity it's not Bundy,' Avalon mused. 'That really rots your gut.'

Kendra watched her pour four fingers of rum into a glass, splash some Diet Coke on top and then finish it in several large gulps. 'Feel better?'

Avalon blinked and then burped. 'No,' she said in a small voice. 'I think I'm going to chuck.'

Kendra had already had 'chuck' and 'chunder' explained to her. She jumped to her feet and grabbed the ice bucket.

'No, it's all right,' Avalon said. 'I think it passed.'

'Well, take the ice bucket, anyway,' Kendra said, tipping the ice into a Russell Wright bowl.

Avalon held it in her lap and stared forlornly into space.

'Here, put your head on my shoulder.' Taking it easy: it was too soon for *put your head in my lap*.

'Gee, you're so nice,' Avalon said as Kendra stroked her hair. (God, it feels like rough twine, Kendra thought. I must get her up to Garren immediately.) 'Cheyne's never stroked my hair.'

'Never?'

'It's all rooting to him.'

'He's a keen gardener?'

'No, rooting. Fucking. I mean, he could fuck me all day and then make like it was my idea.'

'Typical man.'

'As if I was the one chasing him. I admit I was a bit sloshed in that pub in Tassie and went right up to him and grabbed his willy, but I'd been sitting in a fucking tent watching those makeup girls cover him with body paint all week. I mean, you should have seen where they put their hands! He didn't seem to mind. And I was his co-star, sort of, even if I only had five lines. And he looked at me during the scene with those misty eyes of his and that funny broken eyebrow and that mouth that always smirks and I knew he wanted me. So I wasn't doing anything he didn't agree to, you know? It was like two fucking incredible weeks! And before we leave Tassie I say, "Cheyne, are you thinking what I'm thinking?" and he says, "What?" like he doesn't know and I say, "You know" and I put my hand down his jeans and he says, really sweetly, "Yes, Avalon, I know what you're thinking but I have to catch a plane" and I say, "I could do this for the rest of my life" and he says, "Yes, I bet you could" and kisses me on the forehead and it's like we're engaged. Didn't see him for months because he had all this publicity to do and then I did *Star Wars* but when Phil told me he was missing me…'

Kendra was horrified to see tears streaming down her face, taking a few spiky black lashes with them. 'Look, it's not your fault. He clearly has the usual male problem with commitment.'

Avalon sniffed. 'The trouble with Cheyne is he's such a snob. He went to some fancy private school where they wore stupid little straw boaters, and his dad's a multi-millionaire, and he can speak with this posh accent when he wants to, so he thinks I'm not good enough for him. Like he's an actor and I'm just an extra. He's got such a swelled head. But I've seen his Dad on telly and he's no different to me! I don't know where Cheyne gets off with all this cultured stuff, like he's ashamed to be Australian or something. He doesn't even like sport!'

'Goodness,' said Kendra.

'And he's screwing American girls because he thinks it'll make him more international or something. Like he's fucking James Bond.'

'You might be right Avalon, but you have to stop thinking about him and start thinking about you. You've got a lot of potential. Why don't you start looking for an agent? I know some people who could help.'

'Yeah, but I'll be lonely here without Cheyne. What will I do?'

'You've got me.'

'It's not the same thing.'

'It could be.'

'Gee, Kendra, that's nice and all but you don't understand.'

'I think I do.'

'I'm talking about action in the bed department. I mean, I've got to have a root a day or I get aggro. And you don't have a dick.'

'My dear,' Kendra said soothingly, running her right hand up a taut inner thigh. 'I think I might be able to do something about that.'

Cheyne brushed the pale pastry crumbs off his dark coat as he strode morosely away from Natalie's place.

What happened up there? He couldn't work it out. She'd been positively flirtatious with him all along and then—pow—the tray on the side of the head. He rubbed his right temple. He could feel a lump coming up. His bruised eye was tenderer to the touch, but Natalie's blow had been the one that had hurt the most.

He couldn't believe the words 'I love you' had come out of his mouth. He hadn't said them before, to anyone, unless you counted the moment in Taliesin when Rhiannon washes the pig's blood off his face. He must have been convincing on film because Avalon had chased him halfway around the world. When he hadn't meant it he was believed. And now, when it was suddenly as true and real as anything he had ever felt, he got a tray of hors d'oeuvres for his trouble.

She'd called him surfer scum. That, he felt, was at the root of it. He had told her this lie because he was afraid she'd think he was sucking up to her if she found out he was a film actor. But that was bloody stupid—no one sucked up to a caterer. Caterers had just about as much power in Hollywood as sixty-year-old screenwriters. It had been a mistake and now he was suffering for it.

He had learned to surf because every kid with a modicum of sporting ability in Australia swam and surfed. He even had a surfing scar high on his brow, under a lock of hair, from some yobbo dropping in on him at Bondi. Five stitches and a course of antibiotics later, he felt he had been blooded. But no one in his or her right mind would ever call him a surfie. He didn't really understand the surfing culture, those guys who wasted their lives lying about smoking bongs and waiting for the wind to come around. As far as he was concerned, surfies were scum—a pack of stoned, drunken, thieving, disease-ridden drifters.

When he was a kid his family had lived at Whale Beach and he'd often come home from school to find surfboards on the verandah and his mother in a bikini sipping gin on a banana lounge while a group of strange young men with pink zinc on their noses raided the poolside refrigerator and sprayed cans of beer on one another. Before Murray put a stop to it and moved his family to a harbourside mansion, away from the tempting South Pacific swell, Gloria's boyfriends had walked off with two television sets and a state-of-the-art Betamax, a drill set from the garage, a portable barbecue, wads of cash and Cheyne's BMX. His mother replaced the bike with something bigger and better but Cheyne was annoyed anyway. Especially when they'd laugh at his school shorts and blazer and call him *little poof* out of his mother's hearing.

She probably would have laughed with them.

Gloria had bought him a top-of-the-line board, wetsuit, surfing lessons, membership to the local surf club. She wanted him to be just like her boyfriends, except she had ambitions for him to go to medical school too. She didn't see it as a paradox. When the board and wetsuit were stolen by his surfing coach he was relieved. He'd rather play Space Invaders anyway.

Later, he felt happier surfing with the hobbyists at Bondi, the big city lawyers and accountants blowing off steam for a couple of hours on the weekends. He could surf, and take advantage of the glamour associated with the sport, the girls sitting on the beach ogling, the interested looks you got carrying your board to the car, but he was not a surfie. Never.

He found himself at the bar without the 'R', had a few whiskies, flirted with the cocktail waitress out of sheer perversity and then stumbled home. He hesitated outside his building, then thought, fuck it, what else can Avalon do to me?

As he crept past Kendra's apartment he heard the orgasmic climax of *Bolero* wafting through the door.

It was a fucking miracle Shane could get up at all, let alone stagger with his board into an Arctic wind along Houston Street with his head screaming and every sinew in his body sobbing with pain. But the alarm had gone off at 5.30 and the act of dragging himself along the floor, where he lay all night after Brian had clocked him, to silence it had awakened in him the furry memory that Finley would be waiting for him on the platform at West 4th Street at 6.15 a.m.

He managed to get his Metrocard into the slot even though three fingers on his right hand weren't functioning. When he hoisted his board over the turnstile, the muscles across his back spasmed. As he stumbled down the stairs to the platform his right knee, where Brian had kicked it repeatedly, gave under him.

'I paid for this fucking knee,' Brian had said between thuds. 'And I can do whatever I fucking like to it.'

Actually, Brian had paid for the left knee.

Shane limped to a seat on the platform and waited for Finley.

The rhythmic clicking of the carriages as they pulled into the station rattled the teeth in his head. It felt like a balloon was inflating inside his skull and would soon push his eyes out through the sockets. A bitter nausea rose in the pit of his stomach and he swallowed hard to keep it down. That would fucking make my day, he thought, to chunder all over Finley's shoes. He'd have to pretend everything was all right, so she wouldn't ask questions. How could he explain Brian? He cursed the long train ride, wished he was already at the 67th Street beach, plunging between the bobbing ice floes into freezing water. It would either cure his searing headache or kill him. He wouldn't mind being dead. The best way to go was to drown. Everyone said so.

Suddenly there she was at the other end of the platform, running down the ramp in her army jacket and big boots and some kind of furry hat with earflaps, carrying a board. She saw him and gave a wave. He watched her jog towards him as a train pulled in. It was like a fucking romantic movie, the way she sprinted along the platform with the board under her arm and a big smile on her face. He hadn't seen her smile that much before. She was even prettier than when she frowned. He didn't hurt anymore.

As the train stopped and the doors opened, he stepped into the doorway to help her on. A couple of railway workers in fluorescent jackets got on. Finley had caught up with the car and was beaming at him. As the chime sounded for the doors to close, he watched as her smile turned down and her eyebrows pressed inward, squeezing the centre of her face into a tight ball of anger.

'What?' he called out over the chimes, confused, holding his elbows out so that the doors wouldn't close.

'Your face!'

'What about my face?'

'You said you didn't have a black eye!'

'I don't.' Tentatively he touched his left eye with his broken fingers.

'The other one!'

'Ouch!' he said as he felt the bruise.

'Stand clear of the closing doors!' the guard announced. The electric doors opened and closed against his shoulders. The chime sounded repeatedly. Ding. Ding. Ding.

'It's that blonde surfer chick girlfriend of yours. She punched you!'

'No she didn't!'

'You see! You admit she exists!'

'Stand clear of the closing doors!'

Ding. Ding.

'It's not what you think!' Shane spread his legs to wedge the doors open.

'Oh, isn't it?' said Finley, thrusting a perfectly aimed boot at the target between his legs.

'Shit, why did you do that?' he screamed as he went down.

Ding. And then the doors closed on him.

When Kendra left for the day Avalon quickly showered and dressed in yellow and black exercise clothes. She'd heard Cheyne come in

last night and wanted to go straight up and have it out, but Kendra
had said, 'No, it isn't wise. If the urge to see him is so overwhelming I'm going to have to tie you to the bed.' Which was very sweet
and caring of her.

Kendra had her best interests at heart. Avalon had been a bit
surprised when the back rub Kendra had given her to calm her down
had progressed to her stomach, bum and inner thighs. Kendra was
only trying to help Avalon forget Cheyne, she said, but Avalon
couldn't help giggling when she brought out that plastic massage
thing.

'Cheyne's not that big, Kendra,' she had chortled and Kendra had
seemed a bit annoyed, so Avalon had let Kendra use it on Avalon's
nipples which was kind of silly but seemed to keep Kendra happy.
Avalon wanted to keep Kendra happy because she'd been so ace.

But now that Kendra had gone to work, Avalon couldn't sit down
here on her bum wondering what Cheyne was up to for another
whole day. She hated being cooped up. Cheyne would come downstairs to apologise soon for having that slut up there, but he could
stew in his own juices for a few hours longer.

She picked up from the kitchen counter the notice she'd torn off
the board at the health food shop a couple of days before. Exactly
what she needed. A good fucking workout at one of those Mo Bo
places.

Blossom tried to make herself scarce while Finley rampaged through
the apartment, scattering items of clothing, kicking the stacks of
records, picking up stray mugs and plates and launching them at the
walls. She tipped a jar of shells she'd collected at Rockaway onto

the floor and stomped on them. She picked up her script for *The Importance of Being Earnest*, threw it in the air and watched the pages flutter over the bed.

The dog put her paws over her ears and backed under a chair.

Finley started to feel better. Pumped. Wired. She surveyed the carnage like a general. What she needed now was a fucking good workout.

'Good morning, Sha Mu.' Ra Ke greeted Finley ceremonially and touched his fingers to the floor.

'Yeah, all that,' Finley responded.

Ra Ke drew himself upright and appraised her. 'The little lotus is bringing some bad energy with her again?'

'Let's get on with it. I feel like kicking someone.'

'Now, Sha Mu, you know you are forbidden to practise with ill thoughts in your heart.'

Before Finley could respond, there was a loud bang at the back of the room. The partitions quivered. The women in pink turned and frowned.

'Oh, shit!' a female voice exclaimed. 'Sorry.'

Ra Ke folded his arms. Finley turned and put her hands on her hips.

'I didn't think it would slam like that.' The interloper was gesturing apologetically at the heavy steel door. 'Don't know my own strength.'

The whole class had stopped stretching by now to stare at the vision in yellow and black that had disturbed its tranquillity. She was wearing yellow nylon pants with black lightning bolts down the side, a black cut-off sweatshirt that exposed a golden belly, black leather gloves with the fingers cut out, black and silver Reeboks and a pink towelling headband stretched around a corn yellow head.

God, a throwback to the seventies, Finley noted in disbelief. *She looks like a fucking X-Man in that outfit or an escapee from* Xanadu. *Only the leg warmers are missing.*

'Rick Mord's gym is the next building,' someone called out helpfully.

'Isn't this Mo Bo?' the newcomer asked. 'I saw this ad.' She waved a piece of paper.

'Of course, come in.' Ra Ke said and put his hands together in a gesture of prayer. He bowed his head.

The interloper took a few steps forward. 'Ta,' she said. 'I've only done the Mo Bo on telly before.'

There was quiet snickering from the regulars. But not too much snickering because they were enlightened.

'But in Australia I've done Taekwondo, Karate, Wing-chun, Kung-fu, Judo, Aikido, Kendo, Hapkido and, jees, a lot of other stuff—'

Australia! Shit, Finley thought, *they're coming out of the woodwork. All I need today is to run into another one, a surfer chick with blonde hair and big tits.*

Shit. That's how Natalie had described her.

Could it be?

'You must forget all those disciplines,' Ra Ke was telling the newcomer. 'Mo Bo is far more spiritually integrated.'

'Yeah?' She started digging into the bag around her waist. 'I'll give it a go. Why not? Who do I pay around here?' She dug out a few crumpled notes.

'Later,' Ra Ke said.

'Oh, OK. Is there somewhere I can get out of this stuff?'

'I'll show you,' Finley volunteered.

She took Avalon to the dressing room and pulled the curtain. The Australian threw down her bag, unzipped it, pulled out some purple bicycle shorts.

Finley watched her, arms folded.

'Thanks for showing me the ropes,' Avalon said. 'I'm new in town.'

'Really?'

'You couldn't tell?'

'Not at all.' Finley rolled her eyes.

'Oh, good. It's just there's a greater chance of me being mugged if I look like a tourist.'

'No one could ever mistake you for a tourist,' Finley reassured her.

'Well, you never know. You have guns here. I keep all my money in this bumbag.' She held up a zippered belt. 'Although, I wouldn't mind being mugged, but. It'd be a great story to tell everyone back at home.'

'Where are you from exactly?' Finley tried to sound nonchalant.

'Oh, I'm from Brissie but I spent some time in Tassie and now I live in Sinnie.'

'Sydney?' Finley interpreted. 'Not Melbourne?'

'No way! I had to go there for work once. It's too bloody cold. You wouldn't have a snowball's chance in hell of getting me back.'

So maybe she didn't know Shane after all. Calm down, Finley, there must be more than one Australian blonde wandering around Manhattan right now.

Avalon pulled on the lavender bicycle shorts. 'Shit, do I need this workout today! I had a fight with my boyfriend the night before last. Been stewing in my juices all yesterday.'

'Oh, yeah?' said Finley, only vaguely interested now.

'Punched him right out. He deserved it. He was fooling around with another woman. A negro, can you believe? I bet he's got a beautiful black eye but!'

'Black eye?' The artery in Finley's neck started twitching.

'Yeah, he was two-timing me. Can you believe it? I mean Cheyne and me are virtually engaged.'

'Shane?'

'Yeah, he asks me to come all the way over here to New York and then he goes play hide the sausage with this black person.'

Blender had said he'd left Contaminated with some Afro babe. And Esther had overheard the Australian chick say she'd given Shane a black eye. And there was Shane all messed-up at West 4th Street this morning. It was coming together.

And it was coming together in the form of this…this…yellow tulip.

'I'm ready,' the girl was saying, adjusting her headband. 'Let's get started.'

'No!' Finley launched herself at her and pushed her against the wall.

'Hey! Why did you do that?'

'He's my fucking boyfriend!' Finley held her fists up, ready to punch.

'What do you mean? Who's your boyfriend?'

'Shane!'

'My Cheyne?'

'Not your fucking Shane. Mine! How dare you give him a black eye! I wanted to give him that black eye!'

The girl cringed, flattened herself against the wall. Great Kung-fu champion she looks like, Finley sneered. I'm going to send her back to Australia in a fucking box.

'But I've been engaged to him for nine months!'

'Liar! He didn't say anything about you!'

'That doesn't mean I don't exist,' Avalon said reasonably. 'I didn't know about you but you exist. Cheyne's a bit of a fibber. That's why he's an actor.'

'He sure is a fucking actor!' Finley thought of the sweet hangdog look he always gave her, making her believe she was the only girl for him.

'So he's been playing around behind my back with the darkie and you?' the girl was asking.

'Not behind your back,' Finley pointed out. 'Behind mine. He's been playing around behind my back with you!'

'But he's my boyfriend! He's only been here a few weeks. I had him first!'

'You may have had him first but I had him last!'

'I think the negro had him last.' Avalon put her hands up in a conciliatory gesture. 'Look, I'm sorry about this. I'm going to give him another bloody black eye when I see him. I've told him he's got to control his willy. But Cheyne loves me. I've got the wedding all planned. We're going to get married jumping out of a small plane over Uluru. Did you know you can even get white satin parachutes? So you see—'

'Shut up! I don't even know what you're talking about!' Finley slid a hand down her leg looking for her box cutter and then realised she'd unbuckled it before class. She moved swiftly into the position of the Wary Monkey, elbows and knees bent, hands flattened like blades, ready to chop.

Avalon immediately assumed a position, her arms moving back and forth like pistons.

This one has seen too many Jackie Chan movies, Finley thought. Let's see her go to water when I give her my Ferocious Yak.

Finley bent at the waist, raised a knee and an arm and charged. Instead of ducking, the blonde girl stood her ground. Before Finley knew what was happening, she put the heel of one hand under Finley's chin and pushed her face up and backwards, at the same time clawing at her brow. Finley flew backwards and Avalon kicked her legs from underneath her.

She went down, a jumble of backpacks and exercise bags breaking her fall. Thinking quickly, she hooked a foot around Avalon's ankle and pulled her knee up. The girl tripped and began to fall back. Finley jumped up and got ready to grapple her, but all she could do was stare in amazement as the blonde threw her arms backward to break her fall and then sprang back into a standing position. She shot a razor-sharp kick to Finley's solar plexus, winding her, and then stretched an arm out, grasping her neck like it was a small bird in an eagle's claw. She raised a fist ready to deliver a knock-out blow. Finley winced, almost blacking out, her arms hanging at her sides like boiled spaghetti.

'Excellent!' Ra Ke had pushed the curtains aside and was standing with a group of horrified pink ladies. 'Who is your teacher?'

'Grandmaster Bruce Packer,' Avalon said, not even winded. 'You should see what I can do when I have some real competition.'

'Hey!' Finley, still hanging loosely in her victor's grip, made a strangled sound.

'Sha Mu, you made some fundamental errors.' Ra Ke's voice was gently scolding. 'What do I always tell you about practising your Hideous Hyena? You could have used it most effectively when your opponent applied the Tiger Claw.'

'Yeah, and the way she came at me with a head-butt,' her

opponent added. 'That's exactly what they teach us not to do.'

'You may let her go now,' Ra Ke said.

Avalon released her grip. Finley stumbled against a bench and flopped down. The pink ladies were all smirking at her. She could feel her face flush red with anger and shame.

'Now, Sha Mu, you relax for a while. I'd like our new member to take your place at the head of the class and give us a demonstration of her many interesting skills.' He bowed deeply.

'Ta,' said the blonde. Then she cast Finley a smug look. 'But I can't stay too long. My boyfriend Cheyne will wonder where I am.'

I hope Finley appreciates all the trouble I've gone to for her sake, Natalie thought, as she tapped the number into her cell phone. Yesterday I allowed her boyfriend to molest me to show her what a no-good jerk he is. And I'm not going to win any awards from the Cowgirl Hall of Fame for doing it.

'Oh, it's you.'

'Thought it was your boyfriend, uh?'

'Fuck off.'

'You sound like you're crying.'

'I'm not. I just got back from Mo Bo.'

'You are crying! I can hear you sniffling.'

'I've got a cold.'

'Well take some echinacea for God's sake. The audition's at two.'

'What audition?'

'For heaven's sake, Finley, it's Wednesday. I've reminded you every day. I even left a note about it at the surf shop this morning.'

'I didn't go to work. I didn't feel like it.'

'Well, stop moping around. I'm leaving for the audition now. Want to meet me at West 4th?'

'I'm not going.'

'Look, you ungrateful little cow, you will go. It's a chance.'

'A chance for what?'

'To do something with your life. You can't drift around waiting for that surfer of yours to come in to shore.'

'I'm not waiting for him.'

'Then why are you crying?'

'I'm not crying.'

'Listen, you idiot, I've been wrestling with my conscience about this all night but I have something to tell you about your boyfriend.'

'I don't want to hear anything!'

'You'll want to hear this.'

'I don't care if you saw him at Balducci's with the whole Dallas Cowboys cheer squad. I don't want to hear about it. I don't care.'

'Well, I'm glad you don't care because I saw him yesterday.'

'So?'

'He was looking much the worse for wear. I gave him some ice for his black eye.'

'Black eye?'

'Well, I could hardly miss it. He told me some girl gave it to him.'

'I know.'

'You do?'

'And she had the nerve to come to my Mo Bo class this morning.'

'The blonde?'

'Yeah. I kicked her head in.'

'Well, good for you.'

'He lied to me! He said he didn't have a black eye! But I saw it!'

'Don't sound so surprised. He's a man.'

'But I really thought…this time. I mean, he's so uncomplicated. He's not writing a novel or starting up a dot-com. He just is…himself.'

'I can tell you he's very complicated. So complicated he took me back to my place and then kissed me.'

'He what?'

'Calm down. I didn't kiss him back.'

'Natalie, if you're playing games—'

'I only went out with him, if you can call it that, for your sake. To show you what a cad he is. He was all over me like the plague. I don't think he can keep his hands off any woman.'

'Why would Shane kiss you? You're a dyke.'

'He didn't seem to notice.'

'And you didn't tell him.'

'Why would I? I was testing him. I only had your interests at heart.'

'And what did he supposedly say when he kissed you?'

'That I was the prettiest, most feminine thing he'd ever seen. I was quite flattered for a minute.'

'Huh! That's unbelievable for a start. You, feminine?'

'Just because I'm same-gender articulated doesn't mean I'm not feminine. Really, Finley, it looks like I wasted all that time explaining it to you. The problem with our relationship was not that I wasn't femme enough, it was that you weren't butch enough.'

'I never said I was.'

'But you come on strong with all that kick-boxing-I've-got-a-tattoo-and-have-a-big-dog stuff and you're really just a little breeder underneath. You go to water whenever any surf bum flexes his muscles at you.'

'I do not.'

'The point is, you should forget him and think about your career.

Look at the time, we better leave. Have you read the script?'

'No.'

'Really, Finley—'

'If I go I'll only be a fucking embarrassment.'

'How could you ever be an embarrassment? You're beautiful, ungrateful and foul-tempered. Who couldn't love you?'

'Hang up, Natalie.'

'I'll see you there in half an hour.'

'Natalie?'

'What?'

'I was wondering...'

'Yes?'

'Did he taste like salt?'

'Peanut butter, actually,' said Natalie.

Finley replaced the receiver, wiped her nose with her hand and put her arm around Blossom. 'If I became a movie star it would serve Shane right.'

Blossom whimpered.

'You're afraid that I'll go away on location and leave you by yourself?'

The dog sighed.

'I'd never do that. You could come too. Think of Natalie's meatballs.'

Blossom, who could not understand why The One Who Brought Meat didn't visit anymore, barked and wagged her tail.

'OK. I'll go to the stupid audition. Natalie's right. I've got to do something about my shitty life. Now where is that script?'

She rolled off the bed and surveyed the debris. Pages of *The Importance of Being Earnest* were scattered far and wide. She started picking them up. 'Come on, Blossom, just don't stand there. You can help me with Gwendolen while I get dressed.'

Shane stared out the diner window at the expanse of metallic water that lay between him and JFK airport. One big fucking oil slick, he thought, watching a duck land on the bleak surface and then take off again. The owners of the diner, with its seafoam vinyl banquettes and mermaid-etched glass, seemed to be under the impression that it offered a view of palm trees, golden sands and girls in string bikinis rather than a highway, a polluted pond and a few oil refineries on the horizon. The ocean side of Rockaway, a jumble of boarded-up game parlours and hot-dog stands, didn't have anything like this. What kind of people would rather eat breakfast looking at aircraft hangars than at six-footers curling onto the shore? If there ever were six-footers in this pissant place.

There'd been a bit of a swell this morning, decent little tubes surprisingly. He managed to struggle into his wetsuit, squeeze his damaged fingers into the thick lobster-claw glove and pull his rubber booties on with one hand.

The water was cold enough to freeze the pain right out of his muscles. But not, he knew, to freeze the pain out of his heart. He thought Finley had ruptured something when she kicked him like that and he'd lain on the train floor for several stops, groaning, while people stepped over him. When he sat up and struggled to a seat he felt worse. Immersing himself in the water for four hours hadn't numbed the ache.

How the fuck did Finley find out about Cassie? 'That blonde surfer chick girlfriend of yours,' she said before she landed the kick. Had she followed him home one night? Or had Brian blabbed? But Brian didn't know about Finley. Neither did Cassie, he was sure. He'd just told Cassie he had a girlfriend. And she'd said she didn't mind. He couldn't imagine Cassie having the brains to find out who Finley was and call her. It didn't make sense. But he couldn't sit here all day wondering either. He had to tell Finley that Cassie didn't mean anything to him. That she was just a root.

He gestured to the waiter and handed him a five-dollar note. The waiter brought back his change.

'Take my advice, young man, and go and talk to her. Get rid of each day's troubles before you go to sleep at night.'

'I suppose you want a tip for that,' Shane said.

Shane hobbled off the train at Chambers Street and dragged himself a few more blocks to Duane.

A balding guy with a stringy ponytail was leaning on the counter at Wipeout reading some girlie magazine. The Japanese girl, Hiromi, wasn't anywhere in sight.

'Is Finley here?'

Stewie didn't look up. 'No, she didn't come in.'

'Do you know where she is?'

'Who ever knows where Finley is, man? Physically or spiritually, you know? Wait a minute.' He looked under the counter and pulled out a sheet of paper. 'Maybe this'll help.'

Shane took the paper. 'She's gone to an audition? At this address?'

Stewie shrugged. 'I suppose so. Her girlfriend stuck it to the store window. Take it if you want. What happened to your eye, man?'

'What girlfriend?'

'You know, that dyke she's screwing around with. Waste of a

good piece of ass if you ask me.'

Shane grabbed him by the shirt. 'Look, you shithead, don't talk about her like that! I'll drop you!'

Stewie shook himself loose. 'Easy, man, I'm just telling it how it is.'

Shane picked up his board and stomped out of the store. He knew there'd been another man. He just didn't know it was a woman.

Cheyne looked at his watch. Damn, it was 1.45. He'd been standing in the queue—he checked himself, in line—at the bank for twenty minutes. And now the teller was taking her own sweet time about running his card through the system. She had been over in a corner hunched over the telephone for about fifteen minutes. If she didn't come back soon, he'd miss the audition. As it was, he'd have to take a taxi once she'd handed over the money. He gave a loud sigh of displeasure and the girl counting out a wad of notes at the teller next door looked up. He smiled at her and shrugged. She lowered her eyes, blushing.

The teller was blushing too when she finally returned. 'I'm sorry, sir, not only was this card declined but there's no record of it in the system. You said it was working last week?'

'Yes, of course. I take cash directly from my Australian bank account with it.'

'Well, there's no record of any bank account, unfortunately. It's linked to Mastercard, so I called them. Do you have any other cards?'

'I've got Visa, but for some bloody reason it's not working either.'

'Do you want me to try it?'

'No,' he said, embarrassed. 'Look, this is ridiculous. I can't get access to my own money?'

'Is there someone in Australia you could call? A parent or girl-friend perhaps?'

'No!' He thumped his fist on the counter. He was aware other customers were looking at him.

'The thing is,' she was saying, her voice turning a fraction chillier. 'I'm sorry about this but they've asked me to keep the card. It's unauthorised.'

'But it's going to take me fucking weeks to get another one!'

'It's for your own protection, sir.'

'How can it be for my protection when you're taking my own card?'

'It's the rules, sir. They've given me an Australian number you can call twenty-four hours a day.' She slid a piece of paper under the bulletproof glass. She smiled. 'It's a free call.'

Fucking lot of good that will do me, Cheyne grumbled as he pocketed the paper and dashed out on to Sixth Avenue. Now I don't have enough money for a cab. He patted his coat pockets, feeling for his Metrocard. Shit, where was it?

'If you just let me through, I'll pay you back tomorrow, I promise,' Cheyne said to the old guy in the subway token booth.

'Move along, buddy,' the clerk growled. 'I've heard that one before.'

For a moment Cheyne thought about jumping the turnstiles, but there was a cop there, his belt weighed down with weapons of deterrence. He ran back up into the street. Maybe he could get a cab, borrow some money from Lara at the other end. He held his hand out and then rejected the idea. Shit, how desperate would that look?

A crowd of people was shuffling onto the Sixth Avenue bus. He got in line, followed them on, sneaking around the passengers running their Metrocards through the machine. The driver wasn't paying attention, anyway. An old woman made a noise at him and pointed her umbrella, but he pushed his way to the back of the bus and found a seat. The bus roared off and then lurched to a halt at a set of red lights.

He was going to be late, but they'd have to wait for him. Lara would make sure of it. He was the whole point of the exercise.

He slumped down in his seat impatiently, closed his eyes. Above him, the grinning face of the Crocodile Hunter watched over him. *Miss Fairfax, ever since I met you I have admired you more than any girl…I have ever met since…I met you.* Jack Worthing sounds about as articulate as I do with Natalie, he thought bitterly. Except that Jack got the girl.

The Mo Bo guy was quite a spunk, if you liked Asians, Avalon thought. But all the way through his class, she was thinking of Cheyne. Two other girlfriends and God knew how many more! No wonder he was always tired when she suggested a root! The truth of the matter was, she just couldn't let him out of her sight.

After the class, she turned down the Mo Bo guy's offer of a frappuchino at Starbucks. She had to get home and confront Cheyne. No more pussy-footing. She had to set him straight. Either he set a date for the parachute wedding and found them a place to live or she'd kill him. It was a fair choice. She couldn't say better than that.

It was 1.45 p.m. when she thumped on Cheyne's door. No response. She put her ear to the lock but couldn't hear anything, not even the tell-tale creak of footsteps scurrying to the bathroom or out the back window. She took her key out and put it in the lock. It turned. He hadn't changed the locks. Maybe that meant that he was hoping she would come back. Maybe he was waiting for her.

The door opened smoothly. Her pulse rate was as slow as a resting goanna.

The apartment seemed empty. She crept into the bedroom first and sniffed the sheets. She upended the wicker basket beside the bed and scrambled through the scrunched-up tissues looking for used condoms. She ran her hand over the bathroom surfaces checking for frizzy, black hairs. She even looked at the toilet roll to see if it had been attached to the holder by a male or female hand. The paper unwound down the back, so Cheyne had obviously put it on. She was always going on at him about this.

In the sitting room, the cushions were thrown all over the floor. She picked them up, punched the stuffing and arranged them back on the sofa. An empty Stoli bottle sat on the coffee table. Judging by the lack of a glass, he'd been drinking straight out of the bottle. She took it into the kitchen and threw it into the trash, first lifting out the plastic bag and combing it for items of a female nature. She clicked her tongue in disgust at the crumpled pizza box and poly-styrene Big Mac container. The minute I turn my back, it's junk food. There's just no excuse, she thought, opening the cupboards and observing her untouched supplies of dried lentils and peas. All he needed to do was soak these overnight, add a few carrots and onions and some peppercorns and boil it all up for a couple of hours. What a lazy dickhead.

She picked up a Metrocard lying by the antique white telephone that sat on the kitchen bench. Underneath it was a scrap of paper. She smoothed it out. In his handwriting was scrawled a message, LARA WEDNESDAY 2 PM, and an address on 45th Street.

Avalon smacked the counter with an open hand. Shit! She vaguely thought he'd mentioned a Lara but she hadn't been listening. Which woman was this? The darkie or the nutcase at Mo Bo or some other woman? Christ, she was acting like a lamb chop short of a barbecue. She was the dickhead, trusting him! She could feel the rage churning through her arteries and singeing the hair on her arms. She picked up a wooden spice rack painted with blue ducks and smashed it on the floor.

That felt better. She looked at her Pokemon watch. It was 1.56 already. If she took the train there was still time to get to him before insertion took place. Cheyne was always too fucking slow about getting down to it anyway. You had to hurry him along. She reckoned she had half an hour, tops.

She pocketed his Metrocard and ran down the stairs. A nice policeman standing by the turnstiles had to remind her how to use it. A train was waiting on the platform. She thrust herself between the closing doors. The other passengers looked warily at her.

God, you'd think I was some kind of lunatic, she thought.

It was against Finley's principles to pay for public transport. It was public, wasn't it? Her taxes, if she ever submitted a tax return, which she hadn't, would be channelled into providing new trains and clean stations and safe tracks. So it was her right to travel on *her* subway system for free. Why use a Metrocard when you were capable of jumping a turnstile?

She evaluated the cop standing by the token booth at West 4th Street. Heavy set, low centre of gravity, facing away from the turnstiles. By the time he'd realised that she'd gone over and he'd ordered the token booth clerk to open the gate, she'd be well on her way down the platform and onto the first passing train. Most times they didn't even bother to chase you, if you were a white girl and gave them a friendly wave from the other side. If they did manage to catch you, you were arrested and fingerprinted and thrown in the slammer for hours until your fingerprints were checked against the computer. All that paperwork and the fingerprints were more than likely to come up clean. But if you were anything darker than toast-coloured...

She hiked her script under her arm and pretended to be digging in her pocket for her card. She made a guarded gesture to suggest she was about to swipe. And then, with a woman carrying a pot plant as cover, she hoisted herself up and over the mechanism.

And straight into the arms of a smirking transit cop.

Natalie handed the tray of meatballs around the room. Derek Grimley declined with the wave of a hand and a sneer but Damian scooped them into his mouth by the handful. 'These are scrumptious, ducky. Who did you say you were?'

'My name's Natalie Myerson and I'm hoping that I'll be doing the catering for your picture. Here's my card.' Damian was licking the ketchup off his fingers so she popped it into his trouser pocket. There was something else in there, wet and tacky to the touch, so she withdrew her hand quickly.

'Lovely,' he said. 'Goodness knows what we would do without you. All this waiting. You don't have any more, do you?'

'I'll be right back,' Natalie said, glad to get out of there. The audition room, painted a curdled cream, was stuffy and smelled of old laundry, specifically, she imagined, Damian Grimley's unwashed socks. There were a few mismatched chairs scattered around and a lumpy sofa on which Lara Dinardo sat with her knees tucked under her, talking into a cell phone and smoking like a filthy oven. Derek Grimley sat Buddha-like on a high stool, knees crossed, cigarette in hand, occasionally casting a glance at the door and sighing 'Oh, really!'

'Hey you!' Lara Dinardo called from the sofa as Natalie walked towards the door.

Natalie turned around. 'Yes?' she asked sweetly.

'Could you check down the hall and see if your girlfriend's there? We're giving her five more minutes and we're out of here.'

'But your actor hasn't turned up, either,' Natalie felt obliged to point out.

'Mr Burdekin's been unavoidably delayed,' Dinardo lied, ruffling.

'Well, I'm sure Miss Rule has been unavoidably delayed too. Maybe they've been unavoidably delayed together.'

Natalie had another stash of food stored in plastic containers in a grimy kitchen she found down the hallway. This included her chocolate cookies with peppermint icing. Damian Grimley would love these. She'd stuff them down his gullet with her own fingers to get that catering job.

She passed a rehearsal room where some kind of wrestling match was going on. Thuds and expletives filled the dusty air. A seven-foot giant with blonde hair to his waist and dark glasses came out of the men's bathroom at the end of the hall, and waved the key at her in greeting. He wore leopard-print tights tucked into boots and a bomber jacket with WSW written on it.

Finley liked that stuff. No wonder Natalie had mistaken her for butch.

Where was the little idiot? Despite her protestations, Natalie had been sure she would be there. Who in their right mind wouldn't want an acting career handed to them on a plate like, well, these cookies? As far as she could see actors just lay around in their trailers having people wait on them with food and drink. The boy they'd dragged out of drama school to be the lead in *Taxi Driver II*, had it written into his contract that he must have seventeen bottles of a certain kind of Lithuanian beer delivered to his trailer every day. Not because he liked Lithuanian beer. But because he could demand it. She didn't mind standing around all day slinging hash herself, but Finley deserved something better.

She arranged some cookies on a plate and walked back up the dingy hallway, her granny shoes making a clattering noise on the dusty floorboards. The wrestlers had turned on a boom box, tuned into something metal. Not heavy, just scratchy.

Both Grimleys looked up as she entered. Damian plunged for a cookie. Derek waved them away. Lara Dinardo snapped her cell phone shut. 'I'm sorry about this, Derek. I thought it was worth taking a chance on the girl…'

Before she could finish there was a noise in the hallway, a thump, a grunt, an expletive and then the sound of the elevator doors dragging themselves closed. Lara looked up. Damian wiped his sticky hands on his trousers. Derek slid off his stool, crossed his arms and started tapping one foot, like a schoolmarm about to chastise a tardy student.

Wrestlers, Natalie sighed.

But it was a shaggy guy with a surfboard.

'Deliveries go backstage,' Derek Grimley instructed him.

'Fuck, am I in the wrong place? Sorry.' The interloper leaned his surfboard against a wall and dug in his pocket for something. It was a piece of paper. He scrutinised it. 'Is this Room 707? I'm looking for Finley Rule.'

'It's her surfboard?' Derek Grimley approached, amused.

'No, it's mine.'

'Really? I think you'll be disappointed to find that there's no surf up here. Maybe if you tried the third floor you might be lucky.'

'Look, you Pommie poonce, do you know Finley or not? I've rushed all the way up here to find her. This note says she's in this room.' He waved the paper.

'Let me take a look at that.' Natalie snatched it off him. 'Where did you get this?'

'What's it matter to you?'

'I wrote it.'

'You couldn't have.'

'And why not?'

'Some dyke wrote it.'

'Say,' Lara Dinardo interrupted, getting up off the sofa, 'haven't I seen you somewhere before?'

'Don't think so.'

'I'm sure I have. Didn't you audition for *The Parent Trap III*?'

'Look, I'm just trying to find my girlfriend.'

'Your girlfriend?' This was Natalie.

'Yeah, Finley, like I said.'

'Well, we're still waiting for her,' Lara said. 'Where are you from?'

'Melbourne.'

'Oh, another of our antipodean friends,' said Derek Grimley. 'You lose one Australian and another pops up to take his place. Wonderful, isn't it? Maybe you can read if Mr Burdekin lets us down.'

'Yes, maybe you can,' said Lara. 'How tall are you? Let me get the video.'

'What's your name, ducky?' Damian asked.

'Shane.'

'Shane?' Natalie put her hands on her hips. 'That's a coincidence!'

'Why is it a coincidence?'

'Because Finley's boyfriend is called Shane.'

'That's what I said. I am her fucking boyfriend.'

'Well, I hate to tell you this buster, but she's already got an Australian boyfriend called Shane. And it's not you.'

'Look, lady, I don't know who you are—'

'I'm her girlfriend.'

'You? No fucking way!'

'And I've met this deadbeat Australian she's been dating. I'm an intimate acquaintance of his.'

'You say your name's Shane?' Lara was a little slow on the uptake. 'Isn't that weird, Derek?'

'And it's giving me an idea.' Derek held one finger up in the air, as if testing for rain and looked heavenwards. 'Rethinking. Rethinking.'

'*The Importance of Being Shane*,' said Damian through a mouthful of crumbs. 'Set on some glorious beach. Lots of bare-chested boys in board shorts. I could work on my tan.' He poked a milky bicep.

'I don't fucking believe it.' Shane was shaking his head, not listening to them. A drift of sand fell on the matted fur of his coat. He brushed a skein of woolly hair out of one eye. 'Finley has another boyfriend and a girlfriend?'

'Say, where did you get that black eye?' Lara asked. 'Were you in a brawl?'

Natalie could now see the bruise, fanning out across his cheek. She was starting to get the picture. 'Do you have a blonde girlfriend with big tits?' she asked.

'I might know someone like that,' the Australian said, cagily. 'What's it to you?'

'Nothing,' she said, subdued. She didn't feel so well. She had kissed the wrong Shane. So who, then, was the other one?

There was another thump and the sound of elevator doors opening and closing again. Everyone stopped chattering.

Finley, thought Shane.

Cheyne, thought Lara.

But it was a blonde in a yellow parka, bouncing up and down as if on a pogo stick and jerking her head around like a member of a SWAT team on a raid. She stopped and raised her hands in a defensive position when she saw everyone looking at her.

Well, well, Natalie said to herself, it's the girlfriend. The one I saw in Balducci's. This will be interesting. And then she had to check herself. No, it's the girlfriend of the other Shane. What the hell is she doing here?

The blonde wasn't after any Shane, as it turned out. 'Which of youse is Lara?' she demanded.

'I'm Lara,' the appropriate person declared.

'Then leave my fucking boyfriend alone!' she roared as she launched her body into the air and landed a thick sole on the startled casting director's throat.

The old elevator seemed to take forever to climb to the seventh floor. Cheyne thumped the control panel in irritation every time it stopped to collect or disgorge other passengers. They were mostly theatre types, teenage girls with their hair in tight buns, primping mothers with sullen brats, a giant in leopard-print tights carrying an armful of pizza and checking his reflection in the elevator mirror. Cheyne checked his reflection too. He tugged at his hair, pulled some long strands over his bruised eye.

The seventh floor was quiet when he reached it, the corridor deserted. He went straight to Room 707 and knocked on the partly closed door.

He pushed it open. No one there. Damn. It was 2.50.

Valerie would have kittens when she found out he'd missed the audition. And then she'd follow those with a litter of puppies.

He stood for a while, cursing himself, the bank, the lumbering Sixth Avenue bus. Then he turned on his heels to walk out. He stepped in something, slipped slightly.

Looked down.

Blood.

Blood?

Why didn't he have a good feeling about this?

Sputnik Records. Esther cradled the phone in her shoulder while she handed a customer some change.

'Esther, it's Finley.'

'Where are you? Rockwell's been asking. Fortunately he's in a good mood about some cheap photo equipment he won on eBay today—'

'Look, I'm down at Central Booking.'

'Central Casting?'

'No, the slammer, idiot. Hang on a minute, there's some homie breathing down my neck…You can call your mother in a minute, all right? Stop blubbering…Tell Rockwell I'm sick, OK? And would you do me a favour and walk Blossom after work? Can you get off early? And you've still got a spare key, haven't you? I could be here all night.'

'You don't sound very unhappy about it.'

'Yeah, well they're trying to frighten me, but I know the game. They caught me jumping a turnstile and now they've got me on some concealed weapons charge for the box cutter. But it's OK, I've convinced them I'm an art student, it's just part of my equipment. But, you know, it's all fucking paperwork.'

'God, Finley, I'd fall to pieces if that happened to me. You're so tough.'

'Right on,' said Finley, hanging up the phone and bursting into tears.

Shane leaned his surfboard against the door of his building and searched for his keys. After everything that had happened that afternoon, he was anxious to get inside and check the damage to his board.

First that blonde chick knocking it out of his hands. Then that stupid Pommy faggot tripping on it trying to get out of the way. The paramedic kicking the fins when he was getting the stretcher out. The domestic-abuse victim at the emergency room landing on it with her 350-pound butt. OK, so her eyes were closed up like two shiny eggplants, but the nurse who guided her to the seat could see, for Christ's sake.

He'd hitched a lift downtown to St Vincents with the paramedics, intending to hop off at the hospital and walk home. Rode in the back of the ambulance with that woman, Lara, but at their destination she had dug her fingers into his arm and begged him to come with her. She looked pretty bad with blood all over her face and the swelling on her neck so he'd said, 'Yes, but just for a fucking few minutes, all right?'

They'd been there for more than three hours. There were at least twenty-five people ahead of them in the emergency room, including a woman who was wailing to anyone who would listen that her right breast implant had exploded on the 110th floor of the World Trade Center and she was going to sue. Didn't even look like she had a left breast implant as far as he could see.

He'd given Lara his knitted cap to mop up the blood and got her a Diet Coke from the drink machine. He didn't think she was hurt too badly, but by the way she was yapping into her cell phone you'd think she was in full-body traction with only a 50-50 chance of survival.

No one knew anything about the girl who attacked her. She'd come straight out of the blue. Lara said she must have had something to do with the actor, Bradford Ford, and she was on her mobile phone to her lawyer before the blood hit the floor. There was some wrestling school down the hall and two fucking enormous wankers, both of them built like refrigerators, had come in and dragged the girl away, but not before she'd given one of them a kick in the balls he wouldn't forget. If he had any balls with all those steroids.

Trouble was, he knew immediately he'd seen that girl before. She was an Aussie, you could pick a scrubber a mile off, didn't even have to open their mouths. At first he couldn't place her. Was she one of the girls from the Pier Hotel? Nah, he would have known her straightaway. He had a vague recollection that the last time he'd seen her she was wearing some kind of plant, some leaves or a tree or something. But he was tripping…Unless. Shit, he worked it out! She was in that telly series his old girlfriend Sharon had taped. What was it called? Something woggy. It was a huge hit but a load of crap as far as he could see. Sharon had the hots for the lead actor, some poof in a cloak. She played the bloody thing over and over again when he wanted to watch *Biggest Wednesday*. The bloke in it was a ponce, looking at his reflection in his shiny sword. And what about that accent? He was fucking Australian but he'd thrown in some Yank for good measure. He hated wankers like that. You are what you are.

But the girl…she was a fox. Reminded him of Sharon, that sharp nose and freckled face, the yellow hair and the blue eyes with spiky lashes. And in the show she hardly wore any clothes, which distracted him a bit from the fact that he wasn't watching Tony Ray and Ross Clarke-Jones getting mown down by a monster wave at Jaws.

Shane didn't tell Lara what he knew. He wasn't going to dob the scrubber in. Let those Pommy bastards scream and flap around, let that dyke with the red lipstick pout. Lara probably deserved what she got. Fooling around with the blonde girl's boyfriend! It just wasn't right.

He turned the key in the lock and picked up his board. He wasn't going to think about Finley, or the dyke who said she was her girlfriend. Or the other Shane, whoever the fuck he was. He was going to check his wounded surfboard and then think about it. First things first.

He pushed into the entrance and pressed the elevator button. He noticed his gloves had blood on them. Some doctor had eventually come and put a plaster on Lara's nose and they'd left. He was glad to get out of there, reminded him too much of the Southampton hospital. Lara had invited him for a drink, seemed keen to exchange more bodily fluids with him. Wasn't his type, though. Too scrawny. Kept on filming him with a stupid little video camera. He just wanted to get away.

'But I've got to discuss Algie with you,' she had said on Seventh Avenue, sticking nails into his arm again.

'Who the fuck is he?' he'd said.

'A character in the film we're casting. I've just spoken to the Grimleys. They think you'll be perfect for him. Why are you looking like that? Don't you want to be an actor?'

'Why the fuck would I want to be one of those?'

'Money. Fame.'

Shane considered this. He'd have thousands next week when the checks started rolling in from his eBay auction. And what use was fame to him unless he was famous as a big-wave board rider? 'Nah.'

'But listen. Derek has this idea, although Damian says it's his, that we shoot it in some exotic location. On a beach, Shane. You can bring your board. You'd like that, wouldn't you?'

'What fucking beach?' Shane asked, wary. 'Jones Beach I suppose?'

'I don't know what beach. Somewhere warm. Somewhere with big waves.'

'They wouldn't consider Spain would they?'

She didn't say no.

The elevator thumped to the bottom of the shaft. Shane got in and pushed his key into the lock. It wouldn't fit. He turned it round, tried again.

'Fuck!' Someone had changed the locks on him.

Avalon jumped off the rubber mat and slapped her hands together to wipe off the grit.

Meathead Mike Rubinek folded his arms, each the size of a small sheep, across his chest and frowned. 'Where did you learn that move?'

'Bruce Packer's Gold Coast Stunt Academy. It took months to perfect. I was the best at it but.'

'It could work,' said the one called Orlando the Oscillator, peering down at her through dark glasses and hardly moving his lips. He tossed his long blond hair aside coquettishly. 'We could write her in as my chick. The fans'll go for it. I've been heartbroken since Mitzi the Manipulator got life for vehicular homicide. And I've rebuffed every ho lookin' to seduce me because I've been true to Mitzi. But the bitch was playin' around with The Eliminator behind my back and he's been bringin' her flowers in jail. So a bit of pussy on the side is justified. When Mitzi's life sentence is overturned in a few weeks, she can come kickin' out of the slammer and challenge this one to a rumble. There's nothin' those teenage boys like better than a tit fight.'

'How come you get all the chicks?' Meathead Mike grumbled. 'Last one I had was that bitch Born Again Joe Barnes' girl. Only waved her ass at me to distract me from the fight, it turns out. What the fuck am I, a freak or something?'

'You're The Man Without a Heart, remember? You Can't Love No Woman.'

'Yeah, OK, but I'm sick of it.'

'What's your name, anyway?' Meathead Mike asked Avalon.

'Avalon Elliot.'

The wrestlers shook their shaven, stubbly and longhaired heads. 'Sounds like a newsreader,' said the third one, a mound of white flesh known as Destructo.

'What about Betty the Ball Cruncher?' offered Mike. 'That was some kick in the balls you gave me before.'

'I explained that. I was after my boyfriend's girlfriend. Gave her a beauty, too.'

'Yeah, righteousness was on your side,' nodded Orlando.

'Who is this jerk, anyway? Want us to fix him?'

'Gosh, thanks Meathead. Can I call you Meathead? But I think I've got him under control.'

'That I can believe!' Mike guffawed and rubbed his crotch.

'Do I have to have a new name?' Avalon asked. 'This is not my real one, anyway. Changed it by deed poll eight years ago. I don't want another one if I can help it. It will be too fucking hard to remember.'

'Do you think my name's really Orlando?' said the blond.

'It isn't?'

'Norman,' he said.

'Larry,' said Mike. 'Meathead Larry didn't work.'

'Frobisher,' said Destructo.

'What is your old name anyway?' Mike/Larry asked Avalon.

'Maxine,' she admitted. 'Horrible, isn't it? It's my dad's name. Max.'

'But that's perfect!' declared Destructo, throwing his towel down on a bench. He rose on surprisingly small feet, wobbled. His grey WSW sweatshirt was the size of a delivery van. 'Gentlemen, meet our new World Star Wrestling champion…Mad Max's little sister— Mad Maxine!'

'Wow, I like that!' said Mike. 'Great fucking movie.'

'Hell, yeah,' said Orlando.

'We dress her up in animal skins…'

'And bring her on in a hot rod…'

Avalon had tuned out. She was thinking of herself striding around the ring in sheepskin boots and rabbit pelts, her hair gelled and sticking out of a headband like a cocky's quill, fifty thousand fans screaming and holding up banners declaring undying love.

Mad Maxine. Fucking ace.

His gammy left knee playing up again, Shane limped the few blocks to Finley's building, still carrying his surfboard and backpack, not wanting to risk leaving them outside his door.

There was no answer when he buzzed her downstairs door. He waited in the entrance of the building opposite, his eyes trained on her greasy window. There was a Roxy decal stuck to the pane. He hadn't noticed it before. At one point Blossom put her soggy nose and paws on the window, leaving a trail of spittle, but she disappeared before he could wave.

It was dark and it had started to snow lightly. He could never get used to the feeling of snow on his cheeks. He was used to hard rain and burning sun, weather that made you wince and shield your face. Snow melted on your skin almost before you could notice it, but there was something creepy about it, like the feeling you got when you slept in the bush, of bugs climbing in and out of your exposed orifices all night.

He pulled his ratty collar up against his neck and thrust his hands into his thin pockets. He'd thrown his bloody gloves in a trash can a couple of blocks away. He'd given his beanie to Lara to clean up the blood. He didn't regret it. It was a habit for the locals, putting on clothes to go outside and then taking them all off again inside. The gloves, the hats, the scarves, the earmuffs, the down vests, the coats. He couldn't stand the ritual. He hated clothes. Even in winter in Melbourne he sometimes only wore rubber thongs on his feet.

But fuck it, he'd be out of there soon. If he could get back in his building. It was Brian's doing, he knew it. Shane didn't give a shit about the place, only how the fuck was he going to get the money from eBay if he was locked out? Maybe he could find another computer, log on. Did Finley have one? Nah, not likely, she even used an old aluminium pot for coffee.

That Lara would have one, though. And she'd have money. Maybe he could say yes to the acting role, get a cash advance. But then he'd probably have to fuck her, and he was all through with rooting neurotic blondes.

The snow turned to wet sleet and he gave up. He'd find some coffee shop or bar to hole up in while he waited for her.

He rejected several Sullivan Street places as too pooncy, full of cigar smoke and the kind of guys who had weekly manicures. Discouraged and wet, he traipsed northward until he at last found the perfect dive, the last bar in the neighbourhood left untouched by an interior decorator's hand. The owners hadn't even bothered to fix the neon sign. The 'R' in BAR sputtered on and off.

Shane pushed the door open.

The cocktail waitress plopped a Samuel Adams down on the bar in front of Cheyne as soon as he sat.

'Hi, Mel. Say, what happened to your eye?'

'Ran into a door.'

'That girlfriend giving you a hard time, uh?'

'Unfortunately.' Cheyne shook his head. How long would he have to stay out tonight before it was safe to go home? But it wasn't Avalon he was avoiding tonight. Valerie would be on the warpath, knowing he'd missed the audition. Avalon's powerful fists were one thing, Valerie's razor-sharp tongue another. He couldn't deal with a multiple assault.

He grabbed the neck of the beer and attempted to pour some of the liquid into his glass. He noticed with alarm his hand was trembling.

'Let me get that,' the waitress offered, speedy with the wipe-up cloth.

'Thanks.'

'A bad day?'

'Not the best.'

'Call if you need anything,' she smiled and sashayed in an exaggerated way to the tables at the front of the bar.

He watched her go. Strange, she looked more attractive to him tonight. Now that he knew there was no way Avalon would let him have her. Or any woman. He'd have to stay out tonight, sneak in early with a locksmith and get the locks changed. Or find a hotel, move out for a while. But until he sorted out what was going on with his bank account, he couldn't even do that.

He downed his beer and knew what he needed was a whisky. A triple. And he didn't even like the stuff.

He motioned to the barman. 'A whisky. Do you make them quadruple?'

'A tall glass?'

'A jug if you've got one. Put it on my tab.' Fortunately he had a running tab with the bar, something the barman had fixed for him. All he had on him was a quarter he'd picked up off the pavement on his long walk downtown. Good for one phone call.

'Hey, Mel.' The waitress sidled up to him and put her tray on the bar. She called out to the barman for a Rolling Rock, a Whisky Sour and a Shirley Temple. 'You know, there's a guy over in the corner who says he's Australian. I picked the accent right up.'

She nodded at a bedraggled creature sitting at a table near the door. A surfboard in a silver cover leaned against the wall behind him.

'You know him?'

'Never seen him before in my life.'

'Want me to ask some more questions? You look like you need a friend tonight.'

If he needed a friend it wouldn't be some Australian surfer glaring at his beer in a Greenwich Village pub. The guy looked liked one of those types whose idea of travel was to get so legless he wouldn't even know what country he was in. He'd start drinking at the airport and wouldn't stop until after his mates took him on a pub-crawl to celebrate his return home.

'Thanks, but I'm not in the mood for conversation.'

He downed three more drinks and suddenly needed fresh air.

'I'll be back in a minute,' he said to the waitress. 'Put an extra ten dollars on my tab for your tip.'

'Hey, thanks,' she said.

As he passed the Australian slouched at the corner table he averted his face. He didn't know what the waitress had told the guy about him and he didn't want to get into any predictable conversation about the lousy weather and the expensive accommodation. The moron would probably hit on him for a place to stay, appealing to Cheyne's sense of compatriotism.

He didn't have anything in common with this wombat at all.

Blossom lifted her velvety ears and whimpered when Esther attached her lead.

'It's all right, Blossom, Mommy's just fine. She's going to be a little late tonight, that's all, so Aunty Esther's come to take you for your walkies. Is that OK?'

Esther wasn't sure Blossom believed her. The dog was reluctant at first to come down the stairs. But once they were on Sullivan Street, she almost pulled Esther's arm out of her socket charging after a rodent. Finley seemed forgotten as Blossom chased after her ball, barked at squirrels and pawed at garbage spilling out of torn trash bags.

Esther jogged with her up to Washington Square. The drizzle had turned back into light snow. Blossom's black coat glistened with moisture. The dark branches overhanging the park closed in on them. Esther could sense movement in the trees, faint rustlings, low whisperings. Enough's enough, she said to herself, I'm taking this puppy home. She gave the dog's collar a sharp tug and tried to turn her around.

But Blossom had seen something and was holding her stance, growling so softly Esther could only feel the vibrations. Esther tugged the lead again, but Blossom had the advantage in size. 'It's only a silly old drug dealer,' she reassured her.

Blossom's low rumble turned into a thundering bark. The lead was torn from Esther's hand as Blossom bounded forward. Esther tried to stomp on it with her foot, but Blossom was too fast. Before Esther could even call out, Blossom had someone bailed up against the fence, barking

'Hey!' cried a male voice. The victim was trying to twist away from the dog, his arm over his face. 'Get that animal off me!'

Esther raced up and grabbed Blossom's collar. She was snarling now, her big paws clawing at the stranger's chest. 'Blossom!' Esther chided. 'What would Mommy say?'

At the mention of 'Mommy' Blossom dropped to four paws and looked around guiltily at Esther. The victim backed away a few paces up Washington Square West.

'What the bloody hell do you think you're doing?' he screamed at her, investigating his arm for teeth marks and brushing dog saliva off his coat. 'This is the second time you've attacked me with that fucking dog!'

'Second time? Look, I'm sorry!' Esther called after him. 'I don't know why she did that.'

'You should have her put down!'

Blossom startled growling again, but this time Esther had her by the choke chain, saddling her. 'I said I was sorry.'

The stranger stepped under a street light. Esther took a closer look at him. He was pretty damn fine—tall, dressed well, light brown hair streaked dirty blonde. Not American.

Black eye.

'Your name wouldn't happen to be Shane, would it?' she asked.

'How do you know?'

'That's what Blossom's got against you, then.'

'That I'm named Cheyne? Why?'

'As if you didn't know,' Esther said and let Blossom off the lead.

The dog had the edge of his coat in its snarling jaws.

Cheyne had his arms around a tree, pulling against its heft, trying to release himself.

The girl was yelling, 'You go, Blossom!'

He tried to kick out but the coat was long and the dog's muzzle was out of reach. He slid in the wet mud and went down on his hip. He could feel his hand tear on the bark, but that was the least of his worries. As he scrambled to his feet, the dog latched onto his left boot and clamped her teeth on it. He grasped the bottom of the tree and pulled his knee up. The boot, which was elastic-sided, came off in the dog's mouth.

Freed, he hobbled away. Across the road and then south, away from the girl, the dog, Avalon, Kendra, Thalia and the spot where he first met Natalie. The lack of a boot meant that he had a gait like the Hunchback of Notre Dame. His sock was soaked with frozen water and his foot felt like a stump. But he didn't look back.

No barks or cries, just the sound of the traffic on Sixth Avenue and a crumpled old alcoholic throwing an empty bottle onto the road from the other side of the street.

Dogs don't go in the subway, he thought, as he spotted the entrance on the corner of West 4th. He limped down the stairs, narrowly missing a coil of excrement at the bottom.

It better be human.

The token clerk looked on blankly as Cheyne patted his pockets, remembering that he *still* didn't have his Metrocard.

He could hear a train pulling in.

Fuck it, he calculated, I'm going over. He jumped the turnstile.

The clerk called out 'Hey!' But no one followed.

He ran down the ramp. The doors opened and he jumped on a car. He hadn't expected it to be so crowded at such a late hour. Most people had an air of tired indifference, although a few cast worried glances in his direction.

Cheyne squeezed himself between a veiled Muslim woman and a Chinese girl reading a book. Both eased away as he sat. He could see in the hard light of the car that the hem of his coat was torn and the knees of his jeans were sloppy with mud. His sock had been pale blue in its pristine state but was now coated in mud. One toe had worked itself out. It looked like the toe of a corpse. When he put a hand to his head to rake his hair out of his eyes, he realised it was sticky with blood from where the bark of the tree scraped it. He wiped his hand on his jeans, then pulled a sleeve down over the wound to make an impromptu bandage.

The train's destination was Mott Street, Far Rockaway. But he didn't care where the train was going. He'd stay on it all night. He had often seen raggedy people curled up on the seats, their old coats pulled over their eyes, feet tucked up under newspapers or garbage bags. He'd wondered if the guards ever moved them along, or whether they allowed them to sleep through the night as the train clattered back and forth along the rails between the Bronx and Queens.

Well, tonight he was going to find out.

Cheyne tucked his wounded hand inside his coat and pulled the fabric tighter around him. He had to remind himself that, despite his derelict state and his empty pockets, he wasn't really a bum. He had an apartment; he was *choosing* not to go there. He patted his pockets to feel his keys. They weren't there. He dug in his jeans— not there either. Oh, well, he'd call Valerie, get another set cut in the morning. But he didn't want to call Valerie. He'd get his keys back from Avalon. But he didn't want to talk to Avalon. Then he'd call a locksmith over to change the locks. *When* he had money.

He felt strangely delirious. He wasn't going to let this bother him. It was only one night. An *experience.* Assaulted by an ex-girlfriend, his credit card confiscated, missed an important audition, attacked by a rabid dog, jumped a turnstile, slumped penniless in a train with a bare toe and a bleeding hand. It was the kind of thing that happened to you in New York. Everyone who was anyone had a story to tell about being down and out in this city.

He slumped lower in his seat, trying to make himself comfortable. People got on and off at various stations. Most gave him a wide berth. As the number of passengers thinned out, the Asian girl next to him stood up and moved to the end of the row. Cheyne knew he probably smelled of beer and whisky from the bar. His head thumped. He wanted to lie down, pull his cold toe into the folds of his coat. A guard kept moving between the cars looking at him suspiciously. He'd move to another carriage when they got to the end of the line.

A stocky little man in a clown's wig came through from the next car, carrying a portable amplifier and a toy trumpet. 'Ladies and genmen. Gut *even-ing*. I play requests for you,' he announced in a thick European accent. 'Any song! I can play!'

Everyone ignored him, so the old man started into a squeaky rendition of something that Cheyne recognised as 'Endless Love'. Suddenly the high he'd felt from jumping the turnstile started to dissipate. What was he doing here anyway, when right now he could be having his usual brunch at Speedos on Bondi Beach, hiding behind dark glasses and his copy of the *Sydney Morning Herald*, dodging autograph hunters and flirting with sassy waitresses?

Because, he reminded himself, he hated how small Australia was, how everyone knew each other, how they talked about the weather or food or sport all the time. He hated the way they pretended to be big-hearted when they were really small-minded, how they dismissed you as a traitor, not a 'mate', if you wanted intellectual stimulation and artistic risk and sought it somewhere else. Everyone was afraid of being branded a 'wanker', of looking like they wanted to be better than anyone else. But of course they did want it and hated you when you went to get it and laughed at you if you came back without it.

Which was why he had to stay. *Wanted* to stay.

And, yet...he missed it. Something about the sky that went forever and the smell of salt and scrub. Fucking odd, that. He'd grown up on a northern beach in Sydney in a mock-Tudor house and he'd studied Latin at school and he'd spent every spare teenage moment at the cinema watching American films, but he missed the landscape. Like he was an Aborigine or something. As if the city towers and the shops and the Thai food and the nightclubs and the sporting arenas and the theatres were all things you could just peel off like those pictures little kids stuck to felt. You could peel those layers from yourself, too, and all you'd find was sand in your bathers and sunburned skin and a kid with his bucket by the sea, digging. Digging to China, they said. But it was really North America.

The Pie King didn't understand him. Best country in the world, son. That's what he and his cronies believed, all of them with their snouts in the trough, fleecing the Japanese while hating them at the same time, hating anything that was 'other'. But they weren't laid back. They were the most anxious people he knew. Insisting too much. Look at Phil, smug about his Sydney lifestyle. But lifestyle was no substitute for a life.

Get a life, they said in New York. He was trying to. But Australia kept butting in, reminding him where he came from, not where he was going. Avalon, turning up like that. Someone in Sydney screwing with his bank account. Producers demanding he be more Australian, whatever that was. Natalie thinking he was *surfer scum*. Even that wombat with the surfboard in the bar. The truth of it— he knew what Americans wanted 'Australian' to be, but he wasn't it. He didn't know what he was.

The man with the toy trumpet was now playing 'Shake Your Booty'. Cheyne tuned out and focused on the bulbous midriff of the person sitting opposite. A platypus, an echidna and a kookaburra danced before his eyes. SYDNEY 2000 was printed across the man's chest. He studied his face, which was dark with stubble. Not Australian, he guessed. Just a guy who bought a tee-shirt off a street stall and wore it even when it was out of date.

The Asian girl at the end of the row snapped her book shut and stood up. As she slipped the book into her bag, he noticed the cover. *Mutant Message Down Under* by Marlo Morgan.

It wouldn't be bloody Stephen King tonight, would it?

The woman opposite, he now saw, was reading a magazine with a brooding photograph of Russell Crowe on the cover.

His eyes scanned the strip of advertisements that ran across the top of the car. Tooth Implants for $750 each. Call 1-800-AMBULANCE CHASER. A cosmetic surgeon who could sandblast your wrinkles off in fifteen minutes. Aussie Moist Shampoo…*Aussie Moist* Shampoo?

The train pulled into Utica station and a few stragglers got on. The man with the toy trumpet went through his spiel again. '*Gut even-ing*, ladies and genmen. I make music for you. Anything you name! I can play!'

'Yeah, I've got a request,' Cheyne called out, belligerent now. 'Can you play "Waltzing Matilda"?'

He expected a shrug but the man broke out into a big smile. 'Gut song,' he said. 'My brudder he lifs in Adelaide. You know him?' He then put the trumpet to his mouth and started playing.

Shit, thought Cheyne. Is this car sponsored by the bloody Australian government?

He had to get away.

He stood up. The other passengers looked at him warily, even a mountain of a guy with a hardware shop of chains around his neck.

The connecting platform between carriages swayed alarmingly as he stepped over it. The next car was almost deserted, except for a teenage boy dry-humping his girlfriend in a corner.

Cheyne flopped on a seat, crossed his arms. No 'Waltzing Matilda'. No Aussie Moist whatever it was. No Russell Crowe.

He yawned and his eyes involuntarily scanned the posters across the top of the car.

The Crocodile Hunter beamed down at him, his tanned arms around the snout of a snapping croc.

Then Cheyne lost it.

Finley saw the surfboard first, leaning against the stoop. He was huddled in the doorway in the cold blue morning light, the matted collar of his jacket turned up, obscuring his face. But she had no doubt who it was.

She kicked him in the thigh. 'Get out of my doorway!'

He woke up, startled. And then he smiled. 'I was worried about you. Where have you been all night?'

'None of your business.'

He looked crestfallen. 'It's that other Shane.'

'What other Shane?'

He sighed. 'You don't have to lie.'

'I'm not lying.'

'I met your girlfriend.'

'I know.'

'I suppose she told you.' He jumped to his feet. 'I can explain everything.'

She went to push past him. 'I don't want an explanation.'

He grasped her hand. His hand was rough, like pumice stone. 'Cassie doesn't mean anything to me.'

'Cassie? Is that her name?'

'I told you. She's just some scrubber I met at the beach. She's chasing me. I don't want her. I want you.'

Finley shook his hand away. 'What about Natalie, then?'

'The girlfriend?'

'You are fucking impossible!' Finley gave him a shove and put her key in the lock. She opened the door and tried to use it to push him away. He was fast and slipped inside as she closed it.

'Get out or I'll scream!'

'Don't scream. We've got things to talk about. Like Spain.'

'Haven't I told you I don't care about fucking Spain! Why are you always talking about Spain?'

'But I've got enough money now. If I could get inside my loft, that is. We could go next week if you want.'

'We?'

'Blossom too.'

He wanted them to go to Spain with him? She stared at him standing there. He had that look Blossom got when Finley held her ball up in the air, ready to throw. If he'd had a tail, he would have wagged it.

But how could she trust him after Natalie?

'I suppose you want to fuck Blossom too!' she sneered and turned on her heels.

'But this chick's offered me a part in a movie. You could be in it too.'

She glared at him. 'A part in a movie? I thought you were a surfer. You said you didn't want to be anything else! Now you want to be an actor like every fucking other person in this town? I suppose you've got an unfinished novel in your back pocket too! Well, fuck you, you fraud!' She started up the stairs, two steps at a time.

'Wait!' he called after her.

'Don't fucking come after me!' she yelled back, not turning. 'You better get your surfer chick girlfriend to teach you some moves before you come near me again. Otherwise I'll...I'll kill you!'

He was on the bottom step, shouting up the stairwell. 'What have I fucking done? You've got another boyfriend and a girlfriend and I'm not getting my knickers in a twist about it! Can't I come up for a minute?'

'Just shut up and leave me alone!'

'But I don't have anywhere to go!'

She stopped and turned around. And gave him the obvious answer.

This is all because of a lie, Shane thought gloomily as he trudged up Sullivan Street with his board. The fucking lie I told her when I first met her about a shark biting my hand. Cut the bloody thing on a dog food can. Why didn't I tell the truth? I was trying to impress her. And look where it's got me.

It's the justice of the sea.

The locksmith didn't look too convinced, even when Cheyne showed him his Australian driver's licence. 'Look, I'm a mess because I've slept in the bloody park most of the night! Why would I sleep in the park if I had my keys?'

'OK buddy, but when we get inside, I want some proof it's your place. Or I call the cops.'

God, is this some kind of police state? Cheyne wondered as he trudged ahead of the locksmith down Sullivan. He couldn't believe the number of transit cops who turned up to defend the Crocodile Hunter advertisement against his frenzied assault. The one time in his life when he lets loose and the whole New York City police department comes down on him. He was still shaken by it. Less by the rough interrogation than the fact Valerie had to come all the way to Brooklyn Central Booking to talk him out of trouble.

He could tell she'd done this sort of thing before.

'This young man needs a hospital! Can't you see he's been savaged by a dog! It might be rabies! That would explain his behaviour! If you don't let me take him to a hospital right now we will sue!' And so on until they gave him his wallet and shoelaces back.

The 'Do Not Smoke Penalty $200' sign on the back window of the cab had not deterred Valerie. She chain-smoked all the way back to Manhattan. She seemed pleased with him. There was no mention of the missed audition.

She had not taken him to a hospital but instead instructed the driver to drop him outside his apartment building. He thought for a moment of admitting everything about his lack of cash and keys, but he already felt humiliated enough having to be rescued by a dumpy sixty-year-old woman in a velvet housecoat.

When he got out of the car he could see the lights in Kendra's sitting room softly glowing. His lights were out. But that didn't mean anything—Avalon was probably planning an ambush. 'Thanks,' he said to Valerie.

'Get the *Post* in the morning,' was her response.

He waved to her and walked towards the door. Maybe he could buzz one of the other tenants into letting him into the building. But he was afraid that yelling into the intercom would alert Avalon. He didn't have the energy to fight her off. He'd be safer in the park.

He found his favourite bench under the Hanging Tree and curled up. Miraculously, he slept.

Now it was 9.30 a.m. and the locksmith was opening the downstairs door for him with a set of keys. 'Fucking easy lock to break into,' he said in disgust, clattering into the lobby.

'Look, do you mind being quiet?' Cheyne whispered as they

ascended. 'And step over that board, will you? We've got invalids in the building.'

Once they'd reached his landing, the locksmith examined the door. 'Hmm, Medeco. Let's see if one of these babies fit.' He started sticking keys in the lock. His key ring rattled. 'You know,' he said, 'doors don't mean nothing no more. They go straight through the wall these days. The neighbours never seem to notice. Funny thing.' He turned a key. 'Yeah, I think we've got it—'

The door opened from the inside. 'Cheyne, what are you doing?'

Avalon stood there in leopard-print leotards, yellow tights and weights in her hands.

The locksmith threw up his hands. 'Look, lady, if this is a domestic problem—'

Avalon smiled at him. 'No, of course not. Cheyne, you know I have a key!'

'You didn't try the intercom?' The locksmith looked at Cheyne in amazement.

'Don't worry about it,' Cheyne said quickly, trying to bundle him away. 'Send me the bill.'

'No, buddy, cash only. Fifty dollars for the call. Thirty-five bucks for the first ten minutes. Plus tax—'

'Avalon, pay the man,' Cheyne said, brushing past her.

'Yeah, will do. Hang on a minute while I get my bag.'

He flopped on the couch, defeated.

When Avalon came back into the room, zipping up her fanny pack, he said, 'Just don't punch me, OK?'

'What happened to you?'

'You punched me, that's what happened—and it started everything. Do you know what happens to a man with a black eye in this town? No one trusts him.'

'Well, you deserved it, Cheyne. Playing around behind my back with those chicks. But you won't be playing around with them any more. I've given them a good going-over.'

'What do you mean?' His stomach did a flip and gave a little growl. When had he last eaten?

'I've punched the fucking daylight out of them. The one at Mo Bo and the other one at that theatre place. They won't be coming near you again. You're lucky I'm in such a good mood, or I'd beat the shit out of you too.'

'Please don't.' He grabbed a cushion for protection. Then it registered. 'Which woman at what theatre place?'

'The one you were meeting yesterday. Lara at two. You left a note, Cheyne. That was pretty silly of you.'

'You attacked Lara?'

'She's all right. Bled like a stuck pig but.'

'Did she know who you were?'

'Course she did. Who else would I be but your girlfriend?'

'Lara's a casting agent, you idiot!'

'There's no need to be like that, Cheyne. I don't care what she does for a living. She needed to be set straight about you, whatever it is.'

He could suddenly feel his head growing heavy on his neck. It was too much. Lara…blood…no movie role. 'Avalon, I need to go to bed.'

'The thing is, Cheyne, I'll go to bed with you and all if you want me to, but I've got something to tell you.'

'Who have you killed now?' he groaned.

She sounded sheepish. 'No, nothing like that. It's just…I have to leave New York.'

'So the cops are finally after you…leave New York?' His head jolted back up off his chest.

'Yeah, well, I've got this bonza new job, you see.'

'You have?'

'Don't get mad with me Cheyne. I can come back and visit. I know it'll be hard to be apart. But you'll manage. If you tidy yourself up. You've really let yourself go, you know. Orlando says it will only be for a few months.'

'Orlando?'

'Yeah, he's this really cute guy I met. He's seven foot two inches tall. I mean, don't look like that, he's not as spunky as you, Cheyne, but he's really nice and I'm going to be his girlfriend.'

'Girlfriend?'

'Not for real. In the World Star Wrestling. I'm going to wrestle on TV! They promised me the women's championship. They can do that, you know. They know who's going to win. I don't know how. But I'll find out when I go to training camp in South Carolina, which is another state somewhere. I'm leaving tomorrow. I'll write. And you can watch me on telly. I'm going to play my euphonium as I come out. I knew all those lessons weren't wasted. Aren't you excited for me? They said I could make a million bucks a year!'

'I'm very happy for you.' Happy? He was ecstatic.

'I knew you would be! I know you'll be a bit lonely—'

'Don't worry about me.' He did his best to sound martyred.

She threw her arms around his neck. 'I knew you wouldn't mind! I'll send you tickets when we play Madison Square Garden.'

She sat on his lap and nuzzled his neck. She took the cushion off him and threw it on the floor. Her hands tugged at his coat, pulling it off his shoulders.

'Jeez, you stink, Cheyne. Now, how about one for the road?'

Shane trudged away from Finley's building. He knew when someone was giving him the bum's rush. But why? He was willing to forgive her for that other Shane if she would forgive him for Cassie. Fair's fair. But then she goes apeshit over that scrawny blonde offering him a film role! He doesn't even know what the fucking film is. He couldn't give a shit about it, only it was going to get them to Spain. She's carrying on about him being a fraud. About not being a *surfer*. As if you could fake riding a board.

He had wanted to tell her that everything he had said and done was true. He wanted to stop her being angry. But she was like the riptide. The more you struggled against her the likelier you were to drown.

He stood on the corner of Houston and Sullivan streets, not knowing where to go. The cool wind felt good on his face. A brisk northwesterly. He licked a finger and held it in the air. Now that he didn't have the computer he had to rely on more primitive measures.

He crossed Houston Street quickly. He could feel the pressure dropping minute by minute. Fuck, there might actually be a wave if he got moving. The wind had been northeast, 35 to 40 knots, the last couple of days. And now it had come round…

Perfect fucking conditions. He'd bet Mavis on it.

MAD MAX?

Is it something in the water? Aussie actors have a reputation for being quick with their fists but newcomer **Cheyne Burdekin**, 27, the loincloth-clad star of last season's TNT sword-and-sorcery potboiler, **Taliesin the Great** appears to have out-Crowed Russell. An

unkempt, bloodied and belligerent Burdekin was
detained late last night by New York City transit police
for disorderly conduct on the A train bound for
Rockaway Beach. Shocked witnesses say the young actor
suddenly jumped from his seat and started kicking a
door between Utica Avenue station and Ralph Avenue.
When a guard approached, Burdekin pushed him out of
the way, jumped on a seat and tried to rip down an
advertisement for the popular Discovery Channel
program, **The Crocodile Hunter**. Burdekin's agent,
Valerie Bone, refused to comment on the incident,
although she did tell Page Six that Burdekin was 'a
normal, enthusiastic young man' and denied any alcohol
or drugs were involved. 'He's just a bit homesick, that's
all,' she explained. No charges were formally laid.

Shane couldn't believe his eyes.

The waves were six feet…more…and barrelling from jetty to jetty.

The sky had opened up to a stinging blue.

A Qantas jet came thundering down over the sea, poised to land
at JFK.

An omen.

There was fucking no one in the water. He had it all to himself.
Wave after wave, not a soul to drop in on him. He cleared his mind
for the first time in months. No thoughts, no before, no after. Just
the memory of his muscles, taking him up and over.

At high tide, he came out of the water for fuel. At the shitty supermarket, he bought Cheese Doodles and a bottle of Coke and a

bruised old banana. He handed over his last twenty and got change.

When he got back in the water two crazy Lebbo guys on boogie boards were swooshing down the face of a wave. Fucking amateurs, he thought.

He didn't really mind. It was their ocean too, wasn't it? Probably more their ocean than his, come to think of it. They probably paid taxes for it. Although, judging by the soggy wad of bandages that just floated past, they didn't pay enough.

He was out of the water as it fell dark. He watched the Lebbos get into a van and drive away. There was no point in going back to the city. Where would he stay? He thought glumly of the thousands of dollars waiting for him if he could get access to Dirk's computer. But fuck it, he'd been poor before. And there'd be another wave in the morning.

He bought a microwaved burrito from the supermarket before it closed and took it back to the dunes. The night was crystalline and he could see the Ambrose lighthouse directly out to sea, blinking. There was a gully underneath the boardwalk and he sat there for shelter.

Later, he unzipped the cover off his board and slipped into it. He was asleep before his head hit his backpack.

CROCODILE DUNDEE?

Following our exclusive report yesterday on Aussie hunk **Cheyne Burdekin**'s tussle with an A train and a poster of **Steve Irwin**, the Discovery Channel's **Crocodile Hunter**, sources close to directors **Derek and Damian Grimley**, the British imports who have been conducting a high-profile search in Manhattan for cast members for a Fox-funded remake of **The Importance of Being Earnest,** tell us that Burdekin is about to be confirmed in the lead role of Jack Worthing in that production. Casting director **Lara Dinardo,** who discovered **Bradford Ford** when he was a bicycle messenger, refuses to confirm or deny the report but says she is impressed by Burdekin's Aussie machismo, which she believes 'works well with the Grimleys' concept of the film'. **Emmylou Kinney,** star of last year's remake of **Rosemary's Baby** is rumoured to have also secured a lead role. Our advice to the Grimley brothers: start taking some of those Mo Bo lessons that are the rage in Hollywood. The film is set to start shooting next May…in Australia.

Finley found Natalie sitting in the window of Cafe Reggio stroking one of the resident cats.

'You look like a witch with that cat,' she said as she took a chair opposite.

'Pity my spells didn't work on you,' Natalie replied.

'I could do with a witch on my side,' Finley sighed. 'Everything's totally fucked.'

'Are you worried about that turnstile-jumping charge? You'll just get a fine. Pretty kooky thing to do, by the way. As if you didn't have a dollar fifty.'

'It's the principle. I pay taxes, so why—'

'Do you pay taxes?'

'Well, you know what I mean. This society's totally screwed up.

I feel like packing up and going somewhere else.'

'Australia perhaps?'

'Very funny.' She leaned over the table and stroked the cat. 'Costa Rica, maybe.'

'Costa Rica? They have giant sloths there, you know. Come to think of it, perhaps it would be the place for you.'

'Bitch.'

A waitress arrived and Finley ordered a double espresso.

'It's a pity you weren't there Wednesday, you know. The actor you were supposed to read with never showed. But it was all very enlightening just the same.' She picked up the cat and dropped it on the floor. It flicked its tail in annoyance and sashayed towards another table. Natalie cleared her throat. 'Your Shane was there.'

'What do you mean my Shane was there?'

'He was there at the audition. Your Shane.'

'The bastard! He said he'd been offered a movie role.'

'Listen to me. That girl was there too. The girl I saw at Balducci's who beat you up.'

'He was there with her? Flaunting her in my face?'

'Actually, he wasn't exactly there with her. You see, there's something I have to tell you and if you hadn't have been in such a foul mood when I called you yesterday I would have told you sooner. So don't blame—'

'Hey, why is that guy tapping on the window? He looks deranged.'

About six inches away, on the other side of the cafe window, a young man with long hair over his eyes was gesticulating. He drew a heart in the air.

'Oh dear,' sighed Natalie.

'He's calling out your name. Do you know him?'

'Yes,' she said, looking away from the window and up at the ceiling in dismay. 'And I think it's time you did too.'

Wednesday everything looked so bleak but today—well, today, Friday, everything was fucking great.

A lead role in a movie! Not any movie. A movie directed by the famous Grimley brothers. No more Avalon. She'd gone to South Carolina. With a bit of luck she'd fall in love for real with this Orlando guy and have a brood of giant babies. And now this. Natalie appearing before him like a vision, sitting in a cafe window, as if she had propped herself there to wait for him.

It was fate that he'd walked up MacDougal at this very moment, on his way to see some photographer for pictures that Valerie had arranged. Cheyne had tried not to think about Natalie after the pigs-in-blankets incident. But now he could see her lovely face circled by the halo of steamy breath that clung to the inside of the window. The coffee cup in her hand had dark red lipstick stains on the rim.

He was smitten all over again.

He tapped on the window. The dark-haired girl sitting opposite Natalie turned and made a face at him. Maybe she was Natalie's assistant. He thought he'd seen her before. She looked like a dyke.

He called out Natalie's name. She looked away, as if she didn't want to see him. He scratched on the window again. She turned back. He traced a heart in the air with his fingers. He could see other people inside the cafe looking at him.

A group of teenagers straggled out. Cheyne scrambled in while they held the door. He bumped the waitress trying to manoeuvre himself around the small tables in the entrance. 'Natalie!'

She gave him a smile he couldn't decipher. But it wasn't discouraging.

He dragged a bentwood chair from another table and sat down. 'Look, I'm sorry about Tuesday. I didn't mean...I think you misunderstood...I don't have that many girlfriends you know.'

'As it turns out, you have one less girlfriend than I thought.'

'She wasn't really a girlfriend. That's what I was trying to tell you. Anyway, she went to South Carolina this morning. And now I'm free to be entirely devoted to you.'

'How heroic. I've got a kitchen full of knives, remember?'

'I wasn't thinking about us being in the kitchen.'

She gave a little grunt that he interpreted as approval. 'You haven't met my friend Finley, have you?'

Cheyne realised that he had his back to the other girl. He turned and smiled. 'I'm sorry.'

'It's OK.' The girl shrugged. She held her coffee cup to her lips and took a sip.

'Finley, I'd like you to meet Shane.'

'Hi, Shane,' Finley said and then suddenly choked, spraying espresso in the air. 'Shane?'

'Interesting, isn't it?' Natalie smiled. 'And he's Australian, too.'

'Aus-tralian?'

'It's a big island in the southern hemisphere,' Cheyne joked.

'You'll also be interested to know Shane has a girlfriend who has blonde hair and big tits and a knock-out punch.'

'Ex-girlfriend,' Cheyne reminded her. 'Let's get off that subject.'

'Knock-out punch?' Finley repeated, blankly. What was wrong with her? Cheyne wondered. The aggressive high colour on her cheeks had drained right out of her.

'She gave him that black eye,' Natalie said.

'Black eye?'

'And he surfs too.'

'Not very much,' he said, trying to make light of it, wondering why Finley's eyes had glazed over. 'I can stand up. That's about it.'

'Remember our conversation about Balducci's, Finley? Well, this is the one. This is the one who tried to rape me.'

So, she was on about that again. He'd heard about Jewish princesses. He wondered if Natalie was one of them. 'Look, it was only a kiss.'

Finley blinked a couple of times and said to him in a small voice. 'Your name is Shane?'

'It was my mother's idea—'

Before he'd finished the sentence she was out of her chair and pounding on his chest.

'Hey!' he cried out, shocked, trying to balance himself against her force and stop his chair from tipping over.

'How dare you be called Shane! You're not allowed to be called Shane!'

'What do you mean?' He put an elbow up to deflect her punches.

'You don't even look like a Shane!'

'Actually, he does,' Natalie commented. 'He convinced me.'

'What's wrong with being called Cheyne?'

Finley's eyes flashed and he jumped to his feet, stumbling when he caught a foot in the hem of his coat. He rattled the cups on the table behind him.

'Because there's only one Shane! If there were two Shanes everything would be all wrong!'

'In fact it would be all right,' Natalie said. 'Think about it.'

She ignored Natalie. 'You've screwed everything up! If you weren't called Shane things would be different.'

'I can't help being called Cheyne.'

'Yes you can. You could change your name.'

'But what if I like it? What if it suits me?'

'I can tell you right now it doesn't suit you!'

'So you'd rather I was called Barry or something?'

'Barry is all right. Shane doesn't belong to you! There's already another Shane. And there's no room in this town for two!' She launched at him with her fists again. He could hear chairs scraping as people at tables nearby stood up.

'Wait!' he said, grabbing one of her arms and twisting it. 'I think you'll find there are more than two Cheynes in New York. You're going to be a very busy girl if you go around thumping every Cheyne you meet.'

She stomped on his foot and twisted out of his grasp. 'I don't care about the other Shanes! You're the one who was at Balducci's. You're the one with the girlfriend who looks like Barbie with a sunburn. I suppose you were at Contaminated too.'

'I've been there once,' he said, carefully.

'And you know Blender.'

'The kid from the video store?'

'And Blossom chased you. Esther told me.'

'The girl who owns that big dog?'

'No, I'm the girl who owns that big dog! You see how you're getting everything confused—just because you're called Shane!'

She leapt at him again, one fist balled tight. He could see the tattoo of the 'F' clearly now. He flashed to the first time the dog attacked him. The girl with the army jacket. Now he could see that same jacket slung over the back of her chair.

Natalie stood up. 'Finley, stop attacking him. It's not his fault he's Australian and he's called Shane.'

'Well, it's not my fault. I've been going mad here with all you people telling me my Shane's been doing this and doing that and it's been this Shane all along!'

'Sit down, Finley,' Natalie said firmly, coming between them.

'What have I done?' Cheyne asked.

Finley pushed him again. 'You've had a black girlfriend and a blonde girlfriend and you've kissed Natalie, that's what you've done! How dare you!'

Cheyne gave Natalie a dirty look, which she ignored. She pushed Finley back into her chair. 'It's all right,' she said to the waitress who was hovering, alarmed. 'It's a misunderstanding.'

'It isn't!' Finley said to Natalie. 'It's a deliberate set-up to break up Shane and me. You hired this person!' she spat at Cheyne.

'I haven't been hired by anyone,' Cheyne protested. 'Who's this other Cheyne anyway?' An idea struck him. 'Or is it Shane? S-H-A-N-E.'

'Of course he's Shane! I hate all Shanes!'

'Well, my name's spelt C-H-E-Y-N-E.'

'Far be it for a dyke like me to suggest you owe a man an apology, but you owe a man an apology,' Natalie said.

'Dyke?' Cheyne asked.

Natalie ignored him. 'You owe Cheyne an apology.'

'Which one?'

'Both, actually.'

'Why should I apologise to him for ruining my life?' She pointed at Cheyne.

'What do you mean, dyke?' Cheyne grasped Natalie's elbow.

Natalie looked at his hand and shook her elbow away. 'It's only an expression.'

'You only kissed me to make her jealous?'

'I'm sure it was very nice for you…if you like that kind of thing. Finley likes that kind of thing.'

'She's not a dyke?'

'No, she's in love with some guy called Shane.'

'I'm not in love with him! Stop talking about me as if I wasn't here!'

Cheyne turned to Finley. The colour had come back in her cheeks. 'Who is this Shane anyway?'

'He's not you!'

'Actually, I'm sorry about that,' Cheyne said. She really was rather cute now that she had calmed down. 'Could I be him?'

Finley narrowed her eyes. 'You're sure you're not a surfer?'

'Cross my heart and hope to die.' He gave her his full-wattage smile. 'I'm an actor.'

This didn't have the effect he wanted. She jumped out of her chair and went at him with her fists. Again. 'Don't fucking tell me you're an actor! I hate fucking actors!'

He grabbed her by the wrists and stood up. A kick landed on his thigh. He let go of her hands and quickly put his chair between them.

He remembered that she had called him yuppie scum once before. 'What's wrong with you? You hate yuppies and you hate actors and you hate surfers and you hate Cheynes. And Shanes. Is there anyone you do like?'

Finley glared at him but didn't answer. He suddenly worried that her dog might be somewhere about. 'Look, I'm getting out of here.'

'Wait a minute,' Natalie commanded. 'You agree, Cheyne, that you're not Finley's Shane?'

'I've never seen her before in my life! Well, once…when her dog attacked me.'

'But you've never fucked her under the boardwalk at Far Rockaway.'

'I think I'd remember if I did.'

'Just a straight yes or no will do.'

'No!'

She turned to Finley, who was still facing Cheyne with her fists up. 'You heard that, Finley?'

'Yes, so?'

'So I believe there's a Shane out there who has been very badly wronged.'

'But he admitted everything!'

'Death row is full of people who have admitted to crimes they never committed.'

Finley dropped her fists, pointed at Cheyne. 'But he's Australian.'

'What's that got to do with it?' he asked.

'Everything!'

'Finley, stop it!' Natalie said. 'Leave this Cheyne to me. I've got a few things to explain to him. You get out of here and find your Shane.'

'But I don't even know where he is!'

'Don't you?'

Cheyne watched Finley grab her jacket and run out the door. Pity he was the wrong Shane. She was rather gorgeous without her dog. He contemplated Natalie calmly. He didn't care for her as much now that she was a lesbian. Besides, she smoked too much.

'Where's she going?' Cheyne asked.

'To the beach,' Natalie said, shaking a cigarette out of a pack. 'Want one?'

He shook his head. 'Isn't it too cold for the beach?'

'Not for her.'

'Will she be all right?'

Natalie passed him the matches. 'Don't worry about her. You know what Shakespeare says?'

He lit her cigarette despite the fact that their table was clearly non-smoking.

She smiled at him over the glow of the ash. 'All's swell that ends swell.'

It was fucking unreal.

The surf had been pumping all day. Shane had only left the water once, to spend his last three bucks on a nuked piece of fried chicken stuffed into a roll so dry you could have thrown it in the air and shot holes in it.

The rest of the time he was in the water. Didn't even need to go out to piss, just filled the legs of his wetsuit with pleasurable warmth. The sets just kept building, barely a lull, seven or eight feet by the afternoon tide. He was out of shape, but he would keep paddling until it killed him or it got dark, whichever came first.

A few faggots had come into the water once the word had got around that the swell was immense. But most of them were way up at the beach at 90th Street where the scenery was more picturesque. Pity he had to look at windowless sheds and ugly red-brick high-rises and rubbish swirling around the carcasses of dead cars in vacant lots. An old blue car was there, nose to nose with a beaten-up Caddie, looking like they were mating. Kids dragged backpacks full of schoolbooks along the boardwalk and occasionally threw them at each other. A couple of them rode those stupid little scooters. An old man with a metal detector ran it over the sand from jetty to jetty.

He sat on his board and watched in dismay as a big sports utility vehicle drove down the sand to the water's edge. Behind it was a jet ski on a trailer.

Wanker! What the fuck was a jet ski doing here? Couldn't the dickhead stay out in the Hamptons where he belonged?

The driver got out of the car, dressed head-to-toe in neoprene. He wrangled the jet ski off the trailer and slid it in the water.

'Get lost, fuckwit!' Shane called out, but the wind took his voice in the other direction. He waved his fist but the pansy was too busy setting up his ride. It was obviously new, judging by the trouble he had starting it. Someone got an early Christmas present, Shane thought, and he's trying it out before he takes it down to the Caribbean to ride round and round in circles with his banker mates and give all the fish a nervous breakdown.

Eventually the poonce got it started and sat on the engine, revving.

'Feel good to have something big throbbing between your legs for once?' Shane shouted.

The jet ski took off, in a wobbly line away from where Shane was paddling. He laughed as it went straight up the face of a big left-hander and flipped upside down on the clown. The poofter somehow clung on. The sound diminished as he roared towards Rockaway. There were more wankers to impress up there.

Shane turned around and paddled up a monster. He shot around and rode it down at dazzling speed, carving through the green jade like a flea on sculptor's trowel. The tunnel ahead narrowed like a shutter and he shot for it, crouching lower, his left index finger drawing a long, thin line in the wall, feeling the rush as the vortex spat him out at the sky, spun him like a top into the next lip and tipped him off his board into the churning white water.

He swam to the surface, pulled his board closer, scrambled back on. He caught five more big ones, his body now so tired the last wave felt like a building coming down on him. His jaw was rattling from the freezing cold. The sky had taken on a bruised hue, the sun dropping violently to the horizon. He suddenly felt melancholy. He would have to come out in fifteen minutes. By tomorrow morning the waves would be blown out.

He faced the shore and drifted for a while. He could hear the buzz of the jet ski somewhere behind him. The kids had gone from the boardwalk. The cars had pulled away. Only the man with his metal detector remained, continuing his relentless shuffling back and forth.

I might have to join you, mate, Shane thought. A bit of buried treasure is just what I need. But what would be buried around here? Rusting car fenders and the thighbones of Russian murder victims.

The old bloke was now waving the rod of his metal detector at a big black blob. The blob started to bark. The man backed away. The blob flopped down on the sand, head between paws. There was a person sitting next to it, arms around knees.

He could see her scowl from where he was floating. He would know that scowl from the moon. He waved both arms in the air. She waved back.

'Pooch!' he called out.

And turned around to paddle into his last wave.

Cheyne's foot creaked on the loose board outside apartment 2B. From habit he stopped breathing and cringed. And then he relaxed. Avalon was gone, off to the south to be a wrestling superstar. He could hear the door open a crack as he passed.

'Oh, Cheyne!'

What now? His mind had struggled with enough loopy concepts this afternoon, enough to last him a lifetime. Two Shanes? A feminine Natalie who was a dyke? A girl with a dog who wasn't the same girl with the dog, even though the dog was the same? Natalie had started to explain and his brain had gone into shutdown.

Kendra stepped into the hallway, holding a glass in her hand. 'I thought you might like to have a drink with me, Cheyne. We can drown our sorrows together. I'm sure you're missing our little friend already. It's funny how a person like that leaves a hole, isn't it?'

'Thanks, Kendra, but I have some things to do.'

'Oh, come on. There isn't anything in life that can't be improved by a little drink.'

'It's very kind of you—'

'The truth is,' she said, linking an arm through his and dragging him into her pristine sitting room, 'Avalon's sudden departure has left me in a bit of a spot. I am making a presentation about Australia to some of my clients on Monday and I was going to bring Avalon along as a sort of…demonstration. But that's all flown out the coop now. If I don't have an Australian as a visual aid I can't do the presentation. And if I don't do the presentation next week, then good Lord, who knows which country will be fashionable the week after! And all that research with Avalon gone to waste. Not to speak of the loss of a good Jeff Koons puppy. So…I was wondering if you'd take her place.'

'Kendra, I'm flattered, but I've got this new role—'

'Oh, yes, I read all about it in the *Post*. That's why I thought you'd be so good for my clients.' She led him to the red sofa and gestured for him to sit. When he hesitated she gave him a little shove. 'Let me get you a Manhattan.'

'Look, Kendra—'

'Now, don't tell me you're going to say no after what I did taking Avalon off your hands. You should be grateful to me, you know.'

Not, thought Cheyne. Not grateful. If it hadn't been for Kendra he would have had Avalon packed off to a hostel in the Bronx long ago. 'I know my agent won't let me do it.'

'Well, you don't have to tell her, do you? It can be our secret. Twist?' She put some lemon peel in a cocktail glass, filled it with something from a jug. 'Here. Now let me run my speech past you. Feel free to make any comments you like.'

She sat beside him on the sofa. 'You know, the main theme of my talk is how the rest of the world is only just beginning to aspire to the Australian lifestyle. You're all so relaxed and healthy down there. Fresh air. Lots of space. Good water. *Great* wine. Everyone plays sport. No stress—'

'Wait a minute,' Cheyne said.

'—I wanted to talk about how *honest* and *primitive* and *uncomplicated* you Australians are. How the rest of the world has lost these qualities and could learn a lot from you.'

'Uncomplicated?' Cheyne looked at her in astonishment.

'Yes, simple. But not simple-minded, of course. What's wrong? Are you choking?'

Cheyne snorted his cocktail out of his nose and started guffawing. Uncomplicated! He rolled on the sofa, chortling.

Kendra jumped up. 'Here—I'll get you some water.'

'No thanks...I'm sorry,' he spat. 'It's an attack...of...the hiccups...' He doubled over, choking. 'I've...got to go.'

'But I've got so much to ask you!'

'Sorry.' He wiped the tears off his cheek and sat up.

'You look like you're going to have a heart attack!'

'I've got some pills upstairs,' he lied, standing up. 'I'm sorry I couldn't help.'

'Well, if you think of anyone.' She took his arm and escorted him to the door. 'Before you go, I've got one more thing to ask...Are you *sure* you're all right? You've gone very pink.'

'I'll be fine when I get those pills.'

'You see, Avalon was going to make me some of those pavlova things for the presentation. And now I'm stuck. I've got to feed them and, at $1500 a head, they won't be satisfied with sandwiches from Balducci's. You don't happen to know someone who could cook up some Australian food for me, do you? Vegemite crackers or whatever you eat.'

He reached for the doorknob. And then he stopped. '*Cook*, you said?'

'You know, cater my presentation? I was thinking of throwing some shrimps on a barbie. Or baking those witchetty grubs or whatever they are.'

Cheyne turned and gave her a wise smile. 'I think I have exactly the woman for you.'

Shane paddled into the wave, no longer aware of the dwindling light or the darkening shadow of water ahead. His head was full of the image of a girl and a dog sitting in the sand, waiting for him, patient as monuments.

The wave was a five-footer, the lip sweetly curling, beckoning him. He looked the wave in the eye and got ready to take off.

He heard it before he saw it, and thought he was hallucinating. It sounded like a hundred Tasmanian devils snarling in unison.

Suddenly, the jet ski came up over the lip of the wave, headed straight for him. He didn't have time to register anything except the rider—*fuckwit*—standing up, screaming, and then diving into the water. The machine flew off the lip, flipped over and plummeted in the direction of Shane's head. He dropped sideways off his board just as the jet ski smashed into it, splitting it in half and body-slamming him with a rush of water and the buoyant fin-end of the board.

He was pushed down into the trough and dragged along the bank. His eyes filled with salt, his mouth with sand, but he knew enough to make himself relax, knowing he wasn't hurt, or at least not fatally, thinking maybe the fin had cut his forehead or smacked into a rib, that was all. He felt the force of the lip crashing over him and kept down on the bank. It wasn't deep down here, maybe three feet, but if he came up now the breaking wave would push him down again and make mincemeat of him.

He felt the rip suck back and turned and swam through the back of the next wave, all the while cursing the jet ski rider and wondering what he'd do without a board. It was only as he emerged for air, and heard the yelling and the barking and saw the jet ski marooned in the shore, its owner looking at it as if it were a horse with a broken leg, that he realised what a gift he had been given.

Fuck it, I'm in America now, he thought. That guy, look at him, look at his car, he's probably got millions. No need to be run over by a truck. I've just made my fortune.

He was pleased to discover he was bleeding from the head. He grabbed at his left shoulder.

'Hey!' Shane called out. 'Help! I've just been seriously wounded! I'll never surf again!'

Blossom barked encouragement. She was looking forward to a warmer climate.

Other outstanding books by Lee Tulloch

FABULOUS NOBODIES
Lee Tulloch

'If you have a taste for frivolity, humor and Manolo Blahnik sling-backs, you will be enthralled. Ms Tulloch's voice is sharp, affectionate and hilarious. She reminds me of the master, P. G. Wodehouse, because although her world is totally unrealistic, it is much more true to life than any of its sordid predecessors.' *New York Times Book Review*

'Who could resist a book that combines an appealingly dizzy Holly Golightly character with all the trashy glamour of New York.' *Sydney Morning Herald*

'Sharp as a knife, *Fabulous Nobodies*…is a witty, pacey parody of a generation obsessed with style, where models are superstars, and gossip columnists are gods.' *Books Magazine*

'A quirky tale of credible young love. As well as proving herself one of the very few fashion writers to have produced a novel at all, she is one of even fewer to have managed it well…she is very funny, and she likes Emma Peel, and if that isn't Fabulous, I can't think what is.' *Sunday Times*

'Lighthearted yet devastatingly accurate and witty social satire…Tulloch's cutting humor suffuses every detail.' *Publishers Weekly*

'Very funny.' *West Australian*

288pp, paperback, rrp$22.00, ISBN 1 876485 05 1

WRAITH
Lee Tulloch

'Stiletto-sharp observations of the racy world of high fashion. Fans of this expatriate Australian journalist's earlier novel, *Fabulous Nobodies*, will find a happy continuum of its social satire and kinetic style…' *Australian*

'Wraith mixes suspense with comedy, plus healthy doses of cynicism and makes for compelling reading.' *Age*

'The style is racy and popular…full of flashes of cynical intimacy with a world where the determination to look glamorous can never really cover up the ugly bumps underneath.' *Good Weekend*

'The novel also has direct, immediate pleasures, moments of deft comedy and knowing one-liners: Tulloch is very good at verisimilitude, at making those Lagerfeld quotes and pieces of fashion industry gossip absurdly believable and believably absurd…Its satire is acute and observant, yet it has feeling and warmth.' *Australian Book Review*

'*Wraith* is full of searing insights into the business of being beautiful, and drips with caustic, cosmopolitan humour…a twisted urban tale full of ghosts, junkies, rock stars, wild sex, cadaverous models, squalid childhoods and designer clothes. For once in the history of fashion-related novels, the author gets all the industry argot and references spot on.' *Harper's Bazaar*

504pp, paperback, rrp$22.00, ISBN 1876485 15 9